"We have always believed that white roses bring happiness."
Page 67.

A Peoples Man

By E. PHILLIPS OPPENHEIM

Author of "The Tempting of Tavernake," "The Mischief Maker," "Peter Ruff and the Double Four," Etc.

With Four Illustrations by
EDMUND FREDERICK

A. L. BURT COMPANY, PUBLISHERS
114-120 East Twenty-third Street - - New York
PUBLISHED BY ARRANGEMENT WITH LITTLE, BROWN & COMPANY

The characters in this story
are entirely imaginary.

A PEOPLE'S MAN

CHAPTER I

"Maraton has come! Maraton! Maraton is here!"

Across Soho, threading his way with devilish ingenuity through mazes of narrow streets, scattering with his hooter little groups of gibbering, swarthy foreigners, Aaron Thurnbrein, bent double over his ancient bicycle, sped on his way towards the Commercial Road and eastwards. With narrow cheeks smeared with dust, yellow teeth showing behind his parted lips, through which the muttered words came with uneven vehemence, ragged clothes, a ragged handkerchief around his neck, a greasy cap upon his head — this messenger, charged with great tidings, proclaimed himself, by his visible existence, one of the submerged clinging to his last spar, fighting still with hands which beat the air, yet carrying the undaunted light of battle in his blazing eyes, deep-sunken, almost cavernous, the last refuge, perhaps, of that ebbing life. Drops of perspiration were upon his forehead, his breath came hard and painfully. Before he had reached his destination, one could almost hear the rattle in his throat. He even staggered as at last he dropped from his bicycle and, wheeling it across a broad pavement, left it reclining against a box of apples exposed in front of a small greengrocer's shop.

The neighbourhood was ugly and dirty, the shop was ugly and dirty. The interior into which he passed was dark, odoriferous, bare of stock, poverty-smitten. A woman, lean, hard-featured, with thin grey hair disordered and unkempt, looked up quickly at his coming and as quickly down again. Her face was perhaps too lifeless to express any emotion whatsoever, but there might have been a shade of disappointment in the swift withdrawal of her gaze. A customer would have been next door to a miracle, but hope dies hard.

" You! " she muttered. " What are you bothering about? "

" I want David," Aaron Thurnbrein panted. " I have news! Is he behind? "

The woman moved away to let him pass.

" He is behind," she answered, in a dull, lifeless tone. " Since you took him with you to Bermondsey, he does no work. What does it matter? We starve a little sooner. Take him to another meeting, if you will. I'd rather you taught him how to steal. There's rest in the prisons, at least."

Aaron Thurnbrein brushed past her, inattentive, unlistening. She was not amongst those who counted. He pushed open an ill-fitting door, whose broken glass top was stuffed with brown paper. The room within was almost horrible in its meagreness. The floor was uncarpeted, the wall unpapered. In a three-legged chair drawn up to the table, with paper before him and a pencil in his hand, sat David Ross. He looked up at the panting intruder, only to glower.

"What do you want, boy?" he asked pettishly. "I am at work. I need these figures. I am to speak to-night at Poplar."

"Put them away!" Aaron Thurnbrein cried. "Soon you and I will be needed no more. A greater than we have known is here — here in London!"

The older man looked up, for a moment, as though puzzled. Then a light broke suddenly across his face, a light which seemed somehow to become reflected in the face of the starveling youth.

"Maraton!" he almost shrieked.

"Maraton!" the other echoed. "He is here in London!"

The face of the older man twitched with excitement.

"But they will arrest him!"

"If they dared," Aaron Thurnbrein declared harshly, "a million of us would tear him out of prison. But they will not. Maraton is too clever. America has not even asked for extradition. For our sakes he keeps within the law. He is here in London! He is stripped for the fight!"

David Ross rose heavily to his feet. One saw then that he was not really old. Starvation and ill-health had branded him with premature age. He was not thin but the flesh hung about him in folds. His cheeks were puffy; his long, hairy eyebrows drooped down from his massive forehead. There was the look about him of a strong man gone to seed.

" They will be all around him like flies over a car-
cass! " he muttered.

" Mr. Foley — Foley — the Prime Minister —
sent for him directly he arrived," Aaron Thurnbrein
announced. " He is to see him to-night at his own
house in Downing Street. It makes no difference."

" Who can tell? " the other remarked despondently.
" The pages of history are littered with the bodies
of strong men who have opened their lips to the poisoned spoon."

Aaron Thurnbrein spat upon the floor.

" There is but one Maraton," he cried fervently.
" There has been but one since the world was shaped.
He is come, and the first step towards our deliverance
is at hand."

The older man, whose trembling fingers still rested
upon the sheets of paper, looked at his visitor curiously.

" You are a Jew," he muttered. " Why do you
worship Maraton? He is not of your race."

The young man's gesture was almost sublime.

" Jew or Christian — what does it matter? " he
demanded. " I am a Jew. What has my religion
done for me? Nothing! I am a free man in my
thoughts. I am one of the oppressed. Men or
women, Jews or Christians, infidels or believers —
what does it matter? We are those who have been
broken upon the wheel. Deliverance for us will come
too late. We fight for those who will follow. It is
Maraton who points towards the light. It is Maraton
whose hand shall press the levers which shall set the
kingdoms rocking. I tell you that our own country,

even, may bite the dust — a conqueror's hand lay
heavy upon her throat; and yet, no matter. Through
the valley of fire and blood and pestilence — one
must pass through these to the great white land."

"Amen!" David Ross cried fervently. "The
gift is upon you to-day, Aaron. Amen!"

The two stood together for a moment, speechless,
carried away out of themselves. Then the door was
suddenly opened. The woman stood there, sour and
withered; behind her, a hard-featured man, official,
malevolent.

"We are for the streets!" the woman exclaimed
harshly. "He's got the order."

"Three pounds thirteen or out you go," the man
announced, pushing his way forward. "Here's the
paper."

David Ross looked at him as one awakened from
a dream.

"Evicted!"

"And d — d well time, too!" the newcomer continued. "You've had all the chance in the world.
How do you expect to make a living, fiddling about
here all day with pencil and paper, and talking Socialist rot at night? Leave that chair alone and be off,
both of you."

They glanced despairingly towards Aaron Thurnbrein. He thrust his hands into his pockets and
exposed them with a little helpless gesture. The
coins he produced were of copper. The official
looked at them and around the place with a grin of
contempt.

"Cut it short," he ordered. "Clear out."

"There's my bicycle," Aaron Thurnbrein said slowly.

They all looked at him — the woman and the man with nervous anxiety, the official with a flicker of interest. Aaron Thurnbrein drew a little sigh. The bicycle had been earned by years of strenuous toil. It was almost a necessity of his existence.

"Aaron's bicycle," David Ross muttered. "No, no! That must not be. Let us go to the streets."

But the woman did not move. Already the young man had wheeled it into the shop.

"Take it," he insisted. "What does it matter? Maraton is here!"

Away again, this time on foot, along the sun-baked pavements, through courts and alleys into a narrow, busy street in the neighbourhood of Shoreditch. He stopped at last before a factory and looked tentatively up at the windows. Through the opened panes came the constant click of sewing machines, the smell of cloth, the vision of many heads bent over their work. He stood where he was for a time and watched. The place was like a hive of industry. Row after row of girls were there, seated side by side, round-shouldered, bending over their machines, looking neither to the right nor to the left, struggling to keep up to time to make sure of the wage which was life or death to them. It was nothing to them that above the halo of smoke the sky was blue; or that away beyond the murky horizon, the sun, which here in the narrow street seemed to have drawn all life from the air, was shining on yellow cornfields bending before the west wind. Here there was simply an intolerable heat, a smell of fish and a smell of cloth.

Aaron Thurnbrein crossed the street, entered the unimposing doorway and knocked at the door which led into the busy but unassuming offices. A small boy threw open a little glass window and looked at him doubtfully.

"I don't know that you can see Miss Thurnbrein even for a minute," he declared, in answer to Aaron's confident enquiry. "It's our busiest time. What do you want?"

"I am her brother," Aaron announced. "It is most important."

The boy slipped from a worn stool and disappeared. Presently the door of the little waiting-room was suddenly opened, and a girl entered.

"Aaron!" she exclaimed. "Has anything happened?"

Once more he raised his head, once more the light that flickered in his face transformed him into some semblance of a virile man.

"Maraton is here! Maraton has arrived!"

The light flashed, too, for a moment in her face, only she, even before it came, was beautiful.

"At last!" she cried. "At last! Have you seen him, Aaron? Tell me quickly, what is he like?"

"Not yet," Aaron replied. "To-night they say that he goes first to visit the Prime Minister. He will come to us afterwards."

"It is great news," she murmured. "If only one could see him!"

The office boy reappeared.

" Guvnor says why aren't you at your work, Miss Thurnbrein," he remarked, as he climbed on to his stool. " You won't get through before closing time, as it is."

She turned reluctantly away. There was something in her face from which even Aaron could scarcely remove his eyes.

" I must go," she declared. " We are busy here, and so many of the girls are away — down with the heat, I suppose. Thank you for coming, Aaron."

" I would like," he answered, " to walk the streets of London one by one, and stand at the corners and shout to the passers-by that Maraton has come. Only I wonder if they would understand. I wonder ! "

He passed out into the street and the girl returned to her work. After a few yards he felt suddenly giddy. There was a little enclosure across the road, called by courtesy a playground — a few benches, a dusty space, and some swings. He threw himself into a corner of one of the benches and closed his eyes. He was worn out, physically exhausted. Yet all the time the sense of something wonderful kept him from collapse. Maraton had come !

CHAPTER II

Westward, the late June twilight deepened into a violet and moonless darkness. The lights in St. James's Park glittered like motionless fireflies; a faint wind rustled amongst the drooping leaves of the trees. Up here the atmosphere was different. It seemed a long way from Shoreditch.

Outside the principal of the official residences in Downing Street, there was a tented passage-way and a strip of drugget across the pavement. Within, the large reception rooms were crowded with men and women. There was music, and many forms of entertainment were in progress; the popping of champagne corks; the constant murmur of cheerful conversation. The Prime Minister was giving a great political reception, and men and women of every degree and almost every nationality were talking and mingling together. The gathering was necessarily not select, but it was composed of people who counted. The Countess of Grenside, who was the Prime Minister's sister and the head of his household, saw to that.

They stood together at the head of the staircase, a couple curiously unlike not only in appearance but in disposition and tastes. Lady Grenside was tall and fair, almost florid in complexion, remarkably well-preserved, with a splendid presence and figure.

She had been one of the beauties of her day, and even now, in the sixth year of her widowhood, was accounted a remarkably handsome woman. Mr. Foley, her brother, was also tall, but gaunt and thin, with a pronounced stoop. His grey imperial gave him an almost foreign appearance. He had the forehead of a philosopher but the mouth of a humourist. His eyes, shrewd and penetrating — he wore no glasses although he was nearly sixty years of age — were perhaps his best feature.

"Tell me, my dear Stephen," she asked, as the tide of incoming guests finally ceased and they found themselves at liberty, "why are you looking so disturbed? It seems to me that every one has arrived who ought to come, and judging by the noise they are making, every one is thoroughly enjoying themselves. Why are people so noisy nowadays, I wonder?"

Mr. Foley smiled.

"What an observant person you are! To tell you the truth, there was just one guest whom I was particularly anxious to see here to-night. He promised to come, but so far I am afraid that he has not arrived."

"Not that awful man Maraton?"

He nodded.

"No use calling him names, Catharine," he continued grimly. "Maraton is one of the most important problems we have to face within the next few weeks. I suppose there is no chance of his having slipped in without our having noticed him?"

Lady Grenside shook her head.

"I should imagine not. I am quite sure that I haven't shaken hands to-night with any one who reminded me in the least of what this man must be. Very likely Elisabeth will discover him if he is here. She has just gone off on one of her tours of inspection."

Mr. Foley shrugged his shoulders. He was, after all, a philosopher.

"I am afraid Elisabeth won't get very far," he remarked. "Carton was in her train, and Ellison and Aubrey weren't far behind. She is really quite wonderful. I never in all my life saw any one look so beautiful as she does to-night."

Lady Grenside made a little grimace as she laid her fingers upon her brother's arm and pointed towards an empty settee close at hand.

"Beautiful, yes," she sighed, "but oh, so difficult!"

Almost at that moment, Elisabeth had paused on her way through the furthest of the three crowded rooms — and Maraton, happening simultaneously to glance in her direction, their eyes met. They were both above the average height, so they looked at one another over the heads of many people, and in both their faces was something of the same expression — the faint interest born of a relieved monotony. The girl deliberately turned towards him. He was an unknown guest and alone. There were times when her duties came quite easily.

"I am afraid that you are not amusing yourself,"

she remarked, with some faint yet kindly note of condescension in her tone.

"You are very kind," he answered, his eyebrows slightly lifted. "I certainly am not. But then I did not come here to amuse myself."

"Indeed? A sense of duty brought you, perhaps?"

"A sense of duty, beyond a doubt," the man assented politely.

She felt like passing on — but she also felt like staying, so she stayed.

"Cannot I help you towards the further accomplishment of your duty, then?" she enquired.

He looked at her and the grim severity of his face was lightened by a smile.

"You could help me more easily to forget it," he replied.

She opened her lips, hesitated and closed them again. Already she had recognised the fact that this was not a man to be snubbed. Neither had she, notwithstanding her momentary irritation, any real desire to do so.

"You do not know many people here?"

"I know no one," he confessed.

"I am Elisabeth Landon," she told him. "Mr. Foley is my uncle. My mother and I live with him and always help him to entertain."

"Hence your interest in a lonely stranger," he remarked. "Please have no qualms about me. I am always interested when I am permitted to watch my fellow creatures, especially when the types are novel to me."

She looked at him searchingly for a moment. As yet she had not succeeded in placing him. His features were large but well-shaped, his cheek-bones a little high, his forehead massive, his deep-set eyes bright and marvellously penetrating. He had a mouth long and firm, with a slightly humorous twist at the corners. His hair was black and plentiful. He might have been of any age between thirty-five and forty. His limbs and body were powerful; his head was set with the poise of an emperor. His clothes were correct and well worn, he was entirely at his ease. Yet Elisabeth, who was an observant person, looked at him and wondered. He would have been more at home, she thought, out in the storms of life than in her uncle's drawing-rooms. Yet what was he? He lacked the trimness of the soldier; of the debonair smartness of the modern fighting man there was no trace whatsoever in his speech or appearance. The politicians who were likely to be present she knew. What was there left? An explorer, perhaps, or a colonial. Her curiosity became imperious.

" You have not told me your name," she reminded him.

" My name is Maraton," he replied, a little grimly.

" You — Maraton ! "

There was a brief silence — not without a certain dramatic significance to the girl who stood there with slightly parted lips. The smooth serenity of her forehead was broken by a frown; her beautiful blue eyes were troubled. She seemed somehow to have dilated, to have drawn herself up. Her air of politeness, half gracious, half condescending, had

vanished. It was as though in spirit she were preparing for battle.

"You seem to have heard of me," he remarked
drily.

"Who has not heard of you!" she answered in a
low tone. "I am sorry. You have made me break
my word."

"I?"

She was recovering herself now. A certain icy
aloofness seemed to have crept into her manner. Her
head was held at a different angle. Even the words
seemed to leave her lips differently. Her tone was
one of measured indignation.

"Yes, you! When Mr. Foley told me that he had
asked you to come here to-night, I vowed that I
would not speak to you."

"A perfectly reasonable decision," he agreed,
without the slightest change of expression, "but am
I really to be blamed for this unfortunate incident?
You cannot say that I thrust myself upon your
notice."

His eyebrows were ever so slightly uplifted. She
was not absolutely sure that there was not something very suggestive of amusement in his deep-set
eyes. She bit her lip. Naturally he was not a gentleman!

"I thought that you were a neglected guest," she
explained coldly. "I do not understand how it is
that you have managed to remain undiscovered."

He shook his head doubtfully.

"I made my entrance with the others. I saw a
very charming lady at the head of the stairs — your

mother, I believe — who gave me her fingers and
called me Mr. Martin. Your uncle shook hands
with me, looking over my head to welcome some one
behind. I passed on with the rest. The fault remains, beyond a doubt, with your majordomo and
my uncommon name."

"Since I have discovered you, then," she declared,
"you had better let me take you to my uncle. He
has been looking everywhere for you for the last
hour. We will go this way."

She laid the extreme tips of her fingers upon his
coat sleeve. He glanced down at them for a moment. Her reluctance was evident.

"Perhaps," he suggested coolly, "we should make
faster progress if I were to follow you."

She took no further notice of him for some time.
Then very suddenly she drew him to one side out of
the throng, into an almost empty anteroom — a dis-
mal little apartment lined with shelves full of blue
books and Parliamentary records.

"I am content to obey my guide," he remarked,
"but why this abrupt flight?"

She hesitated. Then she raised her eyes and
looked at him. Perhaps some instinct told her that
the truth was best.

"Because Mr. Culvain was in that crowd," she
told him. "Mr. Culvain has been looking for you
everywhere. It is only to see you that he came here
this evening. My uncle is anxious to talk with you
first."

"I am flattered," he murmured, smiling.

"I think that you should be," she asserted.

"Personally, I do not understand my uncle's attitude."

"With regard to me?"

"With regard to you."

"You think, perhaps, that I should not be permitted here at all as a guest?"

"I do think that," she replied, looking steadily into his eyes. "I think more than that. I think that your place is in Sing Sing prison."

The corners of his mouth twitched. His amusement maddened her; her eyes flashed. Underneath her white satin gown her bosom was rising and falling quickly.

He became suddenly grave.

"Do you take life seriously, Lady Elisabeth?" he asked.

"Certainly," she answered firmly. "I do not think that human life is a thing to be trifled with. I agree with the *Times*."

"In what it said about me?"

"Yes!"

"And what was that? It is neglectful of me, I know, but I never see the *Times*."

"It held you entirely responsible for the death of those poor men in Chicago," she told him. "It named you as their murderer."

"A very sensible paper, the *Times*," he agreed. "The responsibility was entirely mine."

She looked at him for a moment in horror.

"You can dare to admit that here — to me?"

"Why not?" he answered calmly. "So long as it is my conviction, why not proclaim it? I love the truth. It is the one virtue which has never been denied me."

Her eyes flashed. She made no effort whatever to conceal her detestation.

" And they let you go — those Americans? " she cried. " I do not understand ! "

" There are probably many other considerations in connection with the affair which you do not understand," he observed. " However — they had their opportunity. I walked the streets openly, I travelled to New York openly, I took my steamer ticket to England under my own name. The papers, I believe, chronicled every stage of my journey."

" It was disgraceful ! " she declared. " The people in office over there are cowards."

" Not at all," he objected. " They were very well advised. They acted with shrewd common sense. America is no better prepared for a revolution than England is."

" Do you imagine," she demanded, her voice trembling, " that you will be permitted to repeat in this country your American exploits? "

Maraton smiled a little sadly.

" Need we discuss these things, Lady Elisabeth? "

" Yes, we need ! " she replied promptly. " This is my one opportunity. You and I will probably never exchange another word so long as we live. I have read your book — every word of it. I have read it several times. In that book you have shown just as much of yourself as you chose, and no more. Although I have hated the idea that I might ever have to speak to you, now that you are here, now that it has come to pass, I am going to ask you a question."

He sighed.

"People ask me so many questions!"

"Tell me this," she continued, without heeding his interruption. "Do you, in your heart, believe that you are justified in going about the world preaching your hateful doctrines, seeking out the toilers only to fill them with discontent and to set them against their employers, preaching everywhere bloodshed and anarchy, inflaming the minds of people who in ordinary times are contented, even happy? You have made yourself feared and hated in every country of the world. You have brought America almost to the verge of revolution. And now, just when England needs peace most, when affairs on the Continent are so threatening and every one connected with the Government of the country is passing through a time of the gravest anxiety, you intend, they say, to start a campaign here. You say that you love the truth. Answer me this question truthfully, then. Do you believe that you are justified?"

He had listened to her at first with a slight, tolerant smile upon his lips, a smile which faded gradually away. He was sombre, almost stern, when she had finished. He seemed in some curious way to have assumed a larger shape, to have become more imposing. His attitude had a strange and indefinable influence upon her.

She was suddenly conscious of her youth and inexperience — bitterly and rebelliously conscious of them — before he had even opened his lips.

Her own words sounded crude and unconvincing.

"I am not one of the flamboyant orators of the Socialist party, Lady Elisabeth," he said, "nor am I one of those who are able to see much joy or very much hopefulness in life under present conditions. For every word I have spoken and every line I have written, I accept the full and complete responsibility."

"Those men who were murdered in Chicago, murdered at your instigation because they tried to break the strike — what of them?"

He looked at her as one might have looked at a child.

"Their lives were a necessary sacrifice in a good cause," he declared. "Does one think now of the sea of blood through which France once purged herself? Believe me, young lady, there is nothing in the world more to be avoided than this sentimental and exaggerated reverence for life. It is born of a false ideal, artistically and actually. Life is a sacrifice to be offered in a just cause when necessary. . . . I imagine that this is your uncle."

Mr. Foley was standing upon the threshold of the room, his hand outstretched, his thin, long face full of conviction.

"My niece has succeeded in discovering you, then, Mr. Maraton," he said. "I am glad."

Maraton smiled as he shook hands.

"I have certainly had the pleasure of making your niece's acquaintance," he admitted. "We have had quite an interesting discussion."

Elisabeth turned away without looking towards him.

"I will leave Mr. Maraton to you, uncle," she said. "He will tell you that I have been very candid indeed. We were coming face to face with Mr. Culvain, so I brought him in here."

She did not glance again in Maraton's direction, nor did she offer him any form of farewell salutation. Mr. Foley frowned slightly as he glanced after her. Maraton, too, watched her leave the room. She paused for a moment on the threshold to gather up her train, a graceful but at the same time imperious gesture. She left them without a backward look. Mr. Foley turned quickly towards his companion and was relieved at the expression which he found in his face.

"My niece is a little earnest in her views," he remarked, "too much so, I am afraid, for a practical politician. She is quite well-informed and a great help to me at times."

"I found her altogether charming," Maraton said quietly. "She has, too, the unusual gift of honesty."

Mr. Foley was once more a little uneasy. It was impossible for him to forget Elisabeth's outspoken verdict upon this man and all his works.

"The young are never tolerant," he murmured.

"And quite rightly," Maraton observed. "There is nothing more to be envied in youth than its magnificent certainty. It knows! . . . I am flattered, Mr. Foley, that you should have received me in your house to-night. Your niece's attitude towards me, even if a trifle crude, is, I am afraid, the general one amongst your class in this country."

"To be frank with you, I agree," Mr. Foley assented. "I, personally, Mr. Maraton, am trying to be a dissenter. It is for that reason that I begged you to come here to-night and discuss the matter with me before you committed yourself to any definite plan of action in this country."

"Your message was a surprise to me," Maraton admitted calmly. "At the same time, it was a summons which I could not disregard. As you see, I am here."

Mr. Foley drew a key from his pocket and led the way across the room towards a closed door.

"I want to make sure that we are not disturbed. I am going to take you through to my study, if I may."

They passed into a small inner room, plainly but comfortably furnished.

"My own den," Mr. Foley explained, closing the door behind him with an air of relief. "Will you smoke, Mr. Maraton, or drink anything?"

"Neither, thank you," Maraton answered. "I am here to listen. I am curious to hear what there is that you can have to say to me."

CHAPTER III

Mr. Foley pointed to an easy-chair. Maraton, however, did not at once respond to his gesture of invitation. He was standing, tense and silent, with head upraised, listening. From the street outside came a strange, rumbling sound.

"You permit?" he asked, stepping to the window and drawing the curtain a few inches on one side. "There is something familiar about that sound. I heard it last in Chicago."

Mr. Foley rose slowly from the easy-chair into which he had thrown himself, and stood by his visitor's side. Outside, the pavements were lined by policemen, standing like sentries about half-a-dozen yards apart. The tented entrance to the house was guarded by a solid phalanx of men in uniform. A mounted inspector was riding slowly up and down in the middle of the road. At the entrance to the street, barely fifty yards away, a moving mass of people, white-faced, almost spectral, were passing slowly beneath the pale gas-lamps.

"The people!" Maraton murmured, with a curious note in his tone, half of reverence, half of pity.

"The mob!" Mr. Foley echoed bitterly. "They brawl before the houses of those who do their best to serve them. They bark always at our heels.

Perhaps to-night it is you whom they have come to
honour. Your bodyguard, eh, Mr. Maraton? "

" If they have discovered that I am here, it is not
unlikely," Maraton admitted calmly.

Mr. Foley dropped the curtain which he had taken
from his companion's fingers. Moving back into the
room, he turned on more light. Then he resumed
his seat.

" Mr. Maraton," he began, " we met only once
before, I think. That was four years ago this summer. Answer me honestly — do you see any change
in me? "

Maraton leaned a little forward. His face showed
some concern, as he answered:

" You are not in the best of health just now, I
fear, Mr. Foley."

" I am as well as I shall ever be," was the quiet
reply. " What you see in my face is just the record
of these last four years, the outward evidence of
four years of ceaseless trouble and anxiety. I will
not call myself yet a broken man, but the time is
not far off."

Maraton remained silent. His attitude was still
sympathetic, but he seemed determined to carry out
his rôle of listener.

" If the political history of these four years is
ever truthfully written," Mr. Foley continued, " the
world will be amazed at the calm indifference of the
people threatened day by day with national disaster.
We who have been behind the scenes have kept a stiff
upper lip before the world, but I tell you frankly,
Mr. Maraton, that no Cabinet who ever undertook

the government of this country has gone through what we have gone through. Three times we have been on the brink of war — twice on our own account and once on account of those whom we are bound to consider our allies. The other national disaster we have had to face, you know of. Still, here we are safe up to to-night. There is nothing in the whole world we need now so much as rest — just a few months' freedom from anxiety. Until last week we had dared to hope for it. Now, breathless still from our last escape, we are face to face suddenly with all the possibilities of your coming."

" You fear the people," Maraton remarked quietly.

Mr. Foley's pale, worn face suddenly lit up.

" Fear the people! " he repeated, with a note of passion in his tone. " I fear the people for their own sake; I fear the ruin and destruction they may, by ill-advised action, bring upon themselves and their country. Mr. Maraton, grant, will you not, that I am a man of some experience? Believe, I pray you, that I am honest. Let me assure you of this. If the people be not wisely led now, the Empire which I and my Ministers have striven so hard to keep intact, must fall. There are troubles pressing upon us still from every side. If the people are wrongly advised to-day, the British Empire must fall, even as those other great dynasties of the past have fallen."

Maraton turned once more to the window, raised the curtain, and gazed out into the darkness. There was a little movement at the end of the street. The police had driven back the crowd to allow a carriage to pass through. A hoarse murmur of voices came floating into the room. The people gave way slowly and unwillingly — still, they gave way. Law and order, strenuous though the task of preserving them was becoming, prevailed.

"Mr. Foley," Maraton said, dropping the curtain and returning once more to his place, "I am honoured by your confidence. You force me, however, to remind you that you have spoken to me as a politician. I am not a politician. The cause of the people is above politics."

"I am for the people," Mr. Foley declared, with a sudden passion in his tone. "It is their own fault, the blind prejudice of their ignorant leaders, if they fail to recognise it."

"For the people," Maraton repeated softly.

"Haven't my Government done their best to prove it?" the Prime Minister demanded, almost fiercely. "We have passed at least six measures which a dozen years ago would have been reckoned rank Socialism. What we do need to-day is a people's man in our Government. I admit our weakness. I admit that with every desire to do the right thing, we may sometimes err through lack of knowledge. Our great trouble is this; there is not to-day a single man amongst the Labour Party, a single man who has come into Parliament on the mandate of the people, whose assistance would be of the slightest service to us. I make you an offer which you yourself must consider a wonderful one. You come to this country as an enemy, and I offer you my hand as a friend. I offer you not only a seat in Parliament but a share in the counsels of my party. I ask you to teach us how to legislate for the people of the future."

Maraton remained for a moment silent. His face betrayed no exultation. His tone, when at last he spoke, was almost sad.

"Mr. Foley," he said, "if you are not a great man, you have in you, at least, the elements of greatness. You have imagination. You know how to meet a crisis. I only wish that what you suggest were possible. Twenty years ago, perhaps, yes. To-day I fear that the time for any legislation in which you would concur, is past."

"What have you to hope for but legislation?" Mr. Foley asked. "What else is there but civil war?"

Maraton smiled a little grimly.

"There is what in your heart you are fearing all the time," he replied. "There is the slow paralysis of all your manufactures, the stoppage of your railways, the dislocation of every industry and undertaking built upon the slavery of the people. What about your British Empire then?"

Mr. Foley regarded his visitor with quiet dignity.

"I have understood that you were an Englishman, Mr. Maraton," he said. "Am I to look upon you as a traitor?"

"Not to the cause which is my one religion," Maraton retorted swiftly. "Empires may come and go, but the people remain. What changes may happen to this country before the great and final one, is a matter in which I am not deeply concerned."

The telephone bell upon the table between them

rang. Mr. Foley frowned slightly, as he raised the receiver to his ear.

"You will forgive me?" he begged. "This is doubtless a matter of some importance. It is not often that my secretary allows me to be disturbed at this hour."

Maraton wandered back to the window, raised the curtain and once more looked out upon the scene which seemed to him that night so pregnant with meaning. His mind remained fixed upon the symbolism of the streets. He heard only the echoes of a somewhat prolonged exchange of questions and answers. Finally, Mr. Foley replaced the receiver and announced the conclusion of the conversation. When Maraton turned round, it seemed to him that his host's face was grey.

"You come like the stormy petrel," the latter remarked bitterly. "There is bad news to-night from the north. We are threatened with militant labour troubles all over the country."

"It is the inevitable," Maraton declared.

Mr. Foley struck the table with his fist.

"I deny it!" he cried. "These troubles can and shall be stopped. Legislation shall do it — amicable, if possible; brutal, if not. But the man who is content to see his country ruined, see it presented, a helpless prey, to our enemies for the mere trouble of landing upon our shores,— that man is a traitor and deserves to be treated as such. Tell me, on behalf of the people, Mr. Maraton, what is it that you want? Name your terms?"

Maraton shook his head doubtfully.

" You are a brave man, Mr. Foley," he said, " but
remember that you do not stand alone. There are
your fellow Ministers."

" They are my men," Mr. Foley insisted. " Besides, there is the thunder in the air. We cannot disregard it. We are not ostriches. Better to meet
the trouble bravely than to be crushed by it."

There was a tap at the door, and Lady Elisabeth
appeared upon the threshold. Maraton was conscious of realising for the first time that this was
the most beautiful woman whom he had ever seen
in his life. She avoided looking at him as she addressed her uncle.

" Uncle," she said deprecatingly, " I am so sorry,
but every one is asking for you. You have been in
here for nearly twenty minutes. There is a rumour
that you are ill."

Mr. Foley rose to his feet reluctantly.

" I will come," he promised.

She closed the door and departed silently. At no
time had she glanced towards or taken any notice of
Maraton.

" We discuss the fate of an empire," Mr. Foley
sighed, " and necessity demands that I must return
to my guests! This conversation between us must
be finished. You are a reasonable man; you cannot
deny the right of an enemy to demand your terms
before you declare war? "

Maraton, too, had risen to his feet. He had
turned slightly and his eyes were fixed upon the door
through which Elisabeth had passed. For a moment
or two he seemed deep in thought. The immobility

of his features was at last disturbed. His eyes were wonderfully bright, his lips were a little parted.

" On Saturday," Mr. Foley continued, " we leave for our country home. For two days we shall be alone. It is not far away — an hour by rail. Will you come, Mr. Maraton? "

Maraton withdrew his eyes from the door.

" It seems a little useless," he said quietly. " Will you give me until to-morrow to think it over? "

CHAPTER IV

Maraton made his way from Downing Street on foot, curiously enough altogether escaping recognition from the crowds who were still hanging about on the chance of catching a glimpse of him. He was somehow conscious, as he turned northwards, of a peculiar sense of exhilaration, a savour in life unexpected, not altogether analysable. As a rule, the streets themselves supplied him with illimitable food for thought; the passing multitudes, the ceaseless flow of the human stream, justification absolute and most complete for the new faith of which he was the prophet. For the cause of the people had only been recognised during recent days as something entirely distinct from the Socialism and Syndicalism which had been its precursors. It was Maraton himself who had raised it to the level of a religion.

To-night, however, there was a curious background to his thoughts. Some part of his earlier life seemed stirred up in the man. The one selfishness permitted to rank as a virtue in his sex was alive. His heart had ceased to throb with the loiterers, the flotsam and jetsam of the gutters. For the moment he was cast loose from the absorbed and serious side of his career. A curious wave of sentiment had enveloped him, a wave of sentiment unanalysable and as yet impersonal; he walked as a man in a dream. For the first time he

had seen and recognised the imperishable thing in a
woman's face.

He reached at last one of the large, somewhat
gloomy squares in the district between St. Pancras
and New Oxford street, and paused before one of the
most remote houses situated at the extreme north-
east corner. He opened the front door with a latch-
key and passed across a large but simply furnished
hall into his study. He entered a little abstractedly,
and it was not until he had closed the door behind
him that he realised the presence of another person
in the room. At his entrance she had risen to her
feet.

"At last!" she exclaimed. "At last you have
come!"

There was a silence, prolonged, curious, in a sense
thrilling. A girl of wonderful appearance had risen
to her feet and was looking eagerly towards him.
She was wearing the plain black dress of a working
woman, whose clumsy folds inadequately concealed a
figure of singular beauty and strength. Her cheeks
were colourless; her eyes large and deep, and of a soft
shade of grey, filled just now with the half wondering, half worshipping expression of a pilgrim who
has reached the Mecca of her desires. Her hair —
her shabby hat lay upon the table — was dark and
glossy. Her arms were a little outstretched. Her
lips, unusually scarlet against the pallor of her face,
were parted. Her whole attitude was one of quivering eagerness. Maraton stood and looked at her
in wonder. The little cloud of sentiment in which
he had been moving, perhaps, made him more than

ever receptive to the impressions which she seemed to create. Both the girl herself and her pose were splendidly allegorical. She stood there for the great things of life.

"I would not go away," she cried softly. "They forbade me to stay, but I came back. I am Julia Thurnbrein. I have waited so long."

Maraton stepped towards her and took her hands.

"I am glad," he said. "It is fitting that you should be one of the first to welcome me. You have done a great work, Julia Thurnbrein."

"And you," she murmured passionately, still clasping his hands, "you a far greater one! Ever since I understood, I have longed for this meeting. It is you who will become the world's deliverer."

Maraton led her gently back to the chair in which she had been sitting.

"Now we must talk," he declared. "Sit opposite to me there."

He struck a match and lit the lamp of a little coffee machine which stood upon the table. She sprang eagerly to her feet.

"Let me, please," she begged. "I understand those things. Please let me make the coffee."

He laughed and, going to the cabinet, brought another of the old blue china cups and saucers. With very deft fingers she manipulated the machine. Presently, when her task was finished, she sat back in her chair, her coffee cup in her hand, her great eyes fixed upon him. She had the air of a person entirely content.

"So you are Julia Thurnbrein."

"And you," she replied, still with that note of suppressed yet passionate reverence in her tone, "are Maraton."

He smiled.

"The women workers of the world owe you a great deal," he said.

"But it is so little that one can do," she answered, quivering with pleasure at his words. "One needs inspiration, direction. Now that you have come, it will be different; it will be wonderful!"

She leaned towards him, and once more Maraton was conscious of the splendid mobility of her trembling body. She was a revelation to him — a modern Joan of Arc.

"Remember that I am no magician," he warned her.

"Ah, but your very presence alters everything!" she cried. "It makes everything possible — everything. My brother, too, is mad with excitement. He hoped that you might have been at the Clarion Hall to-night, before you went to Downing Street. You have seen Mr. Foley and talked with him?"

"I have come straight from there," he told her. "Foley is a shrewd man. He sees the writing upon the wall. He is afraid."

She looked at him and laughed.

"They will try to buy you," she remarked scornfully. "They will try to deal with you as they did with Blake and others like him — you — Maraton! Oh, I wonder if England knows what it means, your coming! — if she really feels the breaking dawn!"

"Tell me about yourself?" Maraton asked, a little

abruptly — "your work? I know you only by name, remember — your articles in the reviews and your evidence before the Woman Labour Commission."

"I am a tailoress," she replied. "It is horrible work, but I have the good fortune to be quick. I can make a living — there are many who cannot."

He was leaning back in his chair, his head supported by his hand, his eyes fixed curiously upon her. Her pallor was not wholly the pallor of ill-health. In her beautiful eyes shone the fire of life. She laughed at him softly and held out her hands for his inspection. They were shapely enough, but her finger-tips were scotched and pricked.

"Here are the hall-marks of my trade. Others who work by my side have fallen away. It is of their sufferings I have written. I myself am physically very strong. It is the average person who counts."

He looked at her thoughtfully.

"You have written and worked a great deal for your age. Are you still in employment?"

"Of course! I left off at seven this evening. I have nothing else in my life," she added simply, "but my work, our work, the breaking of these vile bonds. I need no pleasures. I have never thought of any."

Her eyes suddenly dropped before his. A confusion of thought seemed to have seized upon her. Maraton, too, conscious of the nature of his imaginings, although innocent of any personal application, was not wholly free from embarrassment.

"Perhaps you will think," he observed, "that I am asking too many personal questions for a new acquaintance, but, after all, I must know you, must I not? We are fellow workers in a great cause. The small things do not matter."

She looked at him once more frankly. The blush had passed from her cheeks, her eyes were untroubled.

" I don't know what came over me," she confessed. " I was suddenly afraid that you might misunderstand my coming to you like this, without invitation, so late. Somehow, with you, it didn't seem to count."

" It must not! "

More at her ease now she glanced around the room and back at him. He smiled.

" Confess," he said, " that there are some things about me and my surroundings which have surprised you? "

She nodded.

" Willingly. I was surprised at your house, at being received by a man servant — at everything," she added, with a glance at his attire. " Yet what does that matter? It is because I do not understand."

The little lines about his eyes deepened. He laughed softly.

" I only hope that the others will adopt your attitude. I hear that many of them have very decided views about evening dress and small luxuries of any description."

" Graveling and Peter Dale — especially Dale — are terrible," she declared. " Dale is very narrow, indeed. You must bear with them if they are foolish at first. They are uncultured and rough. They do not quite understand. Sometimes they do not see far enough. But to-morrow you will meet them. You will be at the Clarion to-morrow?"

"I am not sure," he answered thoughtfully. "I am thinking matters over. To-morrow I shall meet the men of whom you have spoken, and a few others whose names I have on my list, and consult with them. Personally, I am not sure as to the wisdom of opening my lips until after our meeting at Manchester."

"Oh, don't say that!" she begged. "What we all need so much is encouragement, inspiration. Our greatest danger is lethargy. There are millions who stare into the darkness, who long for a single word of hope. Their eyes are almost tired. Come and speak to us to-morrow as you spoke to the men and women of Chicago."

He smiled a little grimly.

"You forget that this is England. Until the time comes, one must choose one's words. It is just what would please our smug enemies best to have me break their laws before I have been here long enough to become dangerous."

"You broke the laws of America," she protested eagerly.

"I had a million men and women primed for battle at my back," he reminded her. "The warrant was signed for my arrest, but no one dared to serve it. All the same, I had to leave the country with some work half finished."

"It was a glorious commencement," she cried enthusiastically.

"One must not forget, though," he sighed, "that

England is different. To attain the same ends here, one may have to use somewhat different methods."

For the moment, perhaps, she was stirred by some prophetic misgiving. The hard common sense of his words fell like a cold douche upon the furnace of her enthusiasms. She had imagined him a prophet, touched by the great and unmistakable fire, ready to drive his chariot through all the hosts of iniquity; irresistible, unassailable, cleaving his way through the bending masses of their oppressors to the goal of their desires. His words seemed to proclaim him a disciple of other methods. There were to be compromises. His attire, his dwelling, this luxuriously furnished room, so different from anything which she had expected, proclaimed it. She herself held it part of the creed of her life to be free from all ornaments, free from even the shadow of luxury. Her throat was bare, her hair simply arranged, her fingers and wrists innocent of even the simplest article of jewellery. He, on the other hand, the Elijah of her dreams, appeared in the guise of a man of fashion, wearing, as though he were used to them, the attire of the hated class, obviously qualified by breeding and use to hold his place amongst them. Was this indeed to be the disappointment of her life? Then she remembered and her courage rose. After all, he was the Master.

" I will go now," she said. " I am glad to have been the first to have welcomed you."

He held out his hands. Then for a moment they both listened and turned towards the door. There was the sound of an angry voice — a visitor, apparently, trying to force his way in. Maraton strode towards the door and opened it. A young man was in the hall, expostulating angrily with a resolute man servant. His hat had rolled on to the floor, his face was flushed with anger. The servant, on recognising his master, stepped back at once.

" The gentleman insisted upon forcing his way in, sir," he explained softly. " I wished him to wait while I brought you his name."

Maraton smiled and made a little gesture of dismissal. The young man picked up his hat. He was still hot with anger. Maraton pointed to the room on the threshold of which the girl was still standing.

" If you wish to speak to me," he said, " I am quite at your service. Only it is a little late for a visit, isn't it? And yours seems to be a rather unceremonious way of insisting upon it. Who are you? "

The young man stood and stared at his questioner. He was wearing a blue serge suit, obviously ready-made, thick boots, a doubtful collar, a machine-knitted silk tie of vivid colour. He had curly fair hair, a sharp face with narrow eyes, thick lips and an indifferent complexion.

" Are you Maraton? " he demanded.

" I am," Maraton admitted. " And you? "

" I am Richard Graveling, M.P.," the young man announced, with a certain emphasis on those last two letters,—" M.P. for Poplar East. We expected you at the Clarion to-night."

" I had other business," Maraton remarked calmly.

The young man appeared a trifle disconcerted.

"I don't see what business you can have here till we've talked things out and laid our plans," he declared. "I am secretary of the committee appointed to meet and confer with you. Peter Dale is chairman, of course. There are five of us. We expected you 'round to-night. You got our telegram at Liverpool?"

"Certainly," Maraton admitted. "It did not, however, suit my plans to accept your invitation. I had a message from Mr. Foley, begging me to see him to-night. I have been to his house."

The young man distinctly scowled.

"So Foley's been getting at you, has he?"

Maraton's face was inscrutable but there was, for a moment, a dangerous flash in his eyes.

"I had some conversation with him this evening."

"What did he want?" Graveling asked bluntly.

Maraton raised his eyebrows. He turned to the girl.

"Do you know Mr. Graveling?"

The young man scowled. Julia smiled but there was a shadow of trouble in her face.

"Naturally," she replied. "Mr. Graveling and I are fellow workers."

"Yes, we are that," the young man declared pointedly, "that and a little more, I hope. To tell you the truth, I followed Miss Thurnbrein here, and I think she'd have done better to have asked for my escort — the escort of the man she's going to marry — before she came here alone at this time of night."

Mr. Graveling's ill-humour was explained. He was of the order of those to whom the ability to conceal their feelings is not given, and he was obviously in a temper. Maraton's face remained impassive. The girl, however, stood suddenly erect. There was a vivid spot of colour in her cheeks.

"You had better keep to the truth, Richard Graveling!" she cried fearlessly. "I have never promised to marry you, or if I have, it was under certain conditions. You had no right to follow me here."

The young man opened his lips and closed them again. He was scarcely capable of speech. The very intensity of his anger seemed to invest the little scene with a peculiar significance. The girl had the air of one who has proclaimed her freedom. The face of the man who glared at her was distorted with unchained passions. In the background, Maraton stood with tired but expressionless countenance, and the air of one who listens to a quarrel between children, a quarrel in which he has no concern.

"It is not fair," Julia continued, "to discuss a purely personal matter here. You can walk home with me if you care to, Richard Graveling, but all that I have to say to you, I prefer to say here. I never promised to marry you. You have always chosen to take it for granted, and I have let you speak of it because I was indifferent, because I have never chosen to think of such matters, because my thoughts have been wholly, wholly dedicated to the greatest cause in the world. To-night you have forced yourself upon me. You have done yourself harm, not good. You have surprised the truth in my heart. It is clear to me that I cannot marry you; I never could. I shall not change. Now let us go back to our work hand in hand, if you will, but that other matter is closed between us forever."

She turned to say farewell to Maraton, but Graveling interposed himself between them. His voice shook and there were evil things in his distorted face.

"To-night, for the first time," he exclaimed hoarsely, "you speak in this fashion! Before, even if you were indifferent, marriage at least seemed possible to you. To-night you say that the truth has come to you. You look at me with different eyes. You draw back. You begin to feel, to understand. You are a woman to-night! Why? Answer me that! Why? Why to-night? Why not before? Why is it that to-night you have awakened? I will know! Look at me."

She was taken unawares, assailed suddenly, not only by his words but by those curious new sensations, her own, yet unfamiliar to her. It was civil war. A part of herself was in league with her accuser. She felt the blushes stain her cheeks. She looked imploringly at Maraton for help. He smiled at her reassuringly, delightfully.

"Children," he expostulated, "this is absurd! Off with you to your homes. These are small matters of which you speak."

His hands were courteously laid upon both of them. He led them to the door and pointed eastwards through the darkness.

"Think of the morning. Think of the human beings who wake in a few hours, only to bend their bodies once more to the yoke. The other things are but trifles."

She looked back at him from the corner of the Square, a straight, impassive figure in a little halo of soft light. There was a catch in her heart. Her companion's words were surely spoken in some foreign tongue.

"We have got to have this out, Julia," he was saying. "If anybody or anything has come between us, there's going to be trouble. If that's the great Maraton, with his swagger evening clothes and big house, well, he's not the man for our job, and I shan't mind being the first to tell him so."

She glanced at him, for a moment, almost in wonder. Was he indeed so small, so insignificant?

"There are many paths," she said softly, "which lead to the light. Ours may be best suited to ourselves but it may not be the only one. It is not for you or for me to judge."

Richard Graveling talked on, doing his cause harm with every word he uttered. Julia relapsed into silence; soon she did not even hear his words. They rode for some distance on an omnibus through the city, now shrouded and silent. At the corner of the street where she had her humble lodgings, he left her.

"Well, I have had my say," he declared. "Think it over. I'll meet you out of work to-morrow, if I can. We shall have had a talk with Mr. Maraton by that time!"

She left him with a smile upon her lips. His absence seemed like an immense, a wonderful relief. Once more her thoughts were free.

CHAPTER V

But were they free, after all, these thoughts of hers?

Julia rose at daybreak and, fully dressed, stood watching the red light eastwards staining the smoke-hung city. Her little room with its plain deal furniture, its uncarpeted floor, was the perfection of neatness, her bed already made, her little pots of flowers upon the window-sill, jealously watered. In the still smaller sitting-room, visible through the open door, she could hear the hissing of her kettle upon the little spirit lamp. Her hat and gloves were already out. Everything was in readiness for her early start.

She had slept very much as usual, and had got up only a little earlier than she was accustomed to. Yet there was a difference. Only so short a time ago, the incidents of her own daily life, even the possibilities connected with it, had seemed utterly insignificant, so little worthy of notice. Morning and night her heart had been full of the sufferings of those amongst whom she worked. The flagrant, hateful injustice of this ill-arranged world had throbbed in her pulses, absorbed her interests, had occupied the whole horizon of her life. To marry Richard Graveling might sometime be advisable, in the interests of their joint labours. And suddenly it had become impossible. It had become utterly impossible! Why?

The red light in the sky had faded, the sun was now fully risen. Julia looked out of her window and was dimly conscious of the change. The heart which had throbbed for the sorrows of others was to thrill now on its own account. It was something mysterious which had happened to her, something against which she was later on to fight passionately, which was creeping like poison through her veins. With her splendid womanhood, her intense consciousness of life, how was it possible for her to escape?

There was an impatient tap at the door and Aaron came in. She recognised him with a little cry of surprise. He was paler than ever and grim with his night's vigil. The lines under his eyes were deeper, his skin seemed sallower. He had the dishevelled look of one who is still in his attire of the preceding day.

"You have heard?" he exclaimed. "We stayed at the Clarion till three. Maraton never even sent us a message. Yet they say that he is in London. They even declare that he was at Downing Street last night."

"I know that he was there," Julia said quietly.

"You know? You? But they were all sure of it."

He dashed his cap into a corner.

"Maraton is our man," he continued passionately. "No one shall rob us of him. He should have come to us. Downing Street — blast Downing Street!"

"There is no one in this world," she told him gently, "who will move Maraton from his will. I know. I have seen him."

He stared at her, hollow-eyed, amazed.

" You? You have seen him? "

She nodded.

" I heard by accident of the house he had taken —
the house where he means to live. I went there and
I waited. Later, Richard Graveling came there,
too."

The youth struck the table before him. His eyes
were filled with tears.

" All night I waited! " he cried. " I could not sit
still. I could scarcely breathe. Tell me what he is
like, Julia? Tell me what he looks like? Is he
strong? Does he look strong enough for the work? "

She smiled at him reassuringly.

" Yes, he looks strong and he looks kind. For the
rest —"

" There is something! Tell me what it is — at
once? "

" Foolish! Well, he is unlike Richard Graveling
and the others, unlike us. Why not? He is culti-
vated, educated, well-dressed."

The youth, for a moment, was aghast.

" You don't mean — that he is a gentleman? "

" Not in the sense you fear," she assured him.
" Remember that his work is more far-reaching than
ours. It takes him everywhere; he must be fit for
everything. Sit down now, dear Aaron. You are
tired. See, my morning tea is ready, and there is
bread and butter. You must eat and drink. Maraton you will surely see later in the day. I do not
think that he will disappoint you."

Aaron sat down at the table. He ate and drank

ravenously. He was, in fact, half starved but barely conscious of it.

" He spoke of the great things? "

Julia shook her head. She was busy cutting bread and butter.

" Scarcely at all. What chance was there? And then Richard Graveling came."

" They were friends? They took to one another? " the young man asked eagerly.

She hesitated.

" I am not sure about that. Graveling was in one of his tempers. He was rude, and he said things to me which I felt obliged to contradict."

" They did not quarrel? "

She laughed softly.

" Imagine Maraton quarrelling! I think that he is above such pettiness, Aaron."

" Graveling is a good fellow and a hard worker," Aaron declared. " The one thing which he lacks is enthusiasm. He doesn't really feel. He does his work well because it is his work, not because of what it leads to."

" You are right," Julia admitted. " He has no enthusiasm. That is why he never moves people when he speaks. I must go soon, Aaron. Will you lie down and rest for a time here? "

" Rest! " He looked at her scornfully. " How can one rest! Tell me where this house of his is? I shall go and wait outside. I must see him."

She glanced at the clock, and paused for a moment to think.

" Aaron," she decided, " I will be late for once.

Come with me and I will take you to him. He was
kind to me last night. We will go together to his
house and wait till he is down. Then I will tell him
how you have longed for his coming, and perhaps —"

"Perhaps what?" Aaron interrupted. "You
can't escape from it! You have promised. You
shall take me! I am ready to go. Perhaps what?"

"I was only thinking," she went on, "you find it,
I know, impossible to settle down to work anywhere.
But with him, if he could find something —"

Aaron sprang to his feet.

"I would work my fingers to the bone!" he cried.
"It is a glorious idea, Julia. I have to give up the
collecting — my bicycle has gone. · Let us start."

They went out together into the streets, thinly
peopled, as yet, for it was barely six o'clock. Julia
would have loitered, but her brother forced her always
onward. She laughed as they arrived at the Square
where Maraton lived. Every house they passed was
shuttered and silent.

"How absurd we are!" she murmured. "He will
not be up for hours. Very likely even the servants
will not be astir."

"Servants!"

Aaron repeated the word, frowning. She only
smiled.

"You mustn't be foolish, dear. Don't have prejudices. Remember that we are walking along a very
narrow way. We have climbed only a few steps of
the hill. He is more than half-way to the top.
Things are different with him. Don't judge; only
wait."

She rang the bell of the house a little timidly. The door was opened without any delay by a man servant in sombre, every-day clothes.

"We wish to see Mr. Maraton," Julia announced. "He is not up yet, of course, but might we come in and wait?"

"Mr. Maraton is in his study, madam," the man answered.

He disappeared and beckoned them, a moment or so later, to follow him. They were shown into a much smaller apartment at the rear of the house. Maraton was sitting before a desk covered with papers, with a breakfast tray by his side. He looked up at their entrance, but his face was inexpressive. He did not even smile. The sunlight died out of Julia's face, and her heart sank.

"I am sorry," she began haltingly. "I ought not to have come again, I know. But it is my brother. Night and day he has thought of nothing else but your coming."

Aaron seemed to have forgotten his timidity. He crossed the room and stood before Maraton's desk. His face seemed to have caught some of the freshness of the early morning. He was no longer the sallow, pinched starveling. He was like a young prophet whose eyes are burning with enthusiasm.

"You have come to help us," he asserted. "You are Maraton!"

"I have come to help you," Maraton replied. "I have come to do what I can. It isn't an easy task in this country, you know, to do anything, but I think in the end we shall succeed. If you are Julia

Thurnbrein's brother, you should know something
of the work."

"I am only one of the multitude," Aaron sighed.
"I haven't the brains to organise. I talk sometimes
but I get too excited. There are others — many
others — who speak more convincingly, but no one
feels more than I feel, no one prays for the better
times more fervently than I. It isn't for myself — it
isn't for ourselves, even; it's for the children, it's
for the next generation."

Maraton held out his hand suddenly.

"My young friend," he said, "you have spoken
the words I like to hear. Some of my helpers I have
found, at times, selfish. They are satisfied with the
small things that lie close at hand, some material
benefit which really is of no account at all. That
isn't the work for us to engage in. Sit down. Sit
down, Miss Julia. You have breakfasted?"

"Before we left," Julia assured him.

"Never mind, you shall breakfast again," Maraton declared. "It is a good augury that the first
words I have heard from one of ourselves have been
words such as your brother has spoken. To tell
you the truth, I came over here in fear and trembling.
Some of your leaders have frightened me a little."

"You mean —" Aaron began.

"That they don't hold their heads high enough.
I am not for strikes that finish with a shilling a week
more for the men; or for Acts of Parliament which
dole out tardy charity. I am for the bigger things.
Last night I lay awake, thinking — your friend
Richard Graveling set me thinking. We must aim

high. I am here for no man's individual good. I am here to plan not pinpricks but destruction."

The servant brought in more breakfast. They sat and talked, Maraton asking many questions concerning the men whom he would meet later in the day. Then he looked regretfully at the great pile of letters still before him.

" I shall need a secretary," he said slowly.

Aaron sprang to his feet.

" Take me," he begged. " I have been in a newspaper office. I am slow at shorthand but I can type like lightning. I will work morning and night. I want nothing but a little food if I may go about with you and hear you speak. Oh, take me! "

Maraton smiled.

" You are engaged," he declared. " Go out and hire a typewriter and bring it here in a cab. You can start at once, I hope? "

" This minute," Aaron agreed, his voice breaking with excitement.

Maraton passed him money and took them both to the door.

" Tell me about to-night? " Julia asked. " Will you go to the Clarion? Shall you speak? "

Maraton shook his head.

" No. I have written to the men whom I am anxious to meet here, and asked them to come to me. I should prefer not to speak at all until I go to Manchester. I have plans, but I must not speak of them for the moment."

" I had hoped so to hear you speak to-night," she murmured, and her face fell.

They stood together at the door and looked out across the green tree-tops towards the city.

" The time has gone by for speeches," he said quietly. " Perhaps before very long you may hear greater things than words."

They hurried off — Julia to the factory, Aaron to a typewriting depot in New Oxford Street. At the corner of the Square they parted.

" Are you satisfied? " she asked.

His face was all aglow.

" Satisfied! Julia, you told me nothing! He is wonderful — splendid! "

She climbed on to a 'bus with a little smile upon her lips. The long day's work before her seemed like a holiday task. Then she laughed softly as she found herself repeating her brother's fervid words:

" Maraton has come! "

CHAPTER VI

Maraton spent three hours and a half that morning in conclave with the committee appointed for his reception, and for that three hours and a half he was profoundly bored. Every one had a good deal to say except Richard Graveling, who sat at the end of the table with folded arms and a scowl upon his face. The only other man who scarcely opened his lips during the entire time, was Maraton himself. Peter Dale, Labour Member for Newcastle, was the first to make a direct appeal. He was a stalwart, grim-looking man, with heavy grey eyebrows and grey beard. He had been a Member of Parliament for some years and was looked upon as the practical leader of his party.

" We've heard a lot of you, Mr. Maraton," he declared, " of your fine fighting methods and of your gift of speech. We'll hear more of that, I hope, at Manchester. We are, so to speak, strangers as yet, but there's one thing I will say for you, and that is that you're a good listener. You've heard all that we've got to say and you've scarcely made a remark. You won't object to my saying that we're expecting something from you in the way of initiative, not to say leadership? "

Maraton glanced down the table. There were five men seated there, and, a little apart from all of them,

David Ross, who had refused to be shaken off. Excepting him only, they were well-fed and substantial looking men. Maraton had studied them carefully through half-closed eyes during all the time of their meeting, and the more he had studied them, the more disappointed he had become. There was not one of them with the eyes of a dreamer. There was not one of them who appeared capable of dealing with any subject save from his own absolutely material and practical point of view.

Maraton from the first had felt a seal laid upon his lips. Now, when the time had come for him to speak, he did so with hesitation, almost with reluctance.

"As yet," he began, "there is very little for me to talk about. You are, I understand, you five, a committee appointed by the Labour Party to confer with me as to the best means of promulgating our beliefs. You have each told me your views. You would each, apparently, like me to devote myself to your particular district for the purpose of propagating a strike which shall result in a trifling increase of wages."

"And a coal strike, I say," Peter Dale interrupted, "is the logical first course. We've been threatening it for two years and it's time we brought it off. I can answer for the miners of the north country. We have two hundred and seventy thousand pounds laid by and the Unions are spoiling for a fight. Another eighteen-pence would make life a different thing for some of our pitmen. And the masters can afford it, too. Sixteen and a half per cent is the average dividend on the largest collieries around us."

A small man, with gimlet-like black eyes and a heavy moustache, at which he had been tugging nervously during Peter Dale's remarks, plunged into the discussion. His name was Abraham Weavel and he came from Sheffield.

"Coal's all very well," he declared, "but I speak for the ironfounders. There's orders enough in Leeds and Sheffield to keep the furnaces ablaze for two years, and the masters minting money at it. Our wages ain't to be compared with the miners. We've twenty thousand in Sheffield that aren't drawing twenty-five shillings a week and they're about fed up with it. We've our Unions, too, and money to spare, and I tell you they're beginning to ask what's the use of sending a Labour Member to Parliament and having nothing come of it."

A grey-whiskered man, who had the look of a preacher, struck the table before him with a sudden vigour.

"You remember who I am, Mr. Maraton? My name's Borden — Samuel Borden — and I am from the Potteries. It's all very well for Weavel and Dale there to talk, but there's no labour on God's earth so underpaid as the china and glass worker. We may not have the money saved — that's simply because it takes my people all they can do to keep from starvation. I've figures here that'll prove what I say. I'll go so far as this — there isn't a worse paid industry than mine in the United Kingdom."

There was a moment's silence. Abraham Weavel

leaned back in his chair and yawned. Peter Dale made a grimace of dissent. Maraton turned to one of the little company who as yet had scarcely opened his lips — a thin, ascetic-looking, middle-aged man, who wore gold spectacles, and who had an air of refinement which was certainly not shared by any of the others.

"And you, Mr. Culvain," he enquired, "you represent no particular industry, I believe? You were a journalist, were you not, before you entered Parliament?"

"I was and am a journalist," Culvain assented. "Since you have asked my opinion, I must confess that I am all for more peaceful methods. These Labour troubles which inconvenience and bring loss upon the community, do harm to our cause. I am in favour of a vigorous course of platform education through all the country districts of England. I think that the principles of Socialism are not properly understood by the working classes."

"If one might make a comment upon all that you have said," Maraton remarked, "I might point out to you that there is a certain selfishness in your individual suggestions. Three of you are in favour of a gigantic strike, each in his own constituency. Mr. Culvain, who is a writer and an orator, prefers the methods which appeal most to him. Yet even these strikes which you propose are puny affairs. You want to wage war for the sake of a few shillings. We ought to fight, if at all, for a greater and more splendid principle. It isn't a shilling or two more a week that the people want. It's a share — a share to which they are, without the shadow of a doubt, entitled — in the direct product of their labour."

" That's sound enough," Peter Dale admitted. " How are you going to get it? "

" You ask for too much," Weavel observed, " and you get nothing."

" It is never wise," Culvain suggested quietly, " to have the public against one."

Maraton rose a little abruptly to his feet. He had the air of one eager to dismiss the subject.

" Gentlemen," he announced, " I've heard your views. In a few days' time you shall hear mine. Only let me tell you this. To me you all seem to be working and thinking on very narrow lines. Your object seems to be the securing of small individual benefits for your individual constituents. I think that if we get to work together in this country, there must be something more national in our aspirations. That is all I have to say for the present. As I think you know, I intend to make a pronouncement of my own views at Manchester."

They all took their leave a little later. Maraton himself saw them out and watched them across the Square. Somehow or other, his depression had visibly increased as he turned away. He had come into contact lately, on the other side of the world, with a different order of person — men and women, too, passionately, strenuously in earnest. They were well-fed, prosperous individuals, these whom he had just dismissed. Their politics were their business, their position as Members of Parliament a source of unmixed joy to all of them; hard-headed

men, very likely, good each in his own department;
beyond that, nothing.

He returned presently to his study, where Aaron
was already at work, typing letters.

"So that is your committee of Labour Members,"
Maraton remarked, throwing himself into an easy
chair.

Aaron looked up.

"They are all sound men," he declared. "Peter
Dale, too, is a fine speaker."

Maraton sighed.

"Yet it isn't from them," he said quietly, "that
I can take a mandate. I must go to the people. I
couldn't even talk to them to-day. I couldn't take
them into my confidence. I couldn't show them the
things I have seen perhaps only in my dreams. I
don't suppose they would have listened. . . . How
many more letters, Aaron?"

"Thirty-seven, sir."

Maraton rose to his feet.

"I shall walk for an hour or so," he announced.
"Get them ready for me to sign when I come in.
Have you a home, young man?"

"None, sir," Aaron admitted.

"Excellent!" Maraton declared cheerfully.
"These people with homes lose sight of the real
thing. What do you think of your Labour Members, honestly, Aaron? Ah, I can see that they have
been little gods to you! Little tin gods, I am afraid,
Aaron. Do they know what it is to go hungry, I
wonder? Not often! . . . Get on with your letters.
I am going out."

Maraton walked to the Park and sat down underneath the trees. There were a fair number of people about, notwithstanding the hot weather, and very soon he recognised Lady Elisabeth. She was walking back and forth along one of the side-walks, with a little, fussy woman, golden-haired, and wearing a gown of the brightest blue. Maraton watched them, at first idly and then with interest. Lady Elisabeth, in her cool muslin gown and simple hat, seemed to be moving in a world of her own, into which her companion's chatter but rarely penetrated. She walked with a slow and delicate grace, not without a characteristic touch of languor. Once or twice she looked around her — one might almost have imagined that she was seeking escape from her companion — and on one of these occasions her eyes met Maraton's. She stopped short. They were within a few feet of one another, and Maraton rose to his feet. She lowered her parasol and held out her hand.

"Only a very short time ago," she told him, "I was wondering what you were doing. You know that my uncle is expecting to see or hear from you this afternoon?"

"I know," he admitted. "To tell you the truth, I came out here to think. I could not quite make up my mind what to say to him."

"It is strange that we should meet here," she continued, "when Mr. Foley was talking to me about you for so long this morning. He wished that he had laid more emphasis upon the fact that your coming to us at Lyndwood committed you to nothing. No one is the worse off for hearing every point of

view, is he? My uncle will feel so much happier if
he really has had the opportunity of having a long,
uninterrupted talk with you."

Maraton smiled pleasantly. They were standing
in a crowded part of the walk and almost uncon-
sciously they commenced to move slowly along together. Lady Elisabeth turned to her companion.

" You must let me introduce Mr. Maraton to you,"
she said. " This is Mr. Maraton — Mrs. Bollington-Watts."

The little woman leaned forward and looked at
Maraton with undisguised curiosity.

" Forgive my starting at your name, won't you,
Mr. Maraton? " she began. " It is uncommon, isn't
it, and I'm only just over from the States. I dare
say you read about all those awful doings in Chicago."

Maraton, without direct reply, inclined his head.
Mrs. Bollington-Watts continued volubly.

" My brother is a judge out in Chicago. It was
he who signed the warrant for Maraton's arrest. I'm
afraid our people are getting much too scared, nowadays, about that sort of thing. We don't seem
to be able to enforce our laws like you do over here.
They are all saying now that it ought to have been
served and the man shot if there had been any resist-
ance."

" In which case," Maraton remarked, " I should
not have had the pleasure of making your acquaintance, Mrs. Bollington-Watts."

She stared at him for a moment, speechless
through sheer lack of comprehension. Then she

glanced at Lady Elisabeth and the truth dawned upon her. It was more than she could grapple with at first, however.

"You? But Lady Elisabeth —? But you, Mr. Maraton — are you really the man who mur — who was associated with all that trouble in Chicago?"

"I am, without a doubt, the man," Maraton assented cheerfully. "I am an enemy of your class, Mrs. Bollington-Watts. Your husband is the steel millionaire, isn't he? And I am also a Socialist of the most militant and modern type. Nevertheless, I can assure you, for these few moments you are perfectly safe."

Mrs. Bollington-Watts drew a little breath. The remarkable adaptability of her race came to her rescue; her point of view swung round.

"Why," she declared, "I have never been so interested in my life. This is perfectly thrilling. Mr. Maraton, I am having a few friends come in to-morrow evening. I should dearly love to give them a surprise. Couldn't you just drop in for an hour? Or, better still, if you could dine? I have taken Lenchester House for a year. My, it would be good to see their faces!"

Maraton shook his head.

"Thank you very much, Mrs. Bollington-Watts," he said, "but my visit to England is one of business only. To be frank with you, I have no social existence, nor any desire to cultivate one."

"But you know Lady Elisabeth," the little woman protested.

"I have the honour of knowing Lady Elisabeth

incidentally," Maraton replied. "If you will excuse
me now —"

Mrs. Bollington-Watts turned aside to talk vigorously to a passer-by. Lady Elisabeth laid her hand
upon his arm.

"Mr. Maraton," she said softly, "do make up
your mind. Please come to Lyndwood."

Her blue eyes were raised to his, fearlessly, appeal-
ingly. Maraton was more than ever conscious of
the delicate perfection of her person, her clear skin,
her silky brown hair. She was something new to
him in her sex. He knew quite well that a request
from her was an unusual thing.

"I will come, Lady Elisabeth," he promised
gravely. "Beyond that, of course, I can say nothing. But I will come to Lyndwood."

The slight anxiety passed from her face like a
cloud. Her smile was positively brilliant.

"It is charming of you," she whispered.

Mrs. Bollington-Watts was once more free and
by their side. They moved on to the corner and
Maraton was on the point of taking his leave. Just
at that moment Mrs. Bollington-Watts gave a little
cry of amazement. A coach was drawn up by the
side of the path, and a young man who was driving
it, was looking down at them. Mrs. Bollington-
Watts stopped and waved her hand at him almost
frantically.

"Why, it's Freddy Lawes!" she exclaimed.
"Why, Freddy, what on earth are you doing here?
If this isn't a surprise! They told me you never
moved from Paris, and I thought I'd have to come

right over there to see you. . . . Well, I declare!
Freddy! — why, Freddy, what's the matter? "

The words of Mrs. Bollington-Watts seemed as
though they had been spoken into empty air. The
young man was leaning forward in his place, the
reins loosely held in his hand, and a groom was
already upon the path, recovering the whip which
had slipped from his fingers. His eyes were fixed
not upon Mrs. Bollington-Watts nor upon Lady
Elisabeth, but upon Maraton. He was a young man
of harmless and commonplace appearance but his
features were at that moment transformed. His
mouth was strained and quivering, his eyes were lit
with something very much like horror. Some words
certainly left his lips, but they did not carry to the
hearing of any one of those three people. He looked
at Maraton with the fierce, terrified intentness of
one who looks upon a spectre!

CHAPTER VII

Mrs. Bollington-Watts' shrill voice once more broke the silence, which, although it was a matter of seconds only, was not without a certain peculiar dramatic quality.

"Say, what's wrong with you, Freddy? You don't think I'm a ghost, do you? Can't you come down and talk?"

The spell, whatever it may have been, had passed. The young man lifted his hat and leaned over the side of the coach.

"I won't get down just now, Amy," he said. "Tell me where you are and I'll come and see you. How's Richard?"

Maraton, obeying a gesture from Lady Elisabeth, moved away with her, leaving Mrs. Bollington-Watts absorbed in a flood of family questions and answers.

"Come back with me now, won't you?" she asked, a little abruptly. "My uncle is restless and unwell this afternoon, and it will perhaps relieve him to have your decision."

"What about Mrs. Bollington-Watts?"

Lady Elisabeth glanced at him for a moment. Her eyebrows were slightly lifted.

"If you can bear to lose her, I'm sure I can. She is really rather a dear person but she is very intense. She will meet a crowd of people she knows, directly, and quite forget that we have slipped away. Shall we go down Birdcage Walk, or if you are in a hurry, perhaps you would prefer a taxi?"

He shook his head.

"I prefer to walk."

He did not at first prove a very entertaining companion. They proceeded for some distance almost in silence.

"If I were a curious person," Lady Elisabeth remarked, "I should certainly be puzzling my brain as to what there could have been about that very frivolous young man to call such an expression into your face. And how terrified he was to see you!"

Maraton smiled grimly.

"You have observation, I perceive, Lady Elisabeth."

"Powers of observation but no curiosity, thank goodness," Lady Elisabeth declared. "Perhaps that is just as well, for I can see that you are going to turn out to be a very mysterious person."

"In some respects I believe that I am," he assented equably. "My peculiar beliefs are responsible for a good deal, you see — and certain circumstances. . . . But tell me — we have both agreed to be frank — why have you changed your attitude towards me so completely? I scarcely dared to hope even for your recognition this morning."

She was suddenly thoughtful.

"That was the very question I was asking myself when we crossed the street just now," she remarked, with a faint smile.

Maraton was conscious of a curious and undefined

sense of pleasure in her words. In the act of crossing he had held her arm for a few moments, and though her assent to his physical guidance had been purely negative, there was yet something about it which had given him a vague pleasure. Instinctively he knew that she was of the order of women to whom the merest touch from a man whom they disliked would have been torture.

" I think," she went on, " that it is because I am trying to adopt my uncle's point of view towards you."

" And what is your uncle's point of view? "

" He believes you," she declared, " to be a very dangerous person, a rabid enthusiast with brains and also stability — the most difficult order of person in the world to deal with."

" Anything else? "

" He believes you," she continued, " to be harmless enough at a wholesome period of our country's history. Just now, he told me yesterday, that he considered it was within your power to bring something very much like ruin upon the country."

Maraton was silent. He felt singularly indisposed for argument. Every condition of life just then seemed too pleasant. They were walking in the shade, and a soft west wind was rustling in the trees above their heads.

" There are, after all," she said, " so many happy people in the world. Is it worth while to drag down the pillars, to bring so much misery into the world for the sake of a dream? "

" I am no dreamer," he insisted quietly. " It is possible to make absolute laws for the future with the same precision as one can extract examples from the history of the past."

"But human nature," she objected, "is always a shifting quality."

"Only in detail. The heart and lungs of it are the same in all ages."

They crossed the road and turned into St. James's Park. He paused for a moment to look at the front of Buckingham Palace.

"A hateful sight to you, of course," she murmured.

"Not in the least," he assured her. "On the contrary, I think that the actual government of this country is wonderful. I suppose my creed of life would command a halter from any one who heard it, but I raise my hat always to your King."

"It is going to take me ages," she sighed, "to understand you."

"I will supply you with the necessary signposts," he promised. "Perhaps you will find then that the task will become almost too easy. For me I am afraid it will prove too short."

She turned her head and looked at him curiously. There was something provocative in the curl of her lips and in her monosyllabic question.

"Why?"

"Because when you have arrived at a complete understanding," he declared, "I fear we shall have reached the parting of our ways."

She looked steadfastly ahead.

"Wouldn't that rather rest with you?" she asked.

They passed a flower-barrow, wonderfully laden, and she half stopped with a little exclamation.

"Oh, I must have some of those white roses!" she begged. "They fit in at this moment with one of my only superstitions."

He bought her a great handful. She held them in both hands and gave him her parasol to carry.

"Mine is an inherited superstition, so I will not be ashamed of it," she told him. "We have always believed that white roses bring happiness, especially if they come accidentally at a critical moment."

He glanced behind at the retreating figure of the flower woman.

"If happiness is so easily purchased," he said, "what a pity it is that I did not buy the barrowful!"

"It isn't a matter of quantity at all," she assured him. "One blossom would have been enough and you were really frightfully extravagant."

She drifted into silence. They were walking eastwards now, and before them was the great yellow haze which hung over the sun-enveloped city, a haze which stretched across the whole arc of the heavens, and underneath which were toiling the millions to whom his life was consecrated. For a moment the grim inappropriateness of these hours struck him with a pang of remorse. He felt almost like a traitor to be walking with this slim, beautiful girl whose face was hidden from him now in the mass of white blossoms. And then his sense of proportion came to the rescue. He knew that he had but one desire — to work out his ends by the most effective means. It did not even disturb him to reflect that for the first time for many years he had found pleasure in what was merely an interlude.

"We turn here," she directed. "You see, we are close to home now. My uncle will be so glad to see you, Mr. Maraton, and I cannot tell you how delighted I am that you are coming to Lyndwood."

"I only hope," he said a little gravely, "that your uncle will not expect too much from my coming. It seems churlish to refuse, and even though our views are as far apart as the poles, I know that your uncle means well."

She smiled at him delightfully.

"I refuse to be depressed even by your solemn looks," she declared. "It is my twenty-fourth birthday to-day and I am still young enough to cling to my optimism."

"Your birthday," he remarked. "I should have brought you an offering."

She held up the roses.

"Nothing in the world," she assured him softly, "could have given me more pleasure than these. Now I am going to take you first into a little den where you will not be disturbed, and then fetch my uncle," she added, as they passed into the house. "I shall pray for your mutual conversion. You won't mind a very feminine room, will you? Just now there are certain to be callers at any moment, and my uncle's rooms are liable to all manner of intrusions."

She threw open the door and ushered him into what seemed indeed to be a little fairy chamber, a chamber with yellow walls and yellow rug, white furniture, oddments of china and photographs, silver-grey etchings, water-colour landscapes, piles of books and

magazines.   On a small table stood a yellow Sèvres
vase, full of roses.

"It's a horrible place for a man to sit in," she
said, looking around her.   "You must take that
wicker chair and throw away as many cushions as
you like.   Now I am going to fetch my uncle, and
remember, please," she concluded, looking back at
him from the door, "if I have seemed frivolous this
morning, I am not always so.   More than anything
I am looking forward, down at Lyndwood, to have
you, if you will, talk to me seriously."

"Shall I dare to argue with you, I wonder?" he
asked.

She smiled at him.

"Why not?   A matter of courage?"

"The bravest person in the world," he declared,
"remembers always that little proverb about dis-
cretion."

CHAPTER VIII

The conference between Mr. Foley and Maraton was brief enough. The former arrived a few moments after his niece's departure.

"I have come," Maraton announced, as they shook hands, "to accept your invitation to Lyndwood. You understand, I am sure, that that commits me to nothing?"

Mr. Foley's expression was one of intense relief.

"Naturally," he replied. "I quite understand that. I am delighted to think that you are coming at all. May I ask whether you have conferred with your friends about the matter?"

Maraton shook his head.

"I have not even mentioned it to them. I met what I understand to be a committee of the Labour Party this morning — a Mr. Dale, Abraham Weavel, Culvain, Samuel Borden and David Ross. Those were the names so far as I can remember. I did not mention my proposed visit to you at all. There seemed to me to be no necessity. I am subject to no one here."

Mr. Foley smiled.

"They won't like it," he declared frankly.

"Their liking or disliking it will not affect the situation in the least," Maraton assured him. "I shall come, without a doubt. It will interest me to hear what you have to say, although unfortunately I cannot hold out the slightest hope —"

"That is entirely understood," Mr. Foley interrupted. "Now how will you come? Lyndwood Park is just sixty miles from London. To-day is Friday, isn't it? I shall motor down there sometime to-morrow. Why won't you come down with me?"

Maraton shook his head.

"If you will excuse me," he said, "I will not fix any time definitely. I have a good deal of correspondence still to attend to, and there is one little matter which might keep me in town till the afternoon."

"Let me send a car up for you," Mr. Foley suggested.

"Thank you," Maraton replied, "I have already hired one for a time."

"Then come just at what time suits you," Mr. Foley begged,— "the sooner the better, of course. Apart from that, I shall be about the place all day."

In Buckingham Gate, Maraton came slowly to a standstill. The coach which he had seen in the Park an hour ago was drawn up in front of a large hotel. The young man who was driving it had just come down the steps and was drawing on his gloves. They met almost face to face.

"Am I to speak to you?" the young man asked.

"You had better," Maraton assented. "Tell me what you are doing here?"

"I was bored with Paris," the young man answered.

"My friends were all coming here. I had no idea that we were likely to meet."

Maraton looked at him thoughtfully. As they stood face to face at that moment, there was a certain strange likeness between them, a likeness of the husk only.

"I do not wish to interfere with your movements," Maraton said calmly. "Where you are is nothing to me. I proposed that you should remain away from London simply because I fancied that it would be easier for you to observe the conditions which exist between us. So long as you remember them, however, your whereabouts are indifferent to me."

The young man laughed a little nervously.

"You're not over-cordial!"

Maraton shrugged his shoulders.

"The world in which you live," he remarked, "is a training school, I suppose, for false sentiment. The slight kinship that there is between us is of no account to me. I simply remind you once more that it is to your advantage to neither know me or to know of me. Remember that, and it may be London or Paris or New York — wherever you choose."

The young man remounted his coach, and Maraton passed on. He walked without a pause to the square in which his house was situated. Here he found Aaron hard at work and, sitting down at once, he began to sign his letters.

"No end of people have been here," Aaron announced. "I have got rid of them all."

"Good!" Maraton said shortly. "By-the-bye, Aaron, isn't there a meeting to-night at the Clarion?"

Aaron nodded.

"David Ross is going to speak. He can move them when he starts. My sister is going to call here for me, and I thought if you didn't want me, I'd like to go."

"We will all go together," Maraton decided. "We can creep in somewhere at the back, I suppose. I want to hear how they do it."

The young man's face lit up with joy.

"There's sure to be lots of people there," he declared, "but we can find a seat at the back quite easily."

"What's it all about?" Maraton asked.

"The proposed boiler-maker's strike," Aaron replied eagerly. "The meeting is really a meeting of the workpeople at Boulding's. But are you sure you won't go on the platform, sir?"

Maraton shook his head.

"That is just what I don't want to do. I want to see what these meetings are like, what sort of arguments are used, what the spirit of the people is, if I can. That is what I would really like to find out, Aaron — the spirit of the people."

The young man looked up from his work. He was greatly changed during the last few hours. He was wearing a new suit of clothes and clean linen; his hair had been cut, his face shaved. Yet in some respects he was unaltered. His eyes still burned in their sockets, his lips still quivered.

"I will tell you what the people are like," he said. "They are like dumb animals, like sheep. They have suffered so long and so much that their nerve power is numbed. They lack will, they lack initiative. They are narrowed down to a daily life which makes of them something little different from an animal. Yet they can be roused. David Ross himself has done it, done it like none of those other M.P.'s. I have seen him carried out of himself. He is like some of these Welshmen and Salvation Army people when they're half drunk with religion — the words seem to come to them in a stream. That's how David Ross is sometimes. But it isn't often any one can get at them."

"That is what they say over on the other side," he remarked softly.

"They've got to be in such a state," Aaron continued, "that nothing appeals to them except some material benefit; a pipe of tobacco or a mug of beer will stir them more than any dream of freedom. Oh! it's sad to see them, often. I used to go to the gates at the shipbuilding yard and watch them come out. Ten years about does for a man there. It's a short spell."

Maraton sighed.

"Yet they endure," he muttered to himself.

"Yet they endure," Aaron echoed. "Can't you see why? Don't you know that it is because they haven't heard the word — the one great word? That's what they're waiting for — for the prophet to open their eyes and lead them out of the wilderness. Only just at first it may be that even his voice will sound in vain. You are sure you won't mind my sister coming with us, sir? She is so interested and they all know her down there."

" It will be an advantage to have your sister,"
Maraton replied. " There are many things I should
like to ask her."

CHAPTER IX

At twenty minutes past eight, Maraton, with his two companions, reached the building in which the meeting was to take place — a plain, unimposing-looking edifice, built for a chapel, whitewashed inside, but with plastered walls and bare floors. The room was almost packed, and it was with some difficulty that they found seats in the back row. David Ross, Peter Dale and Graveling occupied chairs on the platform. Between them, Julia and Aaron kept Maraton informed as to the identity of each newcomer.

"That's Mr. Docker, who is going to speak now," the latter declared in an excited whisper. "He is a fighting man. It's he who has manœuvred this strike, they say. Now he's off."

Mr. Docker has risen to his feet amidst a little hoarse cheering. For a quarter of an hour or more, he spoke fluently and convincingly. It appeared from his statements that boiler-makers were the worst paid mechanics in the universe, that it was he who had discovered this, that it was he who had drawn up the ultimatum which had been presented to the masters and refused. His peroration was friendly but appealing.

"There are some amongst Boulding's people," he wound up, "who, they tell me, are satisfied. If so, I hope they are not here. They haven't any place

here. To them I would say — ' If you are satisfied
with twenty-four shillings a week, well, don't waste a
penny in subscribing to the Unions, but go and spend
your twenty-four shillings a week and live on it and
enjoy it, and get fat on it if you can.' But to those
others I want to say that it's just as easy to get
twenty-eight. The masters don't want you to strike
just now. You only have to be firm and you can get
what's fair and right."

A man rose up in the hall.

" Is it true," he asked, " that Boulding's won't pay
the advance? — that they are going to close the doors
to-morrow if we insist upon it? "

" It is true," Mr. Docker answered. " Are you
afraid of that? "

The man hesitated.

" I don't know as ' afraid ' is exactly the word,"
he said, " but I don't fancy being out of work for a
month or so, and perhaps losing my job at the end of
it. Fifteen bob a week from the Union won't keep
my little lot."

There was a murmur of applause. Docker pointed
with threatening forefinger to the man who had just
sat down.

" It's the likes of him," he declared, " who keep
down wages, who make slaves of us! The likes of
him, who haven't the pluck to ask for what they might
get at any time! "

He plunged into facts and figures, and Maraton
more than once yawned. He seemed to find more
interest in watching the faces of the audience than in
listening to the stock arguments which were being

thrown at their heads. A little cloud of tobacco smoke hung about the room. There were few women present, and most of the men were smoking. On the whole they were a very earnest gathering. There were very few there who were not deeply interested. Julia was listening to every word, her head resting upon her hand, her lips a little parted, her eyes full of smouldering fires. At the end of Docker's speech, one of the Union officials got up on his feet. It was for the men themselves to decide, he said. They had subscribed the money; it was for them to say whether it should be used. Was the moment propitious for a blow on behalf of their rights? If they thought so, then let it be war. If they asked for his advice, they were welcome to it. His advice was to fight. The masters had refused their reasonable ultimatum. Let the masters try and carry out their contracts without work people! That was his way of looking at it.

There was a rumble of applause. The militants were certainly in the majority. A man got up from one of the front rows.

" I propose," he said, " that we strike to-morrow. They are working us as hard as they can in shifts on special jobs now, in case they should get left. Every hour we work makes it better for them. I say ' Strike! ' "

There was a thunder of applause. A ballot box was brought and placed on a table in front of the platform.

" They will strike," Aaron muttered,— " three thousand of them! Splendid! "

Maraton shook his head.

"It is piecemeal work, this. They do not understand."

"They do not understand what?" Julia asked him, turning her head swiftly.

He shrugged his shoulders.

"They will ask for five shillings a week more and get half-a-crown," he said. "Half-a-crown a week! What difference can it make? Do you know what Boulding's put on one side for distribution to their shareholders last year? — what they put to their reserve fund? Why, it was a fortune!"

A man from somewhere at the back of the hall climbed on to a seat to get a better view and suddenly pointed out Maraton to his neighbours. A little murmur arose from the vicinity. Some one mentioned his name. The cry was taken up from the other side of the hall.

"Maraton!"

"Maraton!"

Maraton sat back, frowning. The cries, however, became more insistent. The occupants of the platform were leaning forward towards him. The chairman rose to his feet and beckoned. With obvious reluctance, Maraton moved a few steps to the front. From the far corners of the ill-lit hall, white-faced men climbed on to the benches, peering through the cloud of smoke which hung almost like fog about the place. They saluted him in all manner of ways — with cat-calls, hurrahs, stamping of feet, clapping of hands. Maraton, who had climbed up on to the platform, was soon surrounded.

Dale held out his hand.

"Thought you weren't going to honour us here, Mr. Maraton," he remarked gruffly.

"I had not meant to," Maraton replied. "I came as one of the audience. I wanted to hear, to understand if I could."

Dale stretched out his hand.

"This is Mr. Docker," he said, performing the introduction. "Mr. Docker — Mr. Maraton."

"Come to support us, sir, I hope?" the former remarked.

"I came to listen," Maraton answered. "To tell you the truth, it's against my views, this, an individual strike."

They were calling to him now from the front. Mr. Docker's reply was inaudible.

"You'll have to say a few words," Dale insisted. "They'll never leave off until you do."

Maraton nodded and turned towards the audience. He stood looking down at them for a moment or two, without speech. Even after silence had been established he seemed to be at a loss as to exactly what to say. When at last he did speak, it was in an easy and conversational manner. There was no sign of the fire or the frenzy with which he had kindled the enthusiasms of the people of the United States.

"I find it rather hard to know exactly what to say to you," he began. "I am glad to be here and I have come to this country to work for you, if I may. But, you know, I have views of my own, and it isn't a very auspicious occasion for me to stand for the first time upon an English platform. I came as one of the audience to-night and I have listened to all that has been said. I don't think that I am in favour of your strike."

There was a murmur of wonder, mingled with discontent.

" Why not? " some one shouted from the back.

" Aye, why not? " a dozen voices echoed.

" I'll try and tell you, if you like," Maraton continued. " I didn't mean to say anything until after Manchester, but I'll tell you roughly what my scheme is. These individual strikes such as you're planning are just like pinpricks on the hide of an elephant. How many are there of you? A thousand, say? Well, you thousand may get a shilling or two a week more. It won't alter your condition of life. It won't do much for you, any way. You will have spent your money, and in a year or two the masters will be taking it out of you some other way. A strike such as you are proposing causes inconvenience — no more. I'd bigger things in my mind for you."

He hesitated for a moment as though uncertain, even now, whether to go on. Glancing around the hall, his eyes for a moment met Julia's. Something in her still face, the almost passionate enquiry of her wonderful eyes, seemed to decide him. He lifted up his hands, his voice grew in volume.

" Let me tell you what I want, then. Let me tell you the dream which others have had before me, which is laughed to scorn by the enemies of the people, but which grows in substance and shape. you by year. I want to teach you how to smash the individual capitalist. I want to teach you how to frame laws which will bring the wealth of this country into a new and saner distribution. I want to teach you the folly of the old ideas that because of the wretched conditions in which you live, the better educated man, the man better equipped mentally and physically for his job, must gather to himself the wealth and you must become his slaves. What do you suppose, in the course of three or four generations, produces men of different mental and physical calibre? I will tell you. The circumstances of their bringing-up, the life they have to lead, their education, their environment. What chance have you under present conditions? None! For very shame, as the years pass on, you operatives will be better paid. What will it amount to? A few shillings a week more, the same life, the same anxieties, the same daily grinding toil, brainless, machine-like, leading you nowhere because there isn't a way out. There will still remain your masters; there will still remain you, the men. Can't you see what it is that I am aiming at? I want to make a great machine of all the industries of this country. The man with the gift for figures will find himself in the office, and the man with lesser brain power will find himself before a machine. But the two will be working for one aim and one end. They will both be parts of the machine, and for their livelihood they will take what that machine produces, distributed in a scientific and exact ratio. It's co-operation over again, you say? Very well, call it that. Only I tell you why co-operation has failed up till now. It's because you've been in too much of a hurry. I am going to appeal to you presently, not for your own interests but in the interests of your children and your children's children, because the better days that are to come for you won't dawn yet awhile. It may be, even, that you will be called upon to make sacrifices, instead of finding yourselves better off. There are some great changes which time alone can govern."

" What about this strike? " some one shouted from the bottom of the hall.

" You are quite right, sir," Maraton replied swiftly. " I've wandered a little from my point. I think that the first thing I said to you was that this strike, if it took place, would be like the pinprick on an elephant's hide. I want to teach you how to stab ! "

There was a murmur of voices — approving this time, at any rate.

" Can't you see," Maraton continued, " that Society can easily deal with one strike at a time? That isn't the way to make yourself felt. What I want to see in this country is a simultaneous strike of wharfingers, dock labourers, railways, and all the means of communication; a strike which will stop the pulses of the nation, a strike which will cost hundreds of millions, a strike which may cost this country its place amongst the nations, but which will mark the dawn of new conditions. I'd put out your forge fires from Glasgow to Sheffield and Sheffield to London. I'd take the big risks — the rioting, the revolutions, the starvation, the misery that

will surely come. I'd do that for the sake of the
new nation which would start again where the old
one perished."

There was a sudden burst of applause. A little
thrill seemed to have found its way, like zig-zag
lightning, here and there amongst them. But there
were many who sat and smoked in stolid silence.
Maraton looked into their faces and sighed to himself. There were too many hungry people for his
mission.

"We are half starved," a man called from the
back of the hall. "My wage is a pound a week and
four children to keep. It's fine talk, yours, but it
won't feed 'em."

There was a murmur of sullen approval. Maraton's hand shot out, his finger quivered as it pointed
to the man.

"I don't blame you," he said, "but it's the cry
you've just raised which keeps you and a few other
millions exactly in the places you occupy. There are
many generations as yet unborn, to come from your
children and your children's children. Are they,
then, to suffer as you have suffered?"

There was a little stir at the back of the platform.
A tall, broad-shouldered man pushed his way through
to the front. His face was pitted with smallpox;
he had black, wiry hair; small, narrow eyes; a large,
brutal mouth. He took up his position in the middle
of the platform, ignoring Maraton altogether.

"Listen, lads," he began; "you are here to-night
to decide whether or not you want another half-
crown on to your wages. This man who has been

talking to you has done big things in America. I
know nothing about him and I'm not rightly sure
that I know what's at the back of his head. If he
is your friend, he's our friend, and we shall soon fall
into line, but to-night you're here to meet about that
half-crown. It's for you to say whether or no you'll
have it. We've saved the money for the fight, saved
it from your wages, got it with your sweat. You've
given up your beer for it — aye, and maybe your
baccy. We've saved the money and the time's come
to fight. All that he says "— jerking his elbow
towards Maraton — " sounds good enough. That'll
come in later. Are you for the strike? "

There was no doubt about the reply — a roar of
approving voices. Maraton smiled at them and
stepped down from the platform. For the moment
he was forgotten. Only Julia whispered passionately in his ear as they moved out of the place.

"You should have gone on. They didn't understand. They have waited so long, they could have
waited a little longer."

Maraton did not answer until they reached the
street. Then he stood a few steps in the background,
watching the people as they came out.

"I couldn't," he said simply. "I felt as though
I were offering stones for bread. The stones were
better, perhaps, but the cruelty was the same."

CHAPTER X

Maraton walked alone with Elisabeth on the following afternoon in the flower garden at Lyndwood. She was apologising for some unexpected additions to the number of their guests.

"Mother always forgets whom she has asked down for the week-end," she said, "and my uncle is far too sweet about it. I know that he wanted to have as much time as possible alone with you before Monday. It is on Monday you go to Manchester, isn't it?"

"On Monday," he answered, a little absently. "I have to make my bow to the democracy of your country in the evening."

"I wish I could make up my mind, Mr. Maraton," she continued, "whether you have come over here for good or for evil."

"For evil that good may come of it, I am afraid," he rejoined, "would be the kindest interpretation you could put upon my enterprise here."

"The *Spectator* calls you the Missionary of Unrest."

"The *Spectator*, I am afraid, will become more violent later on."

"Let us sit down here for a moment," she suggested, pointing to a seat. "You see, we are just at the top of this long pathway, and we get a view of the roses all the way down."

"It is very beautiful," he admitted,—"far too beautiful."

She raised her eyebrows.

"Too beautiful? Is that possible?"

"Without a doubt," he declared. "Too much beauty is as bad as too little."

"And why is that? Surely it must be good for one to be surrounded by inspiring things?"

"I am not sure that beauty does inspire anything except content," he answered, smiling. "I call this garden of yours, for instance, a most vicious place, a perfect lotus-eater's Paradise. Positively, I feel the energy slipping out of my bones as I sit here."

"Then you shall be chained to that seat," she threatened. "You will not be able to go to Manchester and make trouble, and my uncle will be able to sleep at nights."

"I feel that everything in life is slipping away from me," he protested. "I ought to be thinking over what I am going to say to your country people, and instead of that I am wondering whether there is anything more beautiful in the world than the blue haze over your meadows."

She laughed, and moved her parasol a little so that she could see him better.

"You know," she said, "my uncle declares that if only you could be taught to imbibe a little more of the real philosophy of living, you would become quite a desirable person."

"And what is the real philosophy of living?"

"Just now, with him, it is the *laissez faire*, the non-interference with the essential forces of life, especially the forces that concern other people," she explained.

He looked at her, a little startled. What instinct, he wondered, had led her to place her finger upon the one poison spot in his thoughts?

"I can see," he remarked, "that I have found my way into a dangerous neighbourhood."

She changed her position a little, so as to face him. Her blue eyes were lit with laughter, her lips mocked him. Usually reserved, she seemed at that moment to be inspired with an instinct which was something almost more than coquetry. She leaned a little towards him. The aloofness of her carriage and manner had suddenly disappeared. He was conscious of the perfection of her white muslin gown, of the shape of her neck, the delicate lines and grace of her slim young body.

"You shall be chained here," she repeated. "My uncle has a new theory of individualism. He thinks that if no one tried to improve anybody, the world would be so much more livable a place. Shall we sit at his feet?"

He shook his head.

"I am not brave," he said, "but I am at least discreet."

"Do you think that you are?" she asked him quietly. "Do you think that you are discreet in the sense of being wise? Are you sure that you are using your gifts for the best purpose, for yourself — and other people?"

"No one can be sure," he replied. "I only follow my star."

"Then are you sure that it is your star?"

"No one can ever mistake that," he declared. "Sometimes one may lose one's way, and one may even falter if the path is rugged. But the star remains."

She sighed. Her eyes seemed to have wandered away. He felt that it was a trick to avoid looking at him for the moment.

"I do not want you to go to Manchester on Monday in your present mood," she said. "I hate to think of you up there, the stormy petrel, the apostle of unrest and sedition. If I were a Roman woman, I think that I would poison you to-night at dinner-time."

"Quite an idea," he remarked. "I am not at all sure that our having become too civilised for crime is a healthy sign of the times."

"I do wish," she persisted, "that you would try and see things a little more humanly. My uncle is full of enthusiasms about you. You have had some conversation already, haven't you?"

"We talked for an hour after luncheon," Maraton admitted. "Your uncle's is a very sane point of view. I know just how he regards me — a sort of dangerous enthusiast, a firebrand with the knack of commanding attention. The worst of it is that when I am with him, he almost makes me feel like that myself."

She laughed.

"All men of genius," she declared, "must be im-

pressionable.   We ought to set ourselves to discover
your weak point."

He smiled at her with upraised eyebrows.   There
were times when he seemed to her like a boy.

" Haven't you discovered it? "

She made a little face and swung her parasol
around.   When she spoke again, she was very grave.

" Mr. Maraton," she begged, " please will you
promise that before you go away, you will talk to
me again for a few minutes? "

" It is a promise easily made! " he replied.

" But I mean seriously."

" I will talk to you at any time, anyhow you wish,"
he promised.

She rose to her feet then.

" For the present you have promised to play tennis," she reminded him.   " Please go and change
your things."

" I must have a yellow rosebud for my buttonhole," he begged.

She arranged it herself in his coat.   He laughed
as she swept aside a wisp of her hair which brushed
his cheek.

" What a picture for the photographic Press of
America! " he exclaimed.   " The anarchist of Chicago and the Prime Minister's niece! "

" What is an anarchist? " she asked him abruptly.

He opened the little iron gate which led out of the
garden.

" A sower of fire and destruction," he answered,
" a highly unpleasant person to meet when he's in
earnest."

She looked into his face for a moment with a wistfulness which was almost passionate.

"Please tell me at once, that you aren't —"

He pointed back to the garden.

"We have come out of the land of confessions. On this side of the gate I am your uncle's guest, and I mustn't be teased with questions."

"Before you go," she threatened, "I shall take you back into the rose-garden."

From their wicker chairs drawn under a great cedar tree, Mr. Foley and Lord Armley, perhaps the most distinguished of his colleagues, watched the slow approach of the two from the flower gardens. Lord Armley, who had only arrived during the last half hour, was recovering from a fit of astonishment. He had just been told of his fellow guest.

"Granted, even, that the man is as dangerous as you say," he remarked, "it is certainly creating a new precedent for you to bring him into the bosom of your family. Is it conversion, bribery, or poison that you have in your thoughts?"

"Influence, if possible," Mr. Foley answered. "Somehow or other, I have always detected in his writing a vein of common sense."

"What the dickens is common sense!" Lord Armley growled.

"Shall I say a sense of the fitness of things?" the Prime Minister replied,— "a sense of proportion, perhaps? Notwithstanding his extraordinary speeches in America, I believe that to some extent Maraton possesses it. Anyhow, it seemed to me to be worth trying. One couldn't face the idea of letting him go up north just now without making an effort."

"Things are really serious there," Lord Armley muttered.

"Worse than any of us know," Mr. Foley agreed. "If you hadn't been coming here, I should have sent for you last night. The French Ambassador was with me for an hour after dinner."

"No fresh trouble?"

"It was a general conversation, but his visit had its purpose — a very definite and threatening purpose, too. I do not blame France. We are under great obligations to her already. Half her fleet is there to watch over our possessions. She naturally must be sure of her *quid pro quo*. Everywhere, all over the Continent, the idea seems to be spreading that we are going to be plunged into what really amounts to a civil war. The coming of Maraton has strengthened the people's belief. A country without the sinews of movement, a country in which the working classes laid down their tools, a country whose forges had flickered out and whose railroad tracks were deserted, would simply be the helpless prey of any country who cared to pay off old scores."

Lord Armley was looking curiously at the approaching couple.

"Never saw a man," he said, half to himself, "who looked the part so little. Fellow must be well-bred, Foley."

Mr. Foley nodded.

"No one knows who his people were. It doesn't really matter, does it? Accident has made him a gentleman — accident or fate. Perhaps that is why he has gained such an ascendency over the people. The working classes of the country are most of them sick of their own Labour Members. The practical men can see no further than their noses, and the theorists are too far above their heads. Maraton is the only one who seems to understand. You must have a talk with him, Armley."

Lady Elisabeth, with a little smile, had turned towards the tennis courts, and Maraton came on alone. Mr. Foley turned to his companion.

" Armley," he said, " this is Mr. Maraton — Lord Armley."

" It is a pleasure to meet you, Mr. Maraton," Lord Armley declared, as the two men shook hands, " in such peaceful surroundings. The Press over here has not been too kind to you. Our ideas of your personality are rather based, I am afraid, upon the *Punch* caricature. You've seen it, perhaps? "

Maraton's eyes lit up with mirth.

" Excellent! " he observed. " I have had one framed."

" He is standing," Lord Armley continued, turning to Mr. Foley, " on the topmost of three tubs, his hair flying in the wind, his mouth open to about twice its normal size, with fire and smoke coming out of it. And below, a multitude! It is a splendid caricature. They tell me, Mr. Maraton, that it is your intention to kindle the fires in England, too."

Maraton was suddenly grave.

" Lord Armley," he said, " all the world speaks of me as an apostle of destruction and death. It is because they see a very little distance. In my own thoughts, if ever I do think of myself, it is as a builder, not as a destroyer, that I picture myself. Only in this world, as in any other, one must destroy first to build upon a sound foundation."

"Good reasoning, sir," Lord Armley replied, "only one should be very sure, before one destroys, that the new order of things will be worthy of the sacrifice."

"After dinner," Mr. Foley remarked, as he lit a cigarette, "we are going to talk. At present, Maraton is under a solemn promise to play tennis."

Maraton looked towards the house.

"If I might be allowed," he said, "I will go and put on my flannels. Lady Elisabeth is making up a set, I think."

He turned towards the house. The two men stood watching him.

"Is he to be bought?" Lord Armley asked, in a low tone.

Mr. Foley shook his head.

"Not with money or place," he answered thoughtfully.

"There isn't a man breathing who hasn't his price, if you could only discover what it is," Lord Armley declared, as he took a cigarette from his case and lit it.

"A truism, my friend," Mr. Foley admitted, "which I have always considered a little nebulous. However, we shall see. We have a few hours' respite, at any rate."

CHAPTER XI

Lady Grenside's hospitable instincts were unquenchable. The small house-party to which her brother had reluctantly consented had grown by odd couples until the house was more than half full. Twenty-two people sat down to dinner that night. For the first time in his life, Mr. Foley interfered with the arrangement of the table. He sought his sister out just as the dressing-bell rang.

"My dear Catharine," he asked, a little reprovingly, "was it necessary to have such a crowd here — at any rate until after Monday? You know that I don't interfere as a rule, but there were special reasons why I wanted to be as quiet as possible until after Maraton had left."

Lady Grenside's expression was delightfully apologetic. It conveyed, also, a sense of helplessness.

"What was I to do?" she demanded. "Most of these people were asked, or half asked, weeks ago, and I hate putting any one off. It is quite a weakness of mine, that. And I am sure, Stephen, there isn't a soul who could possibly object to Mr. Maraton. Personally, I think he is altogether charming, and so distinguished-looking. He has quite the air of being used to good society."

Mr. Foley's eyes lit with joyful appreciation of his sister's naïveté. Perhaps one reason why they got on so well together was because she was continually ministering to his sense of humour.

"It wasn't altogether that," he said, "but never mind. We can't send the people away now — that's certain. What I wanted to tell you was that Elisabeth must sit next Maraton to-night."

Lady Grenside was horrified.

"However could I explain such an arrangement to Jack Carton!" she protested. "Apart from a matter of precedence, you know that he is Elisabeth's declared admirer. It is perfectly certain that at a word of encouragement from her, he would propose. A most suitable match, too, in every way, and, you know, Elisabeth is beginning to be just a little anxiety to me. She is twenty-four, and girls marry so young, nowadays."

"Carton and she can make up for lost time later on," Mr. Foley insisted. "Maraton goes to-morrow. To-night I am relying upon Elisabeth to look after him. For some reason or other, they seem to get on together excellently." . . .

Lady Grenside took Lord Carton into one of the corners of her brother's quaint and delightful drawing-room, to explain the matter.

"My dear Jack," she began, "never be a politician."

"I like that!" the young man answered. "Lady Elisabeth has been talking to me for half an hour before dinner, trying to get me to interest myself in what she calls serious objects."

"Oh, it's all right, so far as the man is concerned!" Lady Grenside amended. "I was thinking of my own position. Only an hour ago, my brother comes to me and tells me that I am to send Elisabeth in to dinner to-night with — with whom do you think?"

"With me, I hope," the young man replied promptly, "only I don't know why he should interfere."

"With Mr. Maraton."

"What, the anarchist fellow?"

Lady Grenside nodded several times.

"I can't refuse Stephen in his own house," she said, "and Mr. Maraton is leaving to-morrow."

The young man sighed.

"He is just one of those thoughtful chaps with plenty of gas, that Elisabeth likes to talk to," he complained. "Never mind, it's got to be put up with, I suppose."

"I am sending you in with Lily," Lady Grenside continued. "She'll keep you amused. Only I felt that I must explain."

"I can't think what the fellow's doing here, anyhow," Carton remarked discontentedly. "A few generations ago we should have hung him."

"Hush!" Lady Grenside whispered. "Don't let Elisabeth hear you talk like that. Here she comes. I wonder —"

Lady Grenside stopped short. She was looking steadily at her daughter and her expression of doubt had a genuine impulse behind it. Carton was not so reticent.

"By Jove, she does look stunning!" he murmured.

Elisabeth, who seldom wore colours, was dressed in blue, with a necklace of turquoises. On the threshold she paused to make some laughing rejoinder to a man who was holding open the door for her. Her eyes were brilliant, her face was full of animation. Lady Grenside's face darkened as the unseen man came into sight. It was Maraton.

" Never saw Elisabeth look so ripping," Carton repeated. " Just my luck, not to take her in."

" To-morrow night," Lady Grenside promised.

" That's all very well," Carton grumbled. " I wish she didn't look so thundering pleased with herself."

Lady Grenside leaned a little towards him.

" Elisabeth is a dear girl," she declared. " She is doing all this for her uncle's sake. Mr. Foley is very anxious indeed to conciliate this man, and Elisabeth is helping him. You know how keen she is on doing what she can in that way."

Carton nodded a little more hopefully. His eyes were fixed now upon Maraton.

" Can't think how the fellow learnt to turn himself out like that. I thought these sort of people dressed anyhow."

Lady Grenside shrugged her shoulders.

" I believe," she said, " that this man is full of queer contradictions. Some one once told me that he was enormously wealthy; that he had been to an English public school and changed his name out in America. Rubbish, I expect. . . . Run and find Lily, there's a dear boy. We are going in now."

Dinner was served at a round table, and a good

deal of the conversation was general. On Maraton's left hand, however, was a lady whose horror at his presence, concealed out of deference to her host, reduced her to stolid and unbending silence. Elisabeth, quickly aware of the fact, made swift atonement. While the others talked all around them of general subjects, she conversed with Maraton almost in whispers, lightly enough at first, but with an undernote of seriousness always there. Maraton would have been less than human if he had not been susceptible to the charm of her conversation.

"I cannot tell you," she declared, towards the end of the meal, "how much I am hoping from this brief visit of yours. I know you feel that our class has little feeling for the people whom you represent. If only I could convince you how wrong that idea is! Nothing has interested me so much as the different measures which have been brought in for the sake of the people. And my uncle, too — he is the kindest of men and very broad. He would go even further than he does, but for his colleagues."

"He goes a long way," Maraton reminded her, "when he asks me to his home; invites me — well, why should I not say it? — invites me to join his party."

"He is doing what he believes is sensible," she went on eagerly. "He is doing what I know is right. It is the best, the most splendid idea he has ever had. I think that if nothing comes of it," she added, leaning forward so that her eyes met his, "I think that if nothing comes of it, it will break my heart."

Maraton was a little more serious for a few minutes. She waited in some anxiety for him to speak. When he did so, she realised that there was a new gravity in his face and in his tone.

"Lady Elisabeth," he said, "I am afraid that there is very little hope of our coming to any agreement. You must remember that when I promised to come here —"

"Oh, I know that!" she interrupted. "Only I wish that we had a little longer time. You think that my interest in the people is an amateurish affair, half sentimental and half freakish, don't you? You were probably surprised to hear that I had ever read a volume of political economy in my life. But I have. I have studied things. I have read dozens and dozens of books on Sociology, and Socialism, and Syndicalism, and every conceivable subject that bears upon the relations between your class and ours, and I can't come to any but one conclusion. There is only one logical conclusion. Violent methods are useless. The betterment of the poor must come about gradually. If religion hadn't interfered, things would have been far better now, even."

He looked at her, a little startled.

"It seems strange to hear you say that," he remarked.

"Strange only because you will think of me as a dilettante," she replied swiftly. "I have some sort of a brain. I have thought of these matters, talked of them with my uncle, with many others whom even you would admit to be clever men. I, too, see that charity and charitable impulses have perhaps been

the greatest drawback of the day to a scientific betterment of the people.   I, too, want to see the thing
done by laws and not by impulses."

"You and how many more," he sighed, "and,
alas! this is an age of majorities.   People talk a
good deal.   I wonder how many of your hateful
middle class would give up a tithe of their luxuries
to add to the welfare of the others.   There isn't a
person breathing with so little real feeling for the
slaves of the world, as your middle-class manufacturer, your tradesman.   That is why, in the days to
come, he will be the person who is going to suffer
most."

Maraton was appealed to from across the table
with reference to some of the art treasures which
were reputed to have found their way from Italy
to New York.   He gave at once the information
required, speaking fluently and with the appreciative
air of a connoisseur, of many of the pictures which
were under discussion.   Soon afterwards, Lady
Grenside rose and the men drew up their chairs.
The evening papers had arrived and there was a
general air of seriousness.   Mr. Foley sent one to
Maraton, who glanced at the opening page upon
which his name was displayed in large type:

FIVE MILLION WORKERS WAIT FOR MARATON!

WHAT THE STRIKE MAY MEAN.

HOME SECRETARY LEAVES FOR MANCHESTER TO-MORROW.

ILLEGAL STRIKES BILL TO BE PROPOSED ON MONDAY.

Maraton only glanced at the paper and put it on one side. There was a little constraint. One or two who had not known of his identity were glancing curiously in his direction. Mr. Foley smiled at him pleasantly.

"You may drink your port without fear, Mr. Maraton," he said. "We live in civilised ages. A thousand years ago, you would certainly have had some cause for suspicion!"

Maraton raised his glass to his lips and sipped the wine critically.

"I am afraid," he remarked, with a gleam in his eyes, "that there are a good many of you who may be wishing that they could set back time a thousand years!"

Mr. Foley shook his head.

"No," he decided, "to-day's principles are the best. We argue away what is wrong in the minds of our enemies, and we take unto ourselves what they bring us of good. If you would rather, Mr. Maraton, we will not talk politics at all. On the other hand, the news to-night is serious. Armley here is wondering what the actual results will be if Sheffield, Leeds, and Manchester stand together, and the railway strike comes at the same time."

"I do not know that I wonder at all," Lord Armley declared. "The result will be ruin."

"There is no such thing as permanent destruction," Maraton objected. "The springs of human life are never crushed. Sometimes a generation must suffer that succeeding ones may be blest."

"The question is," Mr. Foley said, holding up his

wine-glass, " how far we are justified in experiments
concerning which nothing absolute can be known,
experiments of so disastrous a nature."

A servant entered and made a communication to
Mr. Foley, who turned at once to Maraton.

" It is your secretary," he announced, " who has
arrived from London with some letters."

Maraton at once followed the servant from the
room. Mr. Foley, too, rose to his feet.

" In ten minutes or so," he declared, " I shall
follow you. We can have our chat quietly in the
study."

Maraton followed the butler across the hall and
found himself ushered into a room at the back of
the house — a room lined with books; with French
windows, wide open, leading out on to the lawn; a
room beautifully cool and odoriferous with the perfume of roses. A single lamp was burning upon a
table; for the rest, the apartment seemed full of the
soft blue twilight of the summer night. Maraton
came to a standstill with an exclamation of surprise.
A tall, very slim figure in plain dark clothes had
turned from the French windows and was standing
there now, her face turned towards him a little
eagerly, a strange light upon her pale cheeks and in
the eyes which seemed to shine at him almost feverishly out of the sensuous twilight.

CHAPTER XII

" Julia! " Maraton exclaimed.

" Aaron was run over just as he was starting," she explained quickly. " He is not hurt badly, but he wasn't able to catch the train. He had an important letter from Manchester and one from the committee for you. We thought it best that I should bring them. I hope we decided rightly."

She was standing out of the circle of the lamp-light, in the shadows of the room. There was a queer nervousness about her manner, a strained anxiety in the way her eyes scarcely left his face, which puzzled him.

" It is very kind of you," he said, as he took the letters. " Please sit down while I look at them."

The first was dated from the House of Commons:

" *Dear Mr. Maraton:*

" At a committee meeting held this afternoon here, it was resolved that I should write to you to the following effect.

" We understood that you were coming over here entirely in the interests of the great cause of labour, of which we, the undersigned, are the accredited representatives in this country. Since your arrival, however, you have preserved an independent attitude which has given cause to much anxiety on our part. After declining to attend a meeting at the Clarion Hall, we find you there amongst the audience, and you address them in direct opposition to the advice which we were giving them authoritatively. We specially invited you to be present at a meeting of this committee to-day, in order that a definite plan of campaign might be formulated before your visit to Manchester. You have not accepted our invitation, and we understand that you are now staying at the private house of the Prime Minister, notwithstanding our request that you should not interview, or be interviewed by any representative of the Government without one of our committee being present.

" We wish to express our dissatisfaction with the state of affairs, and to say that should you be still intending to address the meeting at Manchester on Monday night, we demand an explanation with you before you go on to the platform. We understand that the residence of Mr. Foley is only sixty miles from London. If you are still desirous of acting with us, we beg you, upon receipt of this letter, to ask for a motor car and to return here to London. We shall all be at number 17, Notting Hill, until midnight or later, telephone number 178, so that you can telephone that you are on the way. Failing your coming, some of us will be at the Midland Hotel, Manchester, from mid-day on Monday.

" I am,
" Faithfully yours,

" *For*   " RICHARD GRAVELING,
PETER DALE, Chairman,   " Secretary."
ABRAHAM WEAVEL,
SAMUEL BORDEN,
HENRY CULVAIN.

The second one was from Manchester:

" Dear Sir:

" We understand that you will be arriving in Manchester about mid-day on Monday. We think it would be best if you were to descend from the train either at Derby or any adjacent station, as no police force which could possibly be raised in the county, will be sufficient to control the crowds of people who will gather in the streets to welcome you.

" We beg that you will send us a telegram, informing us by what train you are travelling, and we will send a messenger to Derby, who will confer with you as to the best means of reaching the rooms which we are providing for you.

" Anticipating your visit,
" I am,
" Faithfully yours,
" WILLIAM PRESTON,
" Secretary Manchester Labour Party."

Maraton replaced the letters in their envelopes and turned with them in his hand, towards Julia. She had moved a little towards the open French windows. Every one seemed to have made their way out on to the lawn. Chinese lanterns were hanging from some of the trees and along the straight box hedge that led to the rose gardens. The women were strolling about in their evening gowns, without wraps or covering, and the men had joined them. Servants were passing coffee around, served from a table on which stood a little row of bottles, filled with various

liqueurs. Some one in the drawing-room was singing, but the voice was suddenly silenced. Every one
turned their heads. A little further back in the
woods, a nightingale had commenced to sing.

"You are tired," Maraton whispered.

She shook her head. The strained, anxious look
was still in her face.

"No," she replied in a low tone, "I am not tired."

"There is something the matter," he insisted,
"something, I am sure. Won't you sit down, and
may I not order some refreshment for you? The
people here are very hospitable."

Her gesture of dissent was almost peremptory.

"No!"

The monosyllable had a sting which surprised him.

"Tell me what it is?" he begged.

She opened her lips and closed them again. He
saw then the rising and falling of her bosom underneath that black stuff gown. She stretched out her
hand towards the gardens. Somehow or other, she
seemed to grow taller.

"I do not understand this," she said. "I do
not understand your being here, one of them, dressed
like them, speaking their language, sharing their
luxuries. It is a great blow to me. It is perhaps
because I am foolish, but it tortures me!"

"But isn't that a little unreasonable?" he asked
her quietly. "To accomplish anything in this
world, it is necessary to know more than one side of
life."

"But this — this," she cried hysterically, "is the
side which has made our blood boil for generations!

These women in silk and laces, these idle, pleasure-loving men, this eating and drinking, this luxury in beautiful surroundings, with ears deafened to all the mad, sobbing cries of the world! This is their life day by day. You have been in the wilderness, you have seen the life of those others, you have the feeling for them in your heart. Can you sit at table with these people and wear their clothes, and not feel like a hypocrite?"

"I assure you," Maraton replied, "that I can."

She was trembling slightly. She had never seemed to him so tall. Her eyes now were ablaze. She had indeed the air of a prophetess.

"They are ignorant men, they who sent you that letter," she continued, pointing to it, "but they have the truth. Do you know what they are saying?"

Maraton inclined his head gravely. He felt that he knew very well what they were saying. She did not give him time, however, to interrupt.

"They are saying that you are to be bought, that that is why you are here, that Mr. Foley will pay a great price for you. They are saying that all those hopes we had built upon your coming, are to be dashed away. They say that you are for the flesh-pots. I daren't breathe a word of this to Aaron," she added hurriedly, "or I think that he would go mad. He is blind with passionate love for you. He does not see the danger, he will not believe that you are not as a god."

Maraton looked past her into the gardens, away into the violet sky. The nightingale was singing now clearly and wonderfully. Perhaps, for a mo-

She did not give him time to interrupt. *Page 108.*

ment, his thoughts strayed from the great battle of life. Perhaps his innate sense and worship of beauty, the artist in the man, which was the real thing making him great in his daily work, triumphed apart from any other consideration. The music of life was in his veins. Soft and stately, Elisabeth, standing a little apart, was looking in upon them, an exquisite figure with a background of dark green trees.

" When you faced death in Chicago," Julia went on, her voice quivering with the effort she was making to keep it low, " when you offered your body to the law and preached fire and murder with your lips, you did it for the sake of the people. There was nothing in life so glorious to you, then, as the one great cause. That was the man we hoped to see. Are you that man? "

Maraton's thoughts came back. He moved a little towards her. Her hand shot out as though to keep him at a distance.

" Are you that man? " she repeated.

Her thin form was shaken with stifled sobs.

" I hope so," he answered gravely. " My ways are not the ways to which you have been accustomed. In my heart I believe that I see further into the real truth than some of those very ignorant friends of yours who have been sent into Parliament by the operatives they represent; further even than you, Julia, handicapped by your sex, with your eyes fixed, day by day, only upon the misery of life. You blame me because I am here amongst these people as an equal. Listen. Is one responsible for

their birth and instincts? I tell you now what I
have told to no one, for no one has ever ventured
to ask me twice of my parentage. I was born, in
a sense, as these people were born. I cannot help
it if, finding it advisable to come amongst them, I
find their ways easy. That is all. I came here to
keep a promise to a man who is, in his way, a great
statesman. He is Prime Minister of our country.
He has, without a doubt, so far as it is possible for
such a man to have it there at all, the cause of the
people at his heart. Is it for me to ignore him, to
leave what he would say to me unsaid, to pull down
the pillars which have kept this a proud country for
many hundreds of years, without even listening?
Remember that if I speak at Manchester the things
that are in my heart, this country, for your time
and mine, must perish. Of that I am sure. That
has been made clear to me. Do you wonder, Julia,
that, before I take that last step, I lift every stone,
I turn over every page, I listen to every word which
may be spoken by those who have the right to
speak? That is why I am here. On Monday morning I leave. On Monday night I speak to the people
in Manchester."

She listened to him very much as a prisoner at
the bar might listen to a judge who reasons before
he pronounces sentence, and her face became as the
face of that prisoner might become, who detects
some leniency of tone, some softening of manner,
on the part of the arbiter of his fate. She ceased
to tremble, her lips relaxed, her eyes grew softer and
softer. She came a step nearer, resting her finger-

tips upon a little table, her body leaning towards
him. He had a queer vision of her for a moment —
no longer the prophetess, a touch of the Delilah in
the soft sweetness of her eyes.

"Oh, forgive me!" she begged. "I was foolish.
Forgive me!"

He smiled at her reassuringly.

"There is nothing to forgive," he insisted. "You
asked for an explanation to which you had a right.
I have tried to give it to you. Indeed, Julia, you
need have no fear. Whatever I decide in life will
be what I think best for our cause."

The shadow of fear once more trembled in her
tone.

"Whatever you decide," she repeated. "You will
not — you will not let them call you a deserter? You
couldn't do that."

"There isn't anything in the world," he told her
quietly, "which has the power to tempt me from
doing the thing which I think best. I cannot promise
that it will be always the thing which seems right to
this committee of men," he added, touching the enve-
lope with his forefinger. "I cannot promise you
that, but it should not worry you. You yourself are
different. It is my hope that soon you will understand me better. I think that when that time comes
you will cease to fear."

The light in her face was wonderful.

"Oh, I want to!" she murmured. "I want to
understand you better. There hasn't been anything
in life to me like the sound of your name, like the
thought of you, since first I understood. Perhaps

I am as bad as Aaron," she sighed. "I, too, alas! am your hopeless slave."

He moved a step nearer. This time she made no effort to retreat. Once more she was trembling a little, but her face was soft and sweet. All the pallor, the hard lines, the suffering seemed to have passed miraculously out of it. A soul — a woman's soul — was shining at him out of her eyes. It wasn't her physical self that spoke — in a way he knew that. Yet she was calling to him, calling to him with all she possessed, calling to him as to her master.

He succeeded in persuading her to eat and drink, and she departed, a little grim and unpleased, in the motor car which Mr. Foley had insisted upon ordering round. Then Maraton strolled into the garden to take his delayed coffee. Elisabeth came noiselessly across the turf to his side.

"I hope there was nothing disturbing in your letters?" she said.

"Not very," he replied. "It is only what I expected."

"Every one," she continued, "has been admiring your secretary. We all thought that she had such a beautiful face."

"She is not my secretary," he explained. "She came in place of her brother, who met with a slight accident just as he was starting."

Somehow or other, he fancied that Elisabeth was pleased.

"I didn't think that it was like you to have a woman secretary," she remarked.

He smiled as he replied:

"Miss Thurnbrein is a very earnest worker and a real humanitarian. She has written articles about woman labour in London."

"Julia Thurnbrein!" Elisabeth exclaimed. "Yes, I have read them. If only I had known that that was she! I should have liked so much to have talked to her. Do you think that she would come and see me, or let me come and see her? We really do want to understand these things, and it seems to me, somehow, that people like Julia Thurnbrein, and all those who really understand, keep away from us wilfully. They won't exchange thoughts. They believe that we are their natural enemies. And we aren't, you know. There isn't any one I'd like to meet and talk with so much as Julia Thurnbrein."

He nodded sympathetically.

"They are prejudiced," he admitted. "All of them are disgusted with me for being down here. They look with grave suspicion upon my ability to wear a dress suit. It is just that narrowness which has set back the clock a hundred years. . . . How I like your idea of an open-air drawing-room! Mr. Foley hasn't been looking for me, has he? I am due in his study in three minutes."

Her finger touched his arm.

"Come with me for one moment," she insisted, a little abruptly.

She led him down one of the walks — a narrow turf path, leading through great clumps of rhododendrons. At the bottom was the wood where the nightingale had his home. After a few paces she stopped.

"Mr. Maraton," she said, "this may be our last serious word together, for when you have talked with my uncle you will have made your decision. Look at me, please."

He looked at her. Just then the nightingale began to sing again, and curiously enough it seemed to him that a different note had crept into the bird's song. It was a cry for life, an absolutely pagan note, which came to him through the velvety darkness.

"Isn't it your theory," she whispered, "to destroy for the sake of the future? Don't do it. Theory sometimes sounds so sublime, but the present is actually here. Be content to work piecemeal, to creep upwards inch by inch. Life is something, you know. Life is something for all of us. No man has the right to destroy it for others. He has not even the right to destroy it for himself."

Maraton was suddenly almost giddy. For a moment he had relaxed and that moment was illuminating. Perhaps she saw the fire which leapt into his eyes. If she did, she never quailed. Her head was within a few inches of his, his arms almost touching her. She saw but she never moved. If anything, she drew a little nearer.

"Speak to me," she begged. "Give me some promise, some hope."

He was absolutely speechless. A wave of reminiscence had carried him back into the study, face to face with an accuser. He read meaning in Julia's words now, a meaning which at the time they had not possessed. It was true that he was being tempted. It was true that there was such a thing in the world as temptation, a live thing to the strong as well as to the weak.

"You could be great," she murmured. "You could be a statesman of whom we should all be proud. In years to come, people would understand, they would know that you had chosen the nobler part. And then for yourself —"

"For myself," he interrupted, "for myself — what?"

Her lips parted and closed again. She looked at him very steadily.

"Don't you think," she asked quietly, "that you are, more than most men, the builder of your own life, the master of your own fate, the conqueror — if, indeed, you desired to possess?"

She was gone, disappearing through a winding path amongst the bushes which he had never noticed. He heard the trailing of her skirts; the air around him was empty save for a breath of the perfume shaken from her gown, and the song of the bird. Then he heard her call to him.

"This way, Mr. Maraton — just a little to your left. The path leads right out on to the lawn."

"Is it a maze?" he asked.

"A very ordinary one," she called back gaily. "Follow me and I will lead you out."

CHAPTER XIII

Mr. Foley and Lord Armley were waiting together in the library — not the smaller apartment into which Julia had been shown, but a more spacious, almost a stately room in the front part of the house. Upon Maraton's entrance, Lord Armley changed his position, sitting further back amongst the shadows in a low easy-chair. Maraton took his place so that he was between the two men. It was Lord Armley who asked the first question.

"Mr. Maraton," he enquired, "are you an Englishman?"

"I think that I may call myself so," Maraton replied, with a smile. "I was born in America, but my parents were English."

"I asked," Lord Armley continued, "whether you were an Englishman, for two reasons. One was — well, perhaps you might call it curiosity; the other because, if you are an Englishman, Mr. Foley and I are going to make a strong and I hope successful appeal to your patriotism."

"I am afraid," Maraton replied, "that you will be appealing to a sentiment of which I am ignorant."

"Do you mean," Mr. Foley asked, "that you have no impulse of affection for your own country?"

"For my country as she exists at present, none at all," Maraton answered. "That is where I am afraid we shall find this conference so unsatisfactory. I am not subject to any of the ordinary convictions of life."

"That certainly makes the task of arguing with you a little difficult," Mr. Foley admitted. "We had hoped that the vision of this country overrun by a triumphant enemy, our towns and our pleasant places in the hands of an alien race, our women subject to insults from them, our men treated with scorn — we had an idea that the vision of these things might count with you for something."

"For nothing at all," Maraton replied. "I am not sure that a successful invasion of this country would not be one of the best medicines she could possibly have."

"Are you serious, sir?" Lord Armley asked grimly.

"Absolutely," Maraton answered, without a second's hesitation. "You people have, after all, only an external feeling for the deficiences of your social system. You don't feel, really — you don't understand. To me, England at the present day — the whole of civilisation, indeed, but we are speaking now only of England — is suffering from an awful disease. To me she is like a leper. I cannot think that any operation which could cure her is too severe. She may have to spend centuries in the hospital, but some day the light will come."

"When you talk like that," Mr. Foley declared, "you seem to us, Mr. Maraton, to pass outside the pale of logical argument. But we want to understand you. You mean that for the sake of altering our social conditions, you would, if you thought it necessary, let this country be conquered, plunge her for a hundred years or more into misery deeper than any she has yet known? What good do you suppose could come of this? The poor who are poor now would starve then. From whom would come the mammoth war indemnity we should have to pay?"

"Not from the poor," Maraton replied. "That is one of my theories. It would come from the very class whom I would willingly see enfeebled — the greedy, grasping, middle class. The poor must exist automatically. They could not exist on lower wages; therefore, they will not get lower wages. If there is no employment for them, they will help themselves to the means for life. If there is money in the country, they have a right to a part of it and they will take it. The unfit amongst them will die. The unfit are better dead."

"This is a dangerous doctrine, Mr. Maraton," Lord Armley remarked.

"It is a primitive law," Maraton answered. "Put yourself down amongst the people, with a wife by your side and children crying to you for bread. Would you call yourself a man if you let them starve, if you sent your children sobbing away from you when there was bread to be had for the fighting, bread to be taken from those who had also meat? I think not. I am not afraid of plunging the country into disaster. It is my belief that the sufferings and the loss which would ensue would not fall upon the class who are already dwelling in misery."

Mr. Foley moved nervously to the mantelpiece and helped himself to a cigarette.

"Mr. Maraton," he said, "we will not argue on these lines. I like to feel my feet upon the earth. I like to deal with the things one knows about. Grant me this, at least; that it is possible to reach the end at which you are striving, by milder means?"

"It may be," Maraton admitted. "I am not sure. Milder means have been tried for a good many generations. I tell you frankly that I do not believe it is possible by legislation to redistribute the wealth of the world."

Lord Armley, from his seat amongst the shadows, smiled sarcastically.

"You, too, Mr. Maraton," he murmured. "What is your answer, I wonder, to the oft quoted question? You may redistribute wealth, but how do you propose to keep it in a state of equilibrium?"

Maraton smiled.

"There would have to be three, perhaps half-a-dozen — who can tell how many? — redistributions by violent means," he replied, "but remember that all this time, education, clean living, freedom from sordid anxieties, would be telling upon the lower orders. As their physical condition improved, so would their minds. As the conditions under which men live become more equal, so will their brains become more equal and their power of acquiring wealth. This, remember, may be the work of a hundred years — perhaps more — but it is the end at which we should aim."

"You absolutely mean, then," Mr. Foley persisted, "to destroy the welfare of the country for this genera-

tion and perhaps the next, in order that a new
people may arise, governed according to your methods,
in ages which neither you nor I nor any of us will
ever see? "

" That is what I mean," Maraton assented.
" Need I remind you that if we had not possessed in
the past men who gave their lives for the sake of
posterity, the nations of the world would be even
in a more backward condition than they are to-day? "

Mr. Foley smiled.

" Mr. Maraton," he said, " now I am going to
ask you this question. To-morrow you go to Manchester to pronounce your doctrines. To-morrow
you are going to incite the working people of England practically to revolt. Are you going to tell
them that it is for posterity they must strike? Do
you mean, when you thunder at them from the plat-
forms, to tell them the truth? — to tell them that the
good which you promise is not for them nor for
their children, nor their children's children, but for
the unborn generations? Do you mean to tell them
this? "

Maraton was silent. Lord Armley was watching
him closely. Mr. Foley's eyes were bright, and a
little flush had stained the parchment pallor of his
cheeks. He was feeling all the thrill of the fencer
who has touched.

" I cannot convince you, Mr. Maraton," he went
on, " that yours is not a splendid dream, an idyllic
vision, which would fade from the canvas before even
the colours were dry, but you have common sense, and
I hope at least I can persuade you to see this. You

won't rally the working men of England to your standard under that motto. That's why their leaders are ignorant and commonplace men. They know very well that it's to the pockets of their hearers they must appeal. A shilling a week more now is what they want, not to have their children born to a better life, and their children's children move on the upward plane. Human nature isn't like that, especially the human nature which I admit has suffered from the selfishness and greediness of the middle classes through all these years. The people aren't ready to dream dreams. They want money in their pockets, cash, so much a week — nothing else. I tell you that self-interest is before the eyes of every one of those Lancashire operatives to whom you are going to speak. An hour or so less work a week, an ounce more of tobacco, a glass of beer when he feels inclined, a little more money in the bank — that's what he wants."

"You may be speaking the truth, Mr. Foley," Maraton confessed quietly. "At any rate, you have voiced some of my deepest fears. I know that I cannot bring the people to my standard by showing them the whole of my mind. But why should I? If I know that my cause is just, if I know that it is for the good of the world, isn't it my duty to conceal as much as I find it wise to conceal, to keep my hand to the plough, even though I drive it through the fields of devastation?"

"Then your mission is not an honest one," Lord Armley declared suddenly. "It is dishonest that good things may come of it."

" It is possible to reason like that," Maraton admitted.

" Now, listen," Mr. Foley continued. " I will show you the other way. I will look with you into the future. I cannot agree with all your views but I, too, would like to see the diminution of capital from the hands of the manufacturers and the middle classes, and an increase of prosperity to the operatives. I would like to see the gulf between them narrowed year by year. I would like to see the working man everywhere established in quarters where life is wholesome and pleasant. I would like to see his schools better, even, than they are at present. I would like to see him, in the years to come, a stronger, a more capable, a more dignified unit of the Empire. He can only be made so by prosperity. Therefore, I wish for him prosperity. You want to sow the country red with ruin and fire, and there isn't any man breathing, not even you, can tell exactly what the outcome of it all might be. I want to work at the same thing more gently. Last year for the first time, I passed a Bill in Parliament which interfered between the relations of master and man. In a certain trade dispute I compelled the employers, by Act of Parliament, to agree to a vital principle upon which the men insisted. The night I drove home from the House I said to Lady Elisabeth, my niece, that that measure, small though it was, marked a new era in the social conditions of the country. It did. What I have commenced, I am prepared to go on with. I am prepared by every logical and honest means to legislate for la-

bour. I am prepared to legislate in such a
way that the prosperity of the manufacturer, all the
manufacturers in this country, must be shared
by the workpeople. I am prepared to fight, tooth
and nail, against twenty per cent dividends on capital and twenty-five shillings a week wages for the
operative. There are others in the Cabinet of my
point of view. In a couple of years we must go
to the country. I am going to the country to ask
for a people's government. Go to Manchester, if
you must, but talk common sense to the people.
Let them strike where they are subject to wrongs,
and I promise you that I am on their side, and every
pressure that my Government can bring to bear
upon the employers, shall be used in their favour.
You shall win — you as the champion of the men,
shall win all along the line. You shall improve the
conditions of every one of those industries in the
north. But — it must be done legitimately and without sinister complications. I know what is in your
mind, Mr. Maraton, quite well. I know your pro-
posal. It is in your mind to have the railway strike,
the coal strike, the ironfounders' strike, and the
strike of the Lancashire operatives, all take place
on the same day. You intend to lay the country
pulseless and motionless. You won't accept terms.
You court disaster — disaster which you refer
to as an operation. Don't do it. Try my way.
I offer you certain success. I offer you my alliance, a seat in Parliament at once, a place in my
Government in two years' time. What more
can you ask for? What more can you do for

the people than fight for them side by side with me?"

Maraton had moved a little nearer to the window. He was looking out into the night. Very faintly now in the distant woods he could still catch the song of the nightingale. Almost he fancied in the shadows that he could catch sight of Julia's strained face leaning towards him, the face of the prophetess, warning him against the easy ways, calling to him to remember. His principles had been to him a part of his life. What if he should be wrong? What if he should bring misery and suffering upon millions upon millions, for the sake of a generation which might never be born? There was something practical about Mr. Foley's offer, an offer which could have been made only by a great man. His brain moved swiftly. As he stood there, he seemed to look out upon a vast plain of misery, a country of silent furnaces, of smokeless chimneys, a country drooping and lifeless, dotted with the figures of dying men and women. What an offering! What a sacrifice? Would the people still believe in him when the blow fell? Could he himself pass out of life with the memory of it all in his mind, and feel that his life's work had been good? He remained speechless.

"Let me force one more argument upon you," Mr. Foley continued. "You must know a little what type of mind is most common amongst Labour. I ask you what will be the attitude of Labour towards the starvation of the next ten or twenty years, if you should bring the ruin you threaten upon the country? I ask you to use your common sense. Of what use would you be? Who would listen to you? If they left you alive, would any audience of starving men and women, looking back upon the comparative prosperity of the past, listen to a word from your lips. Believe me, they would not. They would be more likely, if they found you, to rend you limb from limb. The operatives of this country are not dreamers. They don't want to give their wives and children, and their own selves, body and soul, for a dream. Therefore, I come back to the sane common sense of the whole affair. By this time next year, if you use your power to bring destruction upon this country, your name will be loathed and detested amongst the very people for whose sake you do it."

Maraton turned away.

"You have put some of my own fears before me, Mr. Foley," he confessed, "in a new and very impressive light. If I thought that I myself were the only one who could teach, you would indeed terrify me. The doctrines in which I believe, however, will endure, even though I should pass."

"Endure to be discarded and despised by all thinking men!" Lord Armley exclaimed.

"You may be right," Maraton admitted, slowly. "I cannot say. Will you forgive me if I make you no answer at all to-night? My thoughts are a little confused. You have made me see myself with your eyes, and I wish to reconsider certain matters. Before I go, perhaps you will give me ten minutes more to discuss them?"

Mr. Foley was still a little flushed as they shook hands.

"I am glad," he declared, "very glad that you are at least going to think over what I have said. You must have common sense. I have read your book, backwards and forwards. I have read your articles in the American reviews and in the English papers. There is nothing more splendid than the visions you write of, but there is no gangway across from this world into the world of dreams, Mr. Maraton. Remember that, and remember, too, how great your responsibility is. I have never tried to hide from you what I believe your real power to be. I have always said that the moment a real leader was found, the country would be in danger. You are that leader. For God's sake, Mr. Maraton, realise your responsibility! . . . Now shall we go back into the gardens or into the drawing-room? My niece will sing to us, if you are fond of music."

Maraton excused himself and slipped out into the gardens alone. For more than an hour he walked restlessly about, without relief, without gaining any added clearness of vision. The atmosphere of the place seemed to him somehow enervating. The little walk amongst the rhododendrons was still fragrant with perfume, reminiscent of that strange moment of emotion. The air was still languorous. Although the nightingale's song had ceased, the atmosphere seemed still vibrating with the music of his past song. He stood before the window of the room where he had talked with Julia. What would she say, he wondered? Would she think that he had sold his soul if he chose the more peaceful way? It was a night of perplexed thoughts, confused emotions. One thing only was clear. For the first time in his life certain dreams, which had been as dear to him as life itself, had received a shattering blow. Always he had spoken and acted from conviction. It was that which had given his words their splendid force. It was that which had made the words which he had spoken live as though they had been winged with fire. Perhaps it was his own fault. Perhaps he should have avoided altogether this house of the easier ways.

CHAPTER XIV

From the atmosphere of Lyndwood Park and its surroundings — fragrant, almost epicurean — Maraton passed to the hard squalor of the great smoke-hung city of the north. There were no beautiful women or cultured men to bid him welcome. The Labour Member and his companion, who hastened him out of the train at Derby and into an open motor-car, were hard-featured Lancashire men, keen on their work and practical as the day. As they talked together in that long, ugly ride, Maraton almost smiled as he thought of those perfervid dreams of his which had always been at the back of his head; that creed of life, some part of which he had intended to unfold to the people during these few days.

" Plain-speaking is what our folk like," John Henneford assured him, as they sat side by side in the small open car driven by one of the committee; " plain, honest words; sound advice, with a bit o' grit in it."

" ' To hell with the masters! ' is the motto they like best," Preston remarked, moving his pipe to the corner of his mouth. " It's an old text but it's an ever popular one. There's the mill where I work, now, fourteen hundred of us. The girls average from eighteen bob to a pound a week, men twenty-four to twenty-eight, foremen thirty-five to two pounds. It's not much of wages. The house rent's high in these parts, and food, too. The business has just been turned into a company — capital three hundred thousand pounds, profits last year forty-two thousand. That's after paying us our bit. That's the sort of thing turns the blood of the people sour up here. It was the aristocrats brought about the revolution in France. It will be the manufacturers who do it here, and do it quick unless things are altered. They tell me you're a bit of a revolutionist, Mr. Maraton."

"I'm anything," Maraton answered, "that will do away with such profits as you've been speaking of. I am anything which will bring a fair share of the profits of his labour to the operative who now gets none. I hate capital. It's a false quantity, a false value. It's got to come back to the people. It belongs to them."

"You're right, man," Henneford declared grimly. "How are you going to get it back, eh? Show us. We are powerful up here. We could paralyse trade from the Clyde to the Thames, if we thought it would do any good. What's your text to-night, Mr. Maraton?"

"I haven't thought," Maraton replied. "I have plenty to say to the people though."

"You gave 'em what for in Chicago," Preston remarked, with a grin.

"I haven't been used to mince words," Maraton admitted.

"There's four thousand policemen told off to look after you," Henneford informed him. "By-the-bye, is it true that Dale and all of them are coming up to-night? "

Maraton nodded.

"I wired for some of them," he assented. "So long as I am going to make a definite pronouncement, they may as well hear it."

"Been spending the week-end with Foley, haven't you?" Preston enquired, closing his eyes a little.

Maraton nodded.

"Yes," he confessed, "I have been there."

"There are many that don't think much of Foley," Henneford remarked. "Myself I am not sure what to make of him. I think he'd be a people's man, right enough, if it wasn't for the Cabinet."

"I believe, in my heart," Maraton said, "that he is a people's man."

They sped on through deserted spaces, past smoke-stained factories, across cobbled streets, past a wilder-ness of small houses, grimy, everywhere repellent. Soon they entered Manchester by the back way and pulled up presently at a small and unimposing hotel.

"We've taken a room for you here," Henneford announced. "It's close to the hall, and it's quiet and clean enough. The big hotels I doubt whether you'd ever be able to get out of, when once they found where you were."

"As a matter of fact," Preston added, "there's a room taken in your name at the Midland, to put folks off a bit. We'll have to smuggle you out here if there's any trouble to-night. The people are rare and restless."

"It will do very nicely, I am sure," Maraton replied.

The place was an ordinary commercial hotel, clean apparently but otherwise wholly unattractive. Henneford led the way up-stairs and with some pride threw open the door of a room on the first floor.

"We've got you a sitting-room," he said. "Thought you might want to talk to these Press people, perhaps, or do a bit of work. Your secretary's somewhere about the place — turned up with a typewriter early this morning. And there's a young woman —"

"A what?" Maraton asked.

"A young woman," Henneford continued,— "secretary's sister or something."

Maraton smiled.

"Miss Thurnbrein."

"What, the tailoress?" Preston replied. "She's a good sort. Wrote rare stuff, she did, about her trade. They are out together, seeing the sights. Didn't expect you quite so soon, I expect."

Maraton looked around the little sitting-room. It was furnished with a carpet of bright green thrown over a foundation of linoleum, a suite of stamped magenta plush, an overmantel, gilt cornices over the windows, a piano, a table covered with a gaudy table-cloth. On the walls were hung some oleographs. The lighting of the room was of gas with incandescent mantles. There had been, apparently, judging by an odour which still remained, a great deal of beer consumed in the apartment at one time or another.

"Nice room, this," Mr. Henneford remarked approvingly. "Slap up, ain't it? Your bedroom's next door, and your secretary's just round the corner. Done you proud, I reckon. Like a royal suite, eh?"

He laughed good-humouredly. Mr. Preston removed his pipe and rang the bell.

"One drink, I think," he suggested, "and we'll leave Mr. Maraton alone for a bit. You and I'll go down to the station and meet the chaps from London, and we'll have a meeting up here — say at five o'clock. That suit you, Mr. Maraton?"

"Excellently," Maraton assented. "What shall I order?" he asked, as the waiter entered.

Beer, whiskey and cigars were brought. Maraton asked a few eager questions about the condition of one of the industries, and followed Henneford to the door, talking rapidly.

"I know so little about the state of woman labour over here," he said. "In America they are better paid in proportion. Perhaps, if Miss Thurnbrein is here, she will be able to give me some information."

"You'll soon get posted up," Mr. Henneford declared. "I can see you've got a quick way of dealing with things. So long till five o'clock, then. There's a dozen chaps waiting down-stairs to see you. We'll leave it to your judgment just what you want to say to the Press. Ring the bell and have the waiter bring their cards up."

They departed and Maraton returned to his sitting-room. He stood for a moment looking out over the city, the roar of which came to him clearly enough through the open window. He forgot the depressing tawdriness of his surroundings in the exhilaration of the sound. He was back again amongst the people, back again where the wheels of life were crashing. The people! He drew himself up and his eyes sought the furthest limits of that dim yellow haze. Somehow, notwithstanding a vague uneasiness which hung about him like an effort of wounded conscience, he had a still greater buoyancy of thought when he considered his possibly altered attitude towards the multitude who waited for his message. He felt his feet upon the earth with more certainty, with more implicit realism, than in those days when he had spoken to them of the future and had perhaps forgotten to tell them how far away that future must be. There was something more practical about his present attitude. What would they say here in Manchester, expecting fire and thunder from his lips and finding him hold out the olive branch? He shrugged his shoulders; — a useless speculation, after all. He rang the bell and glanced through the cards which the waiter brought him.

"I have nothing of importance to say to any reporters," he declared, "but I will see them all for two minutes. You can show them up in the order in which they came."

The waiter withdrew and Maraton was left for a few moments alone. Then the door was opened and closed again by the waiter, who made no announcement. A man came forward — a small man, very neatly dressed, with gold spectacles and a little black beard. Maraton welcomed him and pointed to a chair.

"I have nothing whatever to say to the newspapers," he explained, "until after I have addressed my first few meetings. You probably will have nothing to ask me then. All the same, I am very pleased to see you, and since you have been waiting, I thought I had better have you come up, if it were only for a moment. No one who has a great cause at their backs, you know, can afford to disregard the Press."

The man laid his hat upon the table. Maraton, glancing across the room at him, was instantly conscious that this newcomer was no ordinary person. He had a strong, intellectual forehead, a well-shaped mouth. His voice, when he spoke, was pleasant, although his accent was peculiar — almost foreign.

"Mr. Maraton," his visitor began, "I thank you very much for your courtesy, but I have nothing to do with the Press. My name is Beldeman. I have come to Manchester especially to see you."

Maraton nodded.

"We are strangers, I believe?" he asked.

"Strangers personally. No thinking man to-day is a stranger to Mr. Maraton in any other way."

"You are very kind," Maraton replied. "What can I do for you?"

Beldeman glanced towards the door so as to be sure that it was closed.

"Mr. Maraton," he enquired, "are you a bad-tempered man?"

"At times," Maraton admitted.

"I regret to see," his visitor proceeded, "that you are a man of superior physique to mine. I am here to make you an offer which you may consider an insult. If you are a narrow, ordinary Englishman, obstinate, with cast-iron principles and the usual prejudices, you will probably try to throw me downstairs. It is part of my living to run the risk of being thrown down-stairs."

"I will do my best," Maraton promised him, "to restrain myself. You have at least succeeded in exciting my curiosity."

"I am, to look at," Mr. Beldeman continued, "an unimportant person. As a matter of fact, I represent a very great country, and I come to you charged with a great mission."

Maraton became a little graver.

"Go on," he said.

"I am anxious — perhaps over-anxious," Mr. Beldeman proceeded, "that I should put this matter before you in the most favourable light. I must confess that I have spent hours trying to make up my mind exactly how I should tell you my business. I have changed my mind so many times that there is nothing left of my original intention. I speak now as the thoughts come to me. I am here on behalf of a syndicate of manufacturers — foreign manufacturers — to offer you a bribe."

Maraton stood quite still upon the hearth-rug. His face showed no emotion whatever.

"You are, I believe," Mr. Beldeman went on, "only half an Englishman. That is why I am hoping that you will behave like a reasonable being, and that my person may be saved from violence. Upon your word rests the industrial future of this country for

the next ten years. If your forges burn out and
your factories are emptied, it will mean an era of
prosperity for my country, indescribable. We are
great trade rivals. We need just the opening.
What we get we may not be able to hold altogether,
when trade is once more good here, but that is of
no consequence. We shall have it for a year or
two, and that year or two will mean a good many
millions to us."

Maraton's eyes began to twinkle.

"The matter," he remarked, "becomes clearer to
me. You are either the most ingenuous person I
ever met, or the most subtle. Tell me, is it a personal bribe you have brought?"

"It is not," Mr. Beldeman replied. "It did not
occur to those in whose employment I am, or to me,
to offer you a single sixpence. I am here to offer
you, if you send your people out on strike within
the next week — the coal strike, the railway strike,
the ironfounders, the smelters, from the Clyde southwards — one million pounds as a subscription to your
strike funds."

"You have it with you?" Maraton enquired, after
a moment.

"I have four drafts for two hundred and fifty
thousand pounds each, in my pocket-book at the present moment," Mr. Beldeman declared. "They are
payable to your order. You can accept my offer and
pay them into your private banking account or the
banking account of any one of your Trades' Unions.
There is not the slightest doubt but that they will
be met."

"Are there any terms at all connected with this little subscription?"

"None," Beldeman replied.

"And your object," Maraton added, "is to benefit through our loss of trade?"

"Entirely," Mr. Beldeman assented, without a quiver upon his face.

Maraton was silent for a moment.

"I do not see my way absolutely clear," he announced, "to recommending a railway strike at the present moment. If I acceded to all the others, what would your position be? The railway strike is of little consequence to a foreign nation. The coal strike, and the iron and steel works of Sheffield and Leeds closed — that's where English trade would suffer most, especially if the cotton people came out."

Mr. Beldeman shook his head slowly.

"My conditions," he said, "embrace the railways."

"Somehow, I fancied that they would," Maraton remarked. "Tell me why?"

Beldeman rose slowly to his feet.

"Are you an Englishman?" he asked.

"I can't deny it," Maraton replied. "I was born abroad. Why are you so interested in my nationality?"

Beldeman shrugged his shoulders.

"I cannot tell you. Just an idea. I do not wish to say too much. I wish you only to consider what a million pounds will do to help your work people. You, they say, are one of those who love the people as your own children. A million pounds may enable them to hold out until they can secure practically what terms they like. Those million pounds are yours to-day, yours for the people, if you pledge your word to a universal strike."

" Including the railways? "

" Including the railways," Mr. Beldeman assented.

Maraton smiled quietly.

" I do not ask you," he said, " what country you represent. I think that it is not necessary. You have come to me rather as though I were a dictator. There are others besides myself with whom influence rests."

" It is you only who count," Mr. Beldeman declared. " I am thankful that at any rate you have met my offer in a reasonable spirit. Accept it, Mr. Maraton. What concern have you for other things save only for the welfare of the people? "

" I have considered this matter," Maraton remarked, " many, many times. A universal strike, absolutely universal so far as regards transport and coal, would place the country in a paralytic and helpless condition. Still, so many people have assured us that an onslaught from any foreign country is never seriously to be considered, that I have come to believe it myself. What is your opinion? "

Mr. Beldeman remained silent for a few moments.

" One cannot tell," he said. " The stock of coal available for your home fleet happens to be rather low just now. One cannot tell what might happen. Do you greatly care? Wasn't it you who, in one of your speeches, pointed out that a war in your country would be welcome? That the class who would suffer would be the class who are your great op-

pressors — the manufacturers, the middle classes —
and that with their downfall the working man would
struggle upwards? Do you believe, Mr. Maraton,
that a war would hurt your own people? "

" My own ideas," Maraton replied, " are in a state
of transition. However, your offer is declined."

" Declined without conditions? " Mr. Beldeman
enquired, taking up his hat.

" For the present it is declined without conditions.
I will be quite frank with you. Your offer doesn't
shock me as it might do if I were a right-feeling
Imperialist of the proper Jingo type. I believe that
a week ago I should have considered it very seriously
indeed. Its acceptance would have been in accord-
ance with my beliefs. And yet, since you have made
it, you have made me wonder more than ever whether
I have been right. I find a revulsion of feeling in
considering it, which I cannot understand."

" I may approach you again," Mr. Beldeman
asked, " if circumstances should change? Possibly
you yourself may, upon reflection, appreciate my
suggestion more thoroughly."

Maraton was silent for a moment. When he
looked up he was alone. Mr. Beldeman had not
waited for his reply.

CHAPTER XV

One by one, Maraton got rid at last of the little crowd of journalists who had been waiting for him below. The last on the list was perhaps the most difficult. He pressed very hard for an answer to his direct question.

"War or peace, Mr. Maraton? Which is it to be? Just one word, that's all."

Maraton shook his head.

"In less than an hour, the delegates from London will be here," he announced. "We shall hold a conference and come to our decision then."

"Will their coming make any real difference?" the journalist persisted. "You hadn't much to say to delegates in America."

"The Labour Party over here is better organised, in some respects," Maraton told him. "I have nothing to say until after the conference."

His persistent visitor drew a little nearer to him.

"There's a report about that you've been staying with Foley."

"And how does that affect the matter?" Maraton enquired.

The journalist looked him in the face.

"The men never had a leader yet," he said, "whom officialdom didn't spoil."

All this time Maraton was standing with the door

in one hand and his other hand upon the shoulder of the man whom he was endeavouring to get rid of. His grasp suddenly tightened. The door was closed and the reporter was outside. Maraton turned to Aaron, with whom, as yet, he had scarcely exchanged a word. The latter was sitting at a table, sorting letters.

"How long will those fellows be?" he asked.

Aaron glanced at the clock.

"On their way here by now, I should say," he replied. "They are all coming. They tried to leave David Ross behind, but he wouldn't have it."

Maraton nodded grimly.

"Too many," he muttered.

Aaron leaned a little forward in his place. His long, hatchet-shaped face was drawn and white. His eyes were full of a pitiful anxiety.

"They were talking like men beside themselves at the Clarion and up at Dale's house last night," he said. "They were mad about your having gone to Foley's. Graveling — he was the worst — he's telling them all that you're up to some mischief on your own account. They are all grumbling like a lot of sore heads. If they could stop your speaking here to-night, I believe they would. They're a rotten lot. Before they got their places in Parliament, they were perfect firebrands. Blast them!"

"And you, Aaron —"

Maraton suddenly paused. The door was softly opened, and Julia stood there. She was wearing her hat and coat, but her hands were gloveless; she had just returned from the street.

"Come in," Maraton invited. "So you're looking after Aaron, are you?"

"I couldn't keep away," Julia said simply. "I thought I'd better let you both know that the street below is filling up. They've heard that you are here. People were running away from before the Midland as I came round the corner."

Maraton glanced out of the window. There was a hurrying crowd fast approaching the front of the hotel. He drew back.

"I was just on the point of asking Aaron," he remarked, "exactly what it is that is expected from me to-night. Tell me what is in your mind?"

Her face lit up as she looked at him.

"We are like children," she replied, "all of us. We have too much faith. I think that what we are expecting is a miracle."

"Is it wise?" Maraton asked quietly. "Don't you think that it may lead to disappointment?"

She considered the thought for a moment and brushed it away.

"We are not afraid, Aaron and I."

"You are belligerents, both of you."

"And so are you," Julia retorted swiftly. "What was it you said in Chicago about the phrase-makers? — the Socialism that flourished in the study while women and children starved in the streets? Those are the sort of things that we remember, Aaron and I."

"This is a country of slow progress," Maraton reminded them. "One builds stone by stone. Listen to me carefully, you two. Since you have had understanding, your eyes have been fixed upon this one immense problem. I have a question to ask you concerning it. Shall I destroy for the sake of the unborn generations, or shall I use all my cunning and the power of the people to lead them a little further into the light during their living days? What would they say themselves, do you think? Would one in a hundred be content to sacrifice himself for a principle?"

"Who knows that the millennium would be so long delayed?" Julia exclaimed. "A few years might see Society reconstituted, with new laws and a new humanity."

Maraton shook his head.

"Don't make any mistake about that," he said. "If I press the levers upon which to-day my hand seems to rest, this country will be laid waste with famine and riot and conquest. An hour ago a little man was here, a little, black-bearded man with a quiet voice, charged with a great mission. He came to offer me, on behalf of a syndicate of foreign manufacturers, a million pounds towards our universal strike."

They both gasped. The thing was surely incredible!

"An incident like that," Maraton continued, "may show you what this country must lose, for her rivals do not give away a million pounds for nothing."

Julia's eyes were fixed upon his. Her face was full of strained anxiety.

"You talk," she murmured, "as though you had doubts, as though you were hesitating. Forgive me

— we have waited so long for to-day — we and all the others."

"Could any one," he demanded, "stand in the position I stand in to-day and not have doubts?"

Her eyes flashed at him.

"Yes," she cried, "a prophet could! A real man could — the man we thought you were, could!"

Aaron leaned forward, aghast. His monosyllable was charged with terrified reproach.

"Julia!"

She turned upon him.

"You, too! You weren't at Lyndwood, were you? . . . Doubts!" she went on fiercely, her eyes flashing once more upon Maraton. "How can you fire their blood if there are doubts in your heart? So long these people have waited. No wonder their hearts are sick and their brains are clogged, their will is tired. Prophet after prophet they have followed blindly through the wilderness. Always it has been the prophet who has been caught up into the easier ways, and the people who have sunk back into misery."

She fell suddenly upon her knees. Before he could stop her, she was at his feet, her face straining up to his.

"Forgive me!" she cried. "For the love of the women and the little children, don't fail us now! If you don't say the word to-night, it will never be spoken, never in your day nor mine. It isn't legislation they want any more. It's revolution, the cleansing fires! The land where the sun shines lies on the other side of the terrible way. Lead them across. Don't try the devious paths. They have filled you with the poison of common sense. It isn't common sense that's wanted. It's only an earthquake can bring out the spirit of the people and make them see and hold what belongs to them."

Maraton lifted her up. Her body was quivering. She lay, for a moment, passive in his arms. Then she sprang away. She stood with her back to him, looking out of the window.

" The streets are full of people," she said quietly. " Their eyes are all turned here. Poor people! "

Maraton crossed the room and stood by her side. He spoke very gently. He even took her hand, which lay like a lump of ice in his.

" Julia," he whispered, " you lose hope and trust too soon."

" You have spoken of doubts," she answered, in a low tone. " The prophet has no doubts."

There was a sound of voices outside, of heavy footsteps on the stairs. They heard Graveling's loud, unpleasant voice. The delegates had arrived!

CHAPTER XVI

Maraton, with the peculiar sensitiveness of the artist to an altered atmosphere, was keenly conscious of the change when Julia had left the room and the delegates had entered. One by one they shook hands with Maraton and took their places around the table. They had no appearance of men charged with a great mission. Henneford, who had met them at the station, was beaming with hospitality. Peter Dale was full of gruff good-humour and jokes. Graveling alone entered with a scowl and sat with folded arms and the air of a dissentient. Borden, who complained of feeling train-sick, insisted upon drinks being served, and Culvain, with a notebook upon his knee, ostentatiously sharpened a pencil. It was very much like a meeting of a parish council. Ross alone amongst the delegates had the absorbed air of a man on the threshold of great things, and Aaron, from his seat behind Maraton, watched his master all the time with strained and passionate attention.

"In the first place," Peter Dale began, " we've no wish to commence this meeting with any unpleasantness. At the same time, Mr. Maraton, we did think that after that letter of ours you'd have seen your way clear to come up to London and cut short that visit to Mr. Foley. We were all there waiting for you, and there were some of us that didn't take it altogether in what I might call a favourable spirit, that you chose to keep away."

"To tell you the truth," Maraton replied calmly, "I did not see the faintest reason why I should shorten my visit to Mr. Foley. We had arranged to meet here to-day and that seemed to me to be quite sufficient."

Peter Dale tugged at his beard for a moment.

"I am not wishful," he reiterated, "to commence a discussion which might lead to disagreement between us. We'll drop the matter for the present. Is that agreeable to everybody?"

There was a little murmur of assent. Graveling only was stolidly silent. Peter Dale struck the table with his fist.

"Now then, lads," he said, "let's get on with it."

"This being mainly my show," John Henneford declared, "I'll come and sit at your right hand, Mr. Maraton. You've got all the papers I've sent you about the cotton workers?"

"I have looked them through," Maraton replied, "but most of their contents were familiar to me. I made a study of the condition of all your industries so far as I could, last year."

"Between you and me," Peter Dale grumbled, "this meeting ought to have been held in Newcastle and not Manchester. These cotton chaps of yours, Henneford, ain't doing so badly. It's my miners that want another leg up."

Henneford struck the table with his fist.

"Rot!" he exclaimed. "Your miners have just had a turn. Half-a-crown a week extra, and a minimum wage — what more do you want? And a piece of plate and a nice fat cheque for Mr. Dale," he added, turning to the others and winking.

Peter Dale beamed good-humouredly upon them.

"Well," he retorted, "I earned it. You fellows should organise in the same way. It took me a good many years' hard work, I can tell you, to bring my lot up to the scratch. Anyway, here we are, and Manchester it's got to be this time. In an hour, Mr. Maraton, the secretary of the Manchester Labour Party will be here. He's got two demand scales made out for you to look through. Your job is to work the people up so that they drop their tools next Saturday night."

"There was an idea," Maraton reminded them quietly, "that I should speak to-night not only to the operatives of Manchester but to Labour throughout the Empire; that I should make a pronouncement which should have in it something of a common basis for all industries — which would, in short, unsettle Labour in every great centre."

They all looked a little blank. Henneford shook his head.

"It can't be done," he affirmed. "One job at a time's our way. You're going to speak to cotton to-night, and we want the mills emptied by the end of the week. We've got a scheme amongst the Unions, as you know, for helping one another, and as soon as we've finished with cotton, then we'll go for iron."

"That's an old promise," Weavel declared sturdily.

"What about the potteries?" Mr. Borden exclaimed. " It's six years since we had any sort of a dust-up, and my majority was the smallest of the lot of you, last election. Something's got to be done down my way. My chaps won't go paying in and paying in forever. We've fifty-nine thousand pounds waiting, and the condition of our girl labour is beastly."

" Iron comes next," Weavel persisted stolidly. " That's been settled amongst ourselves. And as for your fifty-nine thousand, Borden, what about our hundred and thirty thousand? We shall all have to be lending up here, too, to work this thing properly."

" Let's get on," Peter Dale proposed, rapping on the table. " Now listen here, all of you. What I propose is, if we're satisfied with Mr. Maraton's address to-night, as I've no doubt we shall be," he added, bowing to Maraton with clumsy politeness, " that we appoint him kind of lecturer to the Unions, and we make out a sort of itinerary for him, to kind of pave the way, and then he gives one of these Chicago orations of his at the last moment in each of the principal centres. We'd fix a salary — no need to be mean about it — and get to work as soon as this affair's over. And meanwhile, while this strike's on, Mr. Maraton might address a few meetings in other centres on behalf of these fellows, and rope in some coin. There are one or two matters we shall have to have an understanding about, however, and one as had better be cleared up right now. I'll ask you, Mr. Maraton, to explain to us just what you meant down at the Clarion the other night? We

weren't expecting you there and you rather took us
aback, and we didn't find what you said altogether
helpful or particularly lucid. Now what's this business about a universal strike? "

Maraton sat for a moment almost silent. He
looked down the table, along the line of faces, coarse
faces most of them, of varying strength, plebeian,
forceful here and there, with one almost common
quality of stubbornness. They were men of the people, all of them, men of the narrow ways. What
words of his could take them into the further land?
He raised his head. He felt curiously depressed,
immeasurably out of touch with these who should
have been his helpmates. The sight of Julia just
then would have been a joy to him.

" Perhaps," Maraton began, with a little sigh, " I
had better first explain my own position. You are
each of you Members of Parliament for a particular
district. The interests of each of you are bound
up in the welfare of the operatives who send you to
Parliament. It's your job to look after them, and
I've no doubt you do it well. Only, you see, it's a
piecemeal sort of business to call yourselves the representatives of Labour in its broadest sense. I belong more, I am afraid, to the school of theorists.
In my mind I bring all Labour together, all the toilers
of the world who are slaves to the great Moloch,
Capital. You have an immense middle class here in
England, who are living in fatness and content. The
keynote of my creed is that these people have twice
the incomes they ought to have, and Labour half
as much. That, of course, is just the simple, old-

fashioned, illogical Socialism with which you probably all started life, and which doubtless lies in
some forgotten chamber of the minds of all of you.
You've given it up because you've decided that it was
unpractical. I haven't. I believe that if we were
to pull down the pillars which hold up the greatness
of this nation, I believe that if we were to lay her
in ruins about us, that in the years to come — perhaps I ought to say the generations to come — the
rebuilding, stone by stone, would be on the sane
principle which, once established, would last for
eternity, of an absolute partnership between Capital
and Labour, a partnership which I say would be
eternal because, in course of time, the two would
become one."

They all looked at one another a little blankly.
Peter Dale grunted with expressionless face and relit
his pipe, which had gone out during these few moments of intense listening. Graveling reached out his
hand and took a cigar from a box which had been
placed upon the table. Henneford and his neigh-
bour exchanged glances, which culminated in a
stealthy wink. Alone at the table David Ross sat
like a figure of stone, his mouth a little open, something of the light in his face.

"I'm too much of an Englishman, for one,"
Graveling said, "to want to pull the country down.
Now where does this universal strike come in?"

"The universal strike," Maraton explained quietly,
"is the doctrine I came to England to preach. It
is the doctrine I meant to preach to-night. If your
coal strike and your iron strike and your railway

strike were declared within the next few days, the pillars would indeed be pulled down."

"Why, I should say so!" Peter Dale declared gruffly. "Half the people in the country would be starving; there'd be no subscriptions to the Unions; the blooming Germans would be over here in no time, and we should lose our jobs."

"It wouldn't do, Mr. Maraton," Borden said briskly. "It's our job to improve the position of our constituents, but it's jolly certain we shouldn't do that by bringing ruin upon the country."

David Ross suddenly struck the table with his fist.

"You are wrong, all of you," he cried hoarsely. "You are ignorant men, thick-headed, fat, narrow fools, full of self-interest and prejudice. You want your jobs; they come first. I tell you that the man's right. Purge the country; get rid of the poison of ill-distributed capital, start again a new nation and a new morning."

Dale looked across the table, pityingly.

"What you need, Ross, is a drink," he remarked. "I noticed you weren't doing yourself very well coming down."

David Ross rose heavily to his feet. His arm was stretched out towards Dale and it was the arm of an accuser.

"Doing myself well!" he repeated, with fierce contempt. "That's the keynote of your lives, you lazy, self-satisfied swine, who call yourselves people's men! What do you know or care about the people? How many of you have walked by day and night in the wilderness and felt your heart die away within you? How many of you have watched the people hour by hour — the broken people, the vicious people, the cripples, the white slaves of crueller days than the most barbarous countries in history have ever permitted to their children? You understand your jobs, and you do yourselves well; that's your motto and your epitaph. There's only one amongst you who's a people's man and that's him."

He pointed to Maraton and sat down. Peter Dale removed his pipe from his mouth.

" It's just as well, David Ross, for you to remember," he said gruffly, " that you're here on sufferance. Seems to me there's a bit of the dog in the manger about your whining. I don't know as it matters to any one particularly what your opinion is, but if you expect to be taken in along of us, you'll have to alter your style a bit. It's all very well for the platform, but it don't go down here. Now, lads, let's get on with business. What I say is this. If Mr. Maraton is going on the platform to-night to talk anarchy, why then we'd best stop it. We want subscriptions, we want the sympathy of the British public in this strike, and there's nothing would make them button up their pockets quicker than for Mr. Maraton there to go and talk about bringing ruin upon the Empire for the sake of the people who ain't born yet. That's what I call thinking in the clouds. There's nowt of good in it for us," he added, with a momentary and vigorous return into his own vernacular. " Get it out of thy head, lad, or pack thy bag and get thee back to America."

There was a brief silence. Most of those present

had drawn a little sigh of relief. It was obvious that they were entirely in agreement with Dale. Only Ross was leaning across the table, his eyes blinking, drumming upon the tablecloth with the palm of his hand.

"That's right," he muttered, "that's right. Send him away, the only one who sees the truth. Send him away. It's dangerous; you might lose your jobs!"

Then Maraton spoke quietly from his place.

"Gentlemen," he said, "I gather one thing, at least, from our brief conference. You are not extremists. I will bear that in mind. But as to what I may or may not say to-night, I make no promises."

"If you're not going to support the strike," Peter Dale declared sturdily, "then thou shalt never set foot upon the platform. We've had our fears that this might be the result of your spending the week-end with Mr. Foley. There's six of us here, all accredited representatives of great industrial centres, and he's never thought fit to ask one of us to set foot under his roof. Never mind that. We, perhaps," he added, with a slow glance at Maraton, "haven't learnt the knack of wearing our Sunday coats. But just you listen. If Mr. Foley's been getting at you about this cotton strike, and you mean to throw cold water upon it to-night, then I tell ye that you're out for trouble. These Lancashire lads don't stick at a bit. They'll pull you limb from limb if you give them any of Mr. Foley's soft sawder. We're out to fight — in our own way, perhaps, but to fight."

"It is true that I have spent the week-end with Mr. Foley," Maraton admitted. "I had thought, perhaps, to have reported to you to-day the substance of our conversation. I feel now, though," he continued, "that it would be useless. You call yourselves Labour Members, and in your way you are no doubt excellent machines. I, too, call myself a Labour man, but we stand far apart in our ideas, in our methods. I think, Mr. Peter Dale and gentlemen, that we will go our own ways. We will fight for the people as seems best to us. I do not think that an alliance is possible."

They stared at him, a little amazed.

"Look here, young man," Peter Dale expostulated, "what's it all about? What do you want from us? I spoke of a job as lecturer just now. If you've really got the gift of speaking that they say you have, that'll bring you into Parliament in time, and I reckon you'll settle down fast enough with the rest of us then. Until then, what is it you want? We are sensible men. We all know you can't go spouting round the country for nothing, whether it's for the people, or woman's suffrage, or any old game. Open your mouth and let's hear what you have to say."

Maraton rose to his feet.

"I will, perhaps," he said, "come to you with an offer a little later on. For the present I must be excused. I have an appointment which Mr. Henneford has arranged for me with Mr. Preston, Secretary of the Union here. There are a good many facts I need to make sure of before to-night."

Mr. Dale moved his pipe to the other side of his mouth.

"That's all very well for a tale," he muttered,

" but I'm not so sure about letting you go on to the platform at all to-night. We don't want our people fed up with the wrong sort of stuff."

Maraton smiled.

" Mr. Dale," he begged quietly, " listen."

They were all, for a moment, silent. Maraton opened the window. From outside came a low roar of voices from the packed crowds who were even now blocking the street.

" These are my masters, Mr. Dale," Maraton said, " and I don't think there's any power you or your friends could make use of to-night, which will keep me from my appointment with them."

CHAPTER XVII

In the roar of applause which followed Maraton's brilliant but wholly unprepared peroration, a roar which broke and swelled like the waves of the sea, different people upon the platform heard different things. Peter Dale and his little band of coadjutors were men enough to know that a new force had come amongst them. It is possible, even, that they, hardened as they were by time and circumstances, felt some thrill of that erstwhile enthusiasm which in their younger days had brought them out from the ranks of their fellows. To Aaron, listening with quivering attention to every sentence, it seemed like the consummation of all his dreams. Julia alone was conscious of a certain restraint, knew that behind all the deep feeling and splendid hopefulness of Maraton's words, there was a sense of something kept back. It wasn't what he had meant to say. Something had come between Maraton and his passionate dreams of freedom. He, too, had become a particularist. He, too, was content to preach salvation piecemeal. He had spoken to them at first simply, as one worker to another. Then he had drifted out into the larger sea, and for those few moments he had been, at any rate, vigorously in earnest as he had attacked with scorpion-like bitterness the hideous disproportions which existed between the capitalised

corporation and the labour which supported it. Yet
afterwards he had gone back within himself. Almost
she had expected to see him with his hands upraised,
bidding them tear down these barriers for themselves.
Instead he showed them the legalised way, not to free
humanity, but to ensure for themselves a more comfortable place in life. It was all very magnificent.
The strike was assured now, almost the success of it.

It was long before they let him leave the platform.
In the droning impotence of the men who followed
him, the vast audience seemed to realise once more the
splendid perfection of his wholly natural and inspiring oratory. They rose and shouted for him, and
once again, as he said a few words, the spell of silence
lay upon them. Julia sat telling herself passionately that all was well, that nothing more than this
was to have been hoped for, that indeed the liberator
had come. More than once she felt Aaron's hands
gripping her arm, as Maraton's words seemed to
cleave a way towards the splendid truth. Ross, on
her other side, was like a man carried into another
world.

" It is the Messiah," he muttered, " the Messiah
of suffering men and women! No longer will they
cry aloud for bread and be given stones."

Everything that happened afterwards seemed, in
a way, commonplace. When at last they succeeded in
leaving the platform, they had to wait for a long time
in an anteroom while some portion of the immense
crowd dispersed. Peter Dale, as soon as he had lit
his pipe, came up to Maraton and patted him on the
shoulder.

" There's no doubt about thy gift, lad," he said condescendingly. " A man who can talk as you do has no need to look elsewhere for a living."

" Gave it to 'em straight," Mr. Weavel assented, " and what I propose is a meeting at Sheffield — say this day month — and an appeal to the ironfounders. It's all very well, Borden," he went on, a little angrily, " but my people are looking for something from me, in return for their cash. What with these strikes here and strikes there, and a bit out of it for everybody, why, it's time Sheffield spoke."

" There's a question I should like to ask," Graveling intervened, plunging into the discussion, " and that is, why are you so cocksure, Mr. Maraton, of Government support in favour of the men? You said in your speech to-night, so far as I remember, that if the masters wouldn't give in without, Government must force them to see the rights of the matter. And not only that, but Government should compel them to recognise the Union and to deal with it. Now you've only been in this country a few days, and it seemed to me you were talking on a pretty tall order."

" Not at all," Maraton replied. " I have a scheme of my own, scarcely developed as yet, a scheme which I wasn't sure, when I came here, that I should ever make use of, which justified me in saying what I did."

They looked at him jealously.

" Is it an arrangement with Mr. Foley that you're speaking of? " Peter Dale enquired.

" Perhaps so," Maraton assented.

There was a dead silence. Maraton was leaning slightly against a table. Julia was talking to the wife of one of the delegates, a little way off. The others were all spread around, smoking and helping themselves to drinks which had just been brought in. Graveling's face was dark and angry.

"Are we to gather," he demanded, "that there's some sort of an understanding between you and Mr. Foley?"

"If there is," Maraton asked easily, "to whom am I responsible?"

There was a silence, brief but intense. Julia had turned her head; the others, too, were listening. Peter Dale was blowing tobacco smoke from his mouth, Borden was breathing heavily. Graveling's small eyes were bright with anger and distrust. They were all of them realising the presence of a new force which had come amongst them, and already, with the immeasurable selfishness of their class, they were speculating as to its personal effect upon themselves. Peter Dale, with his hands in his trousers pockets, and his pipe between his teeth, elbowed his way to Maraton's side.

"Young man," he began solemnly, "we'd best have an understanding. Ask any of these others and they'll tell you I'm the leader of the Labour Party. Are you one of us or aren't you?"

"One of you, in a sense, I hope, Mr. Dale," Maraton answered simply. "Only you must put me down as an Independent. I don't understand conditions over here yet. Where my own way seems best, I am used to following it."

Peter Dale removed his pipe from his mouth and spoke with added distinctness.

"Politics over here," he said, "are a simpler game than in the States, but there's one class of person we've got to do without, and that's the Independent Member. You can't do anything over here except by sticking together. If you'll come under the standard, you're welcome. I'll say nothing about Parliament for a time, but we'll find you all the talking you want and see that you're well paid for it."

Looking past the speaker's hard, earnest face, Maraton was conscious of the scorn flashing in Julia's eyes. Intuitively he felt her appreciation of the coarse selfishness of these men, terrified at his gifts, resisting stubbornly the unwelcome conviction of a new mastership. Her lips even moved, as though she were signalling to him. At that moment, indeed, he would have been glad of her guidance. He needed the machinery which these men controlled, distasteful though their ideals and methods might be to him.

"Mr. Dale," he declared, "I am a people's man. I cannot enroll myself in your party because I fancy that in many ways we should think differently. But with so many objects in common, it is surely possible for us to be friends?"

Ross leaned suddenly forward in his chair, his grey face passion-stirred, the sweat upon his forehead.

"Aye!" he cried, "it's the greatest friend or the bitterest enemy of the people you'll be. You'll do more with that tongue of yours than a library of books or a century of Parliament, and may it wither in your mouth if they buy you — those others!　God meant you for a people's man.　It'll be hell for you and for us if they buy you away."

Maraton changed his position a little.　He was facing them all now.

"My friends," he said, "that is one thing of which you need have no fear.　Our methods may be different, we may work in different ways, but we shall work towards the same goal.　Remember this, and remember always that whether we fight under the same banner or not, I have told it to you solemnly and from the bottom of my heart.　I am a people's man!"

He turned towards the door and laid his hand upon Aaron's shoulder.　Julia, too, rose and followed him.

"I think," he added, "that the people will have cleared off by now.　I am going to try and get back to the hotel.　I have messages to send away, and an early train to catch in the morning."

They were passing out of the room almost in silence, but Henneford struck the table with his fist.

"Come," he exclaimed, "we seem in a queer humour to-night!　Don't let Mr. Maraton think too hardly of us.　Wherever his place may be in the future, he's done us a grand service to-night, and don't let's forget it.　He's waked these people up as none other of us could have done.　He's started this strike in such a fashion as none other of us could.　Don't let's forget to be grateful.　The education and the oratory isn't all on the other side now.　If we don't see you again to-night, Mr. Maraton, or before you leave for London, here's my

thanks, for one, for to-night's work, and I'll lay
odds that the others are with me."

They crowded around him after that, and though
Graveling stood on one side and Peter Dale still main-
tained his attitude of doubt, they all parted cordially
enough. They reached the back door of the hall
and found the shelter of a four-wheeled cab. Before
they could start, however, they were discovered.
People came running from all directions. Looking
through the window, they could see nothing but a
sea of white faces. The crazy vehicle rocked from
side to side. The driver was lifted from his seat,
the horse unharnessed. Slowly, and surrounded by
a cheering multitude, they dragged the cab through
the streets. Julia, sitting by Maraton's side, felt
herself impelled to hold on to his arm. Her body,
her every sense was thrilled with the hoarse, dramatic roll of their voices, the forest of upraised
caps, the strange calm of the man, who glanced sometimes almost sadly from side to side. She clutched
at him once passionately.

" Isn't it wonderful! " she murmured. " All the
time they call to you — their liberator! "

He smiled, and there was a shadow still of sadness
in his eyes.

" It is a moment's frenzy," he said. " They have
seen a gleam of the truth. When the light goes out,
the old burden will seem all the heavier. It is so
little that man can do for them."

They had flung open the top of the cab, and Maraton's eyes were fixed far ahead at the dull glow
which hung over the city, the haze of smoke and

heat, stretching like a sulphurous pall southwards.
The roar of voices was always in his ears, but for
a moment his thoughts seemed to have passed away,
his eyes seemed to be seeking for some message beyond
the clouds. He alone knew the full meaning of the
hour which had passed.

.   .   .   .

They were sitting alone in the library, the French
windows wide open, the languorous night air heavy
with the perfume of roses and the sweetness of the
cedars, drawn out by the long day's sunshine. Mr.
Foley was sitting with folded arms, silent and pensive
— a man waiting. And by his side was Elisabeth,
standing for a moment with her fingers upon his
shoulder.

"Is that eleven o'clock?" she asked.

"A quarter past," he answered. "We shall hear
in a few minutes now."

She moved restlessly away. There was something
spectral about her in her light muslin frock, as she
vanished through the windows and reappeared almost
immediately, threading her way amongst the flower
beds. Suddenly the telephone bell at Mr. Foley's
elbow rang. He raised the receiver. She came
swiftly to his side.

"Manchester?" she heard him say. . . . "Yes,
this is Lyndwood Park. It is Mr. Foley speaking.
Go on."

There was silence then. Elisabeth stood with
parted lips and luminous eyes, her hand upon his
shoulder. She watched him,— watched the slow
movement of his head, the relaxing of his hard, thin

lips, the flash in his eyes. She knew — from the first she knew!

"Thank you very much, and good night," Mr. Foley said, as he replaced the receiver.

Then he turned quickly to Elisabeth and caught her hand.

"They say that Maraton's speech was wonderful," he announced. "He declared war, but a man's war. Cotton first, and cotton alone."

She gave a little sobbing breath. Her hands were locked together.

"England will never know," Mr. Foley added, in a voice still trembling with emotion, "what she has escaped!"

CHAPTER XVIII

Those wonderful few days at Manchester had passed, and oppressed by the inevitable reaction, Julia was back at work in the clothing factory.

She had given up her place by the window to an anæmic-looking child of seventeen, who had a habit of fainting during these long, summer afternoons. Her own fingers were weary and she was conscious of an increasing fatigue as the hours of toil passed on. No breath of air came in from the sun-baked streets through the wide-flung windows. The atmosphere of the long, low room, in which over a hundred girls closely huddled together, were working, was sickly with the smell of cloth. There was no conversation. The click of the machines seemed sometimes to her partially dulled senses like the beating out of their human lives. It seemed impossible that the afternoon would ever end. The interval for tea came and passed — tea in tin cans, with thick bread and melting butter. The respite was worse almost than the mechanical toil. Julia's eyes ranged over the housetops, westwards. There was another world of trees, flowers, and breezes; another world altogether. She set her teeth. It was hard to have no place in it. A little time ago she had been content, content even to suffer, because she was toiling with these others whom she loved, and for whom, in

her profound pity, she poured out her life and her
talents.   And now there was a change.   Was it the
spell of this cruel summer, she wondered, or was it
something else — some new desire in her incomplete
life, something from which for so many years she
had been free?   She let her thoughts, momentarily,
go adrift.   She was back again in the cab, her fingers
clutching his arm, her heart thrilling with the wonderful passionate splendour of those few hours.   She
recalled his looks, his words, his little acts of kindness.   She realised in those few moments how completely he filled her thoughts.   She began to tremble.

"Better have your place by the window back
again, Miss Thurnbrein," the girl at her side said
suddenly.   "You're looking like Clara, just before
she popped off.   My, ain't it awful!"

Julia came back to herself and refused the child's
offer.

"I shall be all right directly," she declared.
"This weather can't last much longer."

"If only the storm would come!" the child muttered, as she turned back to her work.

If only the storm would come!   Julia seemed to
take these words with her as she passed at last into
the streets, at the stroke of the hour.   It was like
that with her, too.   There was something inside,
something around her heart, which was robbing her
of her rest, haunting her through the long, lonely
nights, torturing her through these miserable days.
Soon she would have to turn and face it.   She shivered with fear at the thought.

In the street a man accosted her.   She looked up

with an almost guilty start. A little cry broke from her lips. It was one of disappointment, and Graveling's unpleasant lips were twisted into a sneer as he raised his cap.

"Thought it was some one else, eh?" he remarked. "Well, it isn't, you see; it's me. There's no one else with a mind to come down here this baking afternoon to fetch you."

"I thought it might be Aaron," she faltered.

"Never mind whom you thought it might have been," he answered gruffly. "Aaron's busy, I expect, typing letters to all the lords and ladies your Mr. Maraton hobnobs with. I'm here, and I want to talk with you."

"I am too tired," she pleaded. "I am going straight home to lie down."

"I'd thought of that," he answered stubbornly. "I've got a taxicab waiting at the corner. Not often I treat myself to anything of that sort. I'm going to take you up to one of those parks in the West End we've paid so much for and see so little of, and when I get you there I'm going to talk to you. You can rest on the way up. There's a breeze blowing when you get out of these infernally hot streets."

She was only too glad to sink back amongst the hard, shiny leather cushions of the taxicab, and half close her eyes. The first taste of the breeze, as they neared Westminster Bridge, was almost ecstatic. Graveling had lit a pipe, and smoked by her side in silence.

"We are coming out of our bit of the earth now,

to theirs," he remarked presently, as they reached
Piccadilly, brilliant with muslin-clad women and
flower-hung windows. "It isn't often I dare trust
myself up here. Makes me feel as though I'd like to
go amongst those sauntering swells and mincing
ladies in their muslins and laces, and parasols, and
run amuck amongst them — send them down like a
pack of ninepins. Aye, I'd send them into hell if
I could!"

She was still silent. She felt that she needed all
her strength. They drove on to the Achilles statue,
where he dismissed the taxicab. The man stared at
the coin which he was offered, and looked at the
register.

"'Ere!" he exclaimed. "You're a nice 'un, you
are!"

Graveling turned upon him almost fiercely.

"If you want a tip," he said, "go and drive some
of these fine ladies and gentlemen about, who've got
the money to give. I'm a working man, and luxuries
aren't for me. Be off with you, or I'll call a policeman!"

He shouldered his way across the pavement, and
Julia followed him. Soon they found a seat in the
shade of the trees. She leaned back with a little sigh
of content.

"Five minutes!" she begged. "Just five minutes!"

He glanced at his watch, relit his pipe, and relapsed
once more into sombre silence. Julia's thoughts
went flitting away. She closed her eyes and leaned
back. She had only one fear now. Would he find

out! He was thick enough, in his way, but he was no fool, and he was already coarsely jealous.

"Ten minutes you've had," he announced at last. "Look here, Julia, I've brought you out to ask you a plain question. Are you going to marry me or are you not?"

"I am not," she answered steadily.

He had been so certain of her reply that his face betrayed no disappointment. Only he turned a little in his chair so that he could watch her face. She was conscious of the cruelty of his action.

"Then I want to know what you are going to do," he continued. "You are thin and white and worn out. You're fit for something better than a tailoress and you know it. And you're killing yourself at it. You're losing your health, and with your health you're losing your power of doing any work worth a snap of the fingers."

"It isn't so bad, except this very hot weather," she protested. "Then I'm secretary to the Guild, you know. I can do my work so much better when I'm really one of themselves. Besides, they always listen to me at the meetings, because I come straight from the benches."

"You've done your whack," he declared. "No need to go on any longer, and you know it. I can make a little home for you right up in Hampstead, and you can go on with your writing and lecturing and give up this slavery. You know you were thinking of it a short time back. You've no one to consider but yourself. You're half promised to me and I want you."

"I am sorry, Richard," she said, "if I have ever misled you, but I hope that from now onward, at any rate, there need be no shadow of misunderstanding. I do not intend to marry. My work is the greatest thing in life to me, and I can continue it better unmarried."

"It's the first time you've talked like this," he persisted. "Amy Chatterton, Rachael Weiss, and most of 'em are married. They stick at it all right, don't they? What's the matter with your doing the same?"

"Different people have different ideas," she pronounced. "Please be my friend, Richard, and do not worry me about this. You can easily find some one else. There are any number of girls, I'm sure, who'd be proud to be your wife. As for me, it is impossible."

"And why is it impossible?" he demanded, in a portentous tone.

"Because I do not care for you in that way," she answered, "and because I have no desire to marry at all."

He smoked sullenly at his pipe for several moments. All the time his eyes were filled with smouldering malevolence.

"Now I am going to begin to talk," he said. "Don't look as though you were going to run away, because you're not. I am going to talk to you about that fellow Maraton."

"Why do you mention his name?" she asked, stiffening. "What has he to do with it?"

"A good deal, to my thinking," was the grim

reply. "It's my belief that you've a fancy for him, and that's why you've turned against me."

"You've no right to say anything of the sort!" she exclaimed.

"And, by God, why haven't I?" he insisted, striking his knee with his clenched fist. "Haven't you been my girl for six years before he came? You were kind of shy, but you'd have been mine in the end, and you know it. Waiting was all I had to do, and I was content to wait. And now he's come along, and I know very well that I haven't a dog's chance. You're a working lass, Julia, fit mate for a working man. Do you think he's one of our sort? Not he! Do you think he's for marrying a girl who works for her bread? If you do, you're a bigger fool than I think you. He's forever nosing around amongst these swell ladies and gentlemen with handles to their names, ladies and gentlemen who live on the other side of the earth to us. He can talk like a prophet, I grant you, but that's all there is of the prophet about him. People's man, indeed! He'll be the people's man so long as it pays him and not a second longer."

"Have you finished?" she asked quietly.

"No, nor never shall have finished," he continued, raising his voice, "while he's playing the rotten game he's at now, and you're mooning around after him as though he were a god. I'll never stop speaking until I've knocked the bottom out of that, Julia. You never used to think anything of fine clothes and all these gentlemen's tricks. It's all come of a sudden."

"Have you finished?" she asked again.

"Never in this life!" he replied fiercely. "I tell you he shan't have you, and you shan't have him. I'm there between, and I'm not to be got rid of. I'll take one of you or both of you by the throat and strangle the life out of you, before I quit. It isn't," he went on, his face once more disfigured by that ample sneer, "it isn't that I'm afraid of his wanting to marry you. He won't do that. But he's one of those who are fond of messing about — philanderer's the word. If he tries it on with you, he'll find hell before his time! Sit down!"

She had risen to her feet. He clutched at her skirt. The sense of his touch — she was peculiarly sensitive to touch —gave her the strength she needed. She snatched it away.

"Now," she declared, "you have had your say. This is what you get for it. You have offended me. Our friendship is forgotten. The less I see of you, the more content I shall be. And as to what I do or what becomes of me, it isn't your business. I shall do with myself exactly as I choose — exactly as I choose, Richard Graveling! You hear that?" she reiterated, with blazing eyes and tone cruelly deliberate. "I haven't much in the world, but my body and my soul are my own. I shall give them where I choose, and on what terms I please. If you try to follow me, you'll put me to the expense of a cab home. That's all!"

She walked away with firm footsteps. She felt stronger, more of a woman than she had done all day. Graveling made no attempt to follow her. He sat and smoked in stolid silence.

CHAPTER XIX

Julia was conscious of a new vitality as she left the Park. She was her own mistress now; her half tie to Graveling was permanently broken. So much the better! The man's personality had always been distasteful to her. She had suffered him only as a fellow worker. His overtures in other directions had kept her in a continual state of embarrassment, but in her ignorance as to her own feelings, she had hesitated to speak out. She put sedulously behind her the question of what had brought this new enlightenment.

She took the Tube to the British Museum and went round to see Aaron. The house was busier than she had ever seen it before; taxicabs were coming and going, and four or five people sat in the waiting-room. Aaron looked up and waved his hand as she entered. He was alone in the study where he worked.

"Come in," he cried eagerly. "Sit down. It's a joy to see you, Julia, but I daren't stop working. I've forty or fifty letters to type before he comes in, and he'll be off again in half-an-hour."

She sank into an easy chair. The atmosphere of the cool room, with its opened windows and drawn Venetian blinds, was most restful.

"Is everything going well, Aaron?" she asked him.

He nodded.

" Better than well. There's a telegram just in from Manchester. We are bound to win there. Did you read Foley's speech? "

" Yes. Did he mean it all, do you think? " she asked doubtfully.

" Every word," he replied confidently. " We've got it here in black and white. There has been a commission appointed. Members of the Government, if you please — nothing less. The masters have got an ultimatum. If they refuse, Mr. Foley has asked Maraton to frame a bill. We've got the sketch of it here already. What do you think of that, Julia? "

" I only wish that I knew," she murmured. " What can have happened to Mr. Foley? "

" They all do as Maraton bids them!" Aaron exclaimed triumphantly. " If only I had four hands! I can't finish, Julia. It's impossible."

She sprang up and tore off her gloves.

" Let me help," she cried eagerly. " You have another typewriter in the corner there. I can work it, and you know I could always read your shorthand."

He accepted her help a little grudgingly.

" You must be careful, then," he enjoined, with the air of one who confers a favour. " There must be no mistakes. Begin here and do those letters. One carbon copy of each. I'll lift the machine on to the table for you."

She propped up the book and very soon there was silence in the room, except for the click of the two typewriters. Presently she stopped short and uttered a little cry.

"What is it?" he demanded, without looking up from his work.

"This letter to the Secretary of the Unionist Association, Nottingham!"

"Well?"

"Mr. Maraton is to go there Thursday, to address a meeting,— a Unionist meeting."

Aaron glowered at her from over his typewriter.

"Why not? It's Mr. Foley's idea. He wants Mr. Maraton in Parliament. Why not?"

"But as a Unionist!" she gasped. "Nottingham isn't a Labour constituency at all."

"He is coming in as a Unionist, so as to have a free hand. We don't want any interference from Peter Dale and that lot."

She looked at him aghast. Peter Dale and his colleagues had been gods a few weeks ago!

"Can't you see," Aaron continued irritably, "that the coming of Maraton has changed many things? A man like that can't serve under anybody, and no man could come as a stranger and lead the Labour Party. He has to be outside. This is a working man's constituency. He is pledged to fight Capital, fight it tooth and nail."

"I suppose it's all right," Julia said. "It seems different, somehow, from what we had expected, and he never goes to the Clarion at all."

"Why should he?" Aaron demanded. "They are all jealous of him, every one of 'em; Peter Dale is the worst of the lot. Didn't you hear how they talked to him at Manchester?"

She nodded, and for a time they went on with their work. She found herself, however, continually returning to the subject of those vital differences; the Maraton as they had dreamed of him — the prophet with the flaming sword, and this wonderfully civilised person.

"Tell me honestly, Aaron," she asked presently, "what do you think of it all? — of him — of his methods? You are with him all the time. Haven't you ever any doubts?"

She watched him closely. She would have been conscious of the slightest tremor in his reply, the slightest hesitation. There was nothing of the sort. He was merely tolerant of her ignorance.

"No one who knows Maraton," he pronounced, "could fail to trust him."

After that she asked no more questions. They worked steadily for another half hour or so. Messages were sometimes brought in to Aaron, which he summarily disposed of. Julia wondered at the new facility, the heart-whole eagerness which he devoted to every trifling matter. Then, just as she was halfway through copying out a pile of figures, Maraton came in. He stood and watched them in the doorway, half amused, half surprised. For a moment she kept her head down. Then she looked up slowly.

"Since when," he asked, "have I been the proud possessor of two secretaries?"

"You left me letters enough for four, sir," Aaron

reminded him. "I wanted to finish them all, so Julia stayed to help me."

Maraton came smiling towards them.

"Why, I am afraid I forgot," he said. "In America I used sometimes to have four typists working. You can't possibly get out all those details by yourself, Aaron."

"We shall have finished this lot, anyhow, in an hour."

"You must get permanent help," Maraton insisted. "Leave off now, both of you. I want to talk to your sister. Do you know," he went on, turning towards her, "that I have scarcely seen anything of you since Manchester?"

"My work keeps me rather a prisoner," she explained, "and after these hot days one hasn't much energy left."

"You are still working at the tailoring?"

She nodded.

"I like to be in the midst of it all, but this weather I am almost afraid I shan't be able to go on. The atmosphere is hateful. It seems to draw all the life out of one."

He glanced over her shoulder at the work she had been doing.

"Why not come to me?" he suggested suddenly. "Aaron needs help. He can't possibly do everything for himself. I have a thirst for information, you know. I want statistics on every possible subject. There are seven or eight big corporations now, whose wages bill I want to compare with the interest they pay on capital. Aaron doesn't have time even to answer the necessary letters. I am in disgrace all round. Do come."

She was sitting quite still, looking at him. It would have been impossible for any one to have guessed that his words were like music to her.

"But there is my trade," she objected. "After all, I am useful there. I keep in touch with the girls."

"You have finished with that," he argued. "You have done your work there. They all know who you are and what you are. You have lots of information which would be useful to me. Aaron must have some one to help him. Why not you? As for the rest, I can afford to pay two secretaries — you needn't be afraid of that."

"I never thought of it," she assured him. "I shouldn't want very much money."

"Leave that to me," he begged, "only accept. Is it a promise? Come, make it a promise and we will have an evening off. All day long I seem to have been moving in a strained atmosphere, talking to men who are only half in sympathy with me, talking to men who are civil because they have brains enough to see the truth. I want an hour or two of rest. Aaron shall telephone to Gardner. I was to have dined with him at his club, but it is of no importance. He was dining there, anyhow, and the other places I was going to this evening don't count. Telephone 1718 Westminster, Aaron, and say that Mr. Maraton is unable to keep his dinner engagement with Mr. Gardner and begs to be excused. Then we'll all go out together. What do you say? I have found something almost like a roof garden. I'll tell you all about New York."

Her face for a moment shone. Then she looked down at her gown. He laughed.

"You have done your day's work and I've done mine," he remarked. "I dare say of the two, yours is the more worthy. We'll go just as we are. Get rid of those people who are waiting, Aaron. I had a look at them. They are all the usual class — cadgers."

"There is one gentleman whom you must see," Aaron declared. "I didn't put him in the waiting-room — a Mr. Beldeman. He came to see you in Manchester."

"Beldeman!"

Maraton repeated the name. Then he smiled.

"A very sensational gentleman," he observed. "Came to offer me — but never mind, I told you about that. Yes, you're right, Aaron. He is always interesting. Take your sister away for a few minutes. You can be getting ready. When I've finished with Mr. Beldeman, we'll start out. I shan't change a thing."

Mr. Beldeman entered the room, carrying his hat in his hand, unruffled by his long wait, to all appearance wearing the same clothes, the same smile, as on his visit to the hotel in Manchester. Maraton greeted him good-humouredly.

"Well, Mr. Beldeman," he began, "you see, I have made things all right for your syndicate of manufacturers, although I couldn't accept your offer. Sit down. You won't keep me long, will you? I have to go out. Perhaps you are going to give me a little for my Lancashire operatives. They can do with it. Strike pay over here is none too liberal, you know."

Mr. Beldeman laid down his hat. He blinked for a moment behind his gold spectacles.

"The Lancashire strike," he said softly, "is of very little service to my principals. As you know, it is more than that for which we were hoping."

Maraton nodded but made no remark.

"My principals," Mr. Beldeman continued, "have watched your career, Mr. Maraton, for some time. They have studied eagerly your speeches and your writings, and when you arrived on this side they expected something more from you. They expected, in fact, the enunciation of a certain doctrine which you have already propounded with singular eloquence in other parts of the world. They expected to find it the text of your first words to Labour in this country. I refer, of course, to the universal strike."

"It was my great theory," Maraton admitted, suddenly grave. "I will not say even now that I have abandoned it. It is in abeyance."

"My principals," Mr. Beldeman remarked slowly, "would like it to take place."

Maraton smiled.

"Your principals, I presume," he said, "do not imagine that I am on the earth to gratify them, even though they did offer me — let me see, how much was it — a million pounds?"

"This time," Mr. Beldeman went on, "it is not a question of money."

"Not a question of money," Maraton repeated. "You don't want to buy me? What do you want to do, then?"

"We threaten," Mr. Beldeman pronounced calmly.

Maraton for a moment seemed puzzled.

"Threaten," he murmured thoughtfully. "Come, do I understand you properly? Is it assassination, or anything of that sort, you're talking about?"

Beldeman shook his head.

"Those are methods for extreme cases," he said. "Yours is not an extreme case. We do not threaten you, Mr. Maraton, with death, but we do threaten you with the death of your reputation, the end of your career as a political power in this country, if you do not see your way clear to act as we desire."

Maraton stood, for a few seconds, perfectly still.

"You have courage, Mr. Beldeman," he remarked.

"Sir," Mr. Beldeman replied, "I have been as near death as most men. That is why I occupy my present position. I am the special agent of the greatest political power in the world. When I choose to make use of my machinery, I can kill or spare, abduct, rob, ruin — what I choose. You I only threaten. I fancy that will be enough. We have our hold upon the press of this country."

Maraton walked to the door and back again.

"I killed a man once, Mr. Beldeman," he said, "who threatened me."

"You will not kill me," Mr. Beldeman declared, with gentle confidence in his tone.

"If I had known," Maraton continued softly, "I'd have wrung your neck at Manchester."

"Quite easy, I should say," Mr. Beldeman agreed. "You look strong. Without a doubt I could make you desperate. Better be reasonable. My people want the railway strike, the coal strike, and the iron strike — want them both within a month. Come, what are you afraid of? Stick to your colours, Mr. Maraton. Wasn't it in the *North American Review* you declared that a war and conquest were the inevitable prelude of social reform in this country?"

"Did I say that?" Maraton asked.

"You did. Now you are here, you are afraid. Never mind, war and conquest are to come. We give you a month in which to deliver your message. You have, I believe, two large meetings to address before that date. Make your pronouncement and all will be well. The million is yours for the people."

"A sort of gigantic blackmail," Maraton remarked drily.

"You can call it what you like. If you have conditions to make, I am prepared to listen. I do not insult you by offering —"

Maraton flung open the door a little noisily.

"That will do, Mr. Beldeman," he said. "I congratulate you upon the manner in which you have conducted this interview. I presume I shall see you again one day before the month is up?"

"You certainly will," Mr. Beldeman replied. "If you should want me before — an advance payment or anything of that sort — I am at the Royal Hotel."

Maraton was alone in the room. For some mo-

ments he remained motionless.   He heard Aaron and
Julia in the hall but he did not hasten to join them.
He moved instead to the window and stood watching
Beldeman's retreating form.

CHAPTER XX

Maraton led the way on to the roof of one of London's newer hotels.

"They won't give us dinner here," he explained. "London isn't civilised enough for that yet, or perhaps it's a matter of climate. But we can get all sorts of things to eat, and some wine, and sit and watch the lights come out. I was here the other night alone and I thought it the most restful spot in London."

He called a waiter and had a table drawn up to the palisaded edge of the roof. Then he slipped something into the man's hand, and there seemed to be no difficulty about serving them with anything they required.

"A salad, some sandwiches, a bottle of hock and plenty of strawberries. We shan't starve, at any rate," Maraton declared. "Lean back in your chairs, you children of the city, lean down and look at your mother. Look at her smoke-hung arms, stretched out as though to gather in the universe; and the lights upon her bosom — see how they come twinkling into existence."

Both of them followed his outstretched finger with their eyes, but Julia only shivered.

"I hate it," she muttered, "hate it all! London seems to me like a great, rapacious monster. Our

bodies and souls are sacrificed over there. For what?
I was in Piccadilly and the parks to-day. Is there
any justice in the world, I wonder? It's just as
though there were a kink in the great wheels and
they weren't running true."

"Sometimes I think," Maraton declared, "that
the matter would right itself automatically but for
the interference of weak people. The laws of life
are tampered with so often by people without understanding. They keep alive the unworthy. They try
to make life easier for the unfit. They endow hos-
pitals and build model dwellings. It's a sop to their
consciences. It's like planting a flower on the grave
of the man you have murdered."

"But these things help," Aaron protested.

"Help? They retard," Maraton insisted. "All
charity is the most vicious form of self-indulgence.
Can't you see that if the poor died in the streets,
and the sick were left to crawl about the face of the
earth, the whole business would right itself automatically. The unfit would die out. A stronger
generation would arise, a generation stronger and
better able to look after itself. But come, we have
been serious long enough. You are tired with your
day's work, Miss Julia, and Aaron, too. I've been
in the committee room of the House of Commons half
the day, and my head's addled with figures. Here
comes our supper. Let us drop the more serious
things of life. We'll try and put a little colour into
your cheeks, young lady."

He served them both and filled their glasses with
wine. Then, as he ate, he leaned back in his chair

and watched them. For all her strange beauty, Julia, too, was one of the suffering children of the world. The lines of her figure, which should have been so subtle and fascinating, were sharpened by an unnatural thinness. Aaron's cheeks were almost like a consumptive's, his physique was puny. There was something in their expression common to both. Maraton was conscious of a wave of pity as he withdrew his eyes.

"Sometimes," he said, "I feel almost angry with you two. You carry on your shoulders the burden of other people's sufferings. It is well to feel and realise them, and the gift of sympathy is a beautiful thing, but our own individualism is also a sacred gift. It is not for us to weaken or destroy it by encouraging a superabundant sympathy for others. We each have our place in the world, whether we owe it to fate or our own efforts, and it is our duty to make the best of it. Our own happiness, indeed, is a present charge upon ourselves for the ultimate benefit of others. A happy person in the world does good always. You two have a leaning towards morbidness. If I had time, I would undertake your education. As it is, we will have another bottle of wine, and I shall take you to a music hall."

It was an evening that lived in Julia's mind with particular vividness for years to come, and yet one which she always found it difficult to piece together in her thoughts. They went to one of the less fashionable music halls, where the turns were frequent and there was no ballet. Aaron was very soon able to re-establish his temporarily lost capacity for enjoyment. Maraton, leaning back in his place with a cigar in his mouth, appreciated everything and applauded constantly. It was Julia who found the new atmosphere most difficult. She laughed often, it is true, but she had always a semi-subjective feeling, as though it were some other person who was really there, and she the instrument chosen to give physical indication of that other person's presence. Only once life seemed suddenly to thrill and burn in her veins, to shoot through her body with startling significance, and in that brief space of time, life itself was transformed for her. Maraton by chance found her hand, as they sat side by side, and held it for a moment in his. There was nothing secret about his action. The firm pressure of his fingers, even, seemed as though they might have been the kindly, encouraging touch of a sympathetic friend. But upon Julia his touch was magical. The rest of the evening faded into insignificance. She understood feelings which had come to her that afternoon in the park with absolute completeness for the first time. From that moment she took her place definitely amongst the women who walk through life but whose feet seldom touch the earth.

When the performance was over, Maraton called a taxicab.

" Aaron," he directed, " you must take your sister back to her lodgings. No, I insist," he added, as she protested. " No 'buses to-night. Go home and sleep well and think about yourself."

She shook her head.

" I will go home in a taxi," she agreed, " if you

will do one thing for me. It won't take long. It
has been in my mind ever since you said what you
did about charity. I want us all to go down to the
Embankment. It isn't late enough really, but I want
you to come."

He sighed.

" You are incorrigible," he declared. " Never
mind, we will go. How good the air is! We'll walk."

They turned along the Strand and descended the
narrow street which led to the Embankment. Then
they walked slowly as far as Blackfriars Bridge.
They neither of them spoke a word. From time to
time they glanced at the silent and motionless figures
on the seats. For the most part, the loiterers there
were either asleep or sitting with closed eyes. Here
and there they caught a glance from some spectral
face, a glance cold and listless. The fires of life were
dead amongst these people. The animal desires alone
remained; their faces were dumb.

They stood together at the corner of Blackfriars
Bridge.

" Well," Maraton said, " I have done your bidding. I have been here before many times, and I
have been here in the winter."

" Tell me," she asked, " there is a girl there on
that third seat, crying. Am I doing wrong if I go
to her and give her money for a night's lodging? "

" Without a doubt," he answered. " And yet, I
expect you'll do it. Principles are splendid — in
the abnegation. If we are to be illogical, let me
be the breaker of my own laws."

He thrust some money into her hand and Julia

disappeared. For some time she remained talking with the figure upon the seat. Aaron and Maraton leaned over the corner of the bridge and looked down the curving arc of lights towards the Houses of Parliament.

"I shall end there, you know, Aaron," Maraton sighed. "I am not looking forward to it. It's a queer sort of a hothouse for a man."

"I wonder," Aaron murmured thoughtfully. "I used to think of you travelling from one to the other of the great cities, and I used to think that when you had spoken to them, the people would see the truth and rise and take their own. I used to be very fond of the Old Testament once," he went on, his voice sinking a little lower. "Life was so simple in those days, and the words of a prophet seemed greater than any laws."

"And nowadays," Maraton continued, "life has become like a huge and complex piece of machinery. Humanity has given way to mechanics. Aaron, I don't believe I can help this people by any other way save by laws."

They both turned quickly around. Julia was standing by their side, and with her the girl.

"I told her," Julia explained, "that it was not my money I was offering, but the money of a gentleman who was the greatest friend the poor people of the world have ever known. She wanted to speak to you."

The girl drew her shawl a little closer around her shoulders. Her face bore upon it the terrible stamp of suffering, without its redeeming purification.

Save for her abundant hair, her very sex would have been unrecognisable. She looked steadily at Maraton.

"You sent me money," she said.

"I did," he admitted.

"Are you one of those soft-hearted fools who go about doing this sort of thing?" she demanded.

"I am not," he replied. "I object to giving money away. I am sorry to see people suffering, but as a rule I think that it is their own fault if they come to the straits that you are in. I sent the money to please this young lady."

"Their own fault, eh?" she muttered.

"I qualify that," he added quickly. "Their own fault because they submit to a heritage of unjust laws. It is your own fault because you don't join together and smash the laws. You would fill the jails, perhaps, but you'd make it easier for those who came after."

She stood quite silent for a moment. When she spoke, the truculent note had departed from her tone.

"I came here," she said, "meaning to chuck this money in your face. I thought you were one of these canting hypocrites who salve their consciences by giving away what they don't want. My baby died this morning in the hospital, and they turned me out. If I keep your money, do you know what I shall do with it? Get drunk."

He nodded.

"Why not?"

She looked at him stolidly.

"When I've spent it, I shall go into the river.

I'm not fit for anything else. I'm too weak to work, and for the rest, look at me. I'm as ugly as sin itself — just a few bones held together."

"Take the money and get drunk," Maraton advised. "You're quite right. There's no help for you. You've no spirit to help yourself. If you hang on to the crust of the world through charity, you only do the world harm. You're better out of it."

She gathered up the money and shivered a little.

"I'll drink yer health," she muttered, as she turned away.

Julia half started to follow her, but Maraton held her arm.

"Useless," he whispered. "She's one of the broken creatures of the world. Whilst you keep her alive, you spread corruption. She'll probably hang on to life until it gives her up."

He called a taxi.

"Now I am going to have my own way," he announced. "Aaron is going to take you home. I came here because you wished it, but it's very amateurish, you know, this sort of thing. It's on a par with district visiting and slumming, and all the rest of it. A disease in the body sometimes brings out scars. A doctor doesn't stare at the scars. He treats the body for the disease. Get these places out of your mind, Julia. They are only useful inasmuch as they remind us of the black truth."

He took her hands.

"Remember," he added, "that you've finished with the tailoring for a time. Aaron will want you to-morrow, or as soon as you can come. We've piles of work to do."

Her eyes shone at him.

"Work," she murmured, "but think of the difference! If it wasn't for what you've just said about individualism, I think that I should be feeling cruelly selfish."

"Rubbish!" he exclaimed. "You're secretary of the Women's Guild, aren't you? You can keep that up. I'll come and talk to your girls some day. Your work has been too narrow down there. There are some other women's industries I want you to enquire into. Till to-morrow!"

He strode vigorously away. The taxicab turned eastward over Blackfriars Bridge.

CHAPTER XXI

On the following morning, Maraton saw Elisabeth for the first time since his return from Manchester. As he rang the bell of Mr. Foley's residence in Downing Street, at a few minutes before the hour at which he had been bidden to luncheon, he found himself wondering with a leaven of resentment in his feelings why he had so persistently avoided the house during the last three weeks. All his consultations with Mr. Foley, and they had been many, had taken place at the House of Commons. He had refused endless invitations of a social character, and even when Mr. Foley had told him in plain words that his niece was anxious to see him, Maraton had postponed his call. This luncheon party, however, was inevitable. He was to meet a great lawyer who had a place in the Government, and two other Cabinet Ministers. No excuse would have served his purpose.

The man who took his hat and coat had evidently received special instructions.

"Mr. Foley is engaged with his secretary, sir," he said. "A messenger has just arrived from abroad. Will you come this way?"

He was taken to Elisabeth's little room. She was there waiting for him. Directly she rose, he knew why he had kept away.

"Are you not a little ashamed of yourself, Mr.

Maraton?" she asked, as the door was closed behind
the departing servant.

"On the contrary," he replied, "I am proud."

She laughed at him, naturally at first, but with a
note of self-consciousness following swiftly, as she
realised the significance of his words.

"How foolish! Really, I know it is only a subter-
fuge to avoid being scolded. Sit down, won't you?
You will have to wait at least ten minutes for
luncheon."

They looked at one another. He took up a volume
of poems from the small table by his side and put it
down again.

"Well?" she asked.

"You have conquered," he declared. "You see,
I came down to earth."

"It isn't possible for me," she said simply, "to
tell you how glad I am. Don't you yourself feel that
you have done the right thing?"

"Since that night at Manchester," he told her, "I
have scarcely stopped to think. Do you know that
your strongest allies were Mr. Peter Dale and his
men?"

She shrugged her shoulders.

"I disclaim my allies. If we arrived at the same
conclusion, we did so by differing lines of thought.
Let me tell you," she went on, "there were two things
for which I have prayed. One was that you might
start your fight exactly as you have done. The other
that you might find no official place amongst the
Labour Members. Of course, I can't pretend to the
practical experience of a real politician, but my uncle

talks to me a great deal, and to me the truth seemed so clear. It is the advanced Unionists who need you. They are really the party from whom progress must come, because it is the middle class which has to be attacked, and it is amongst the middle classes that Liberalism has its stronghold. If you once took your place among the Labour Members, you would be a Labour Member and nothing else. People wouldn't take what you said seriously."

"I am coming into the House, if at all, as an Independent Member," he announced.

She nodded.

"Mr. Foley is quite satisfied with that — in fact he thinks it's best. Do you know, he seems to have gained a new lease of life during the last few weeks. What do you think of his commission on your Manchester strike?"

"He kept his word," Maraton admitted. "I expected no less."

"I can tell you this," she went on, "because I know that he will tell you himself after luncheon. The masters met here this morning. They are simply furious with my uncle, but they have had to give in. The bill you drafted would have been rushed through Parliament without a moment's delay, if they had not. Mr. Foley showed them your draft. They have given in on every point."

"I am afraid I'm going to keep your uncle rather busy," Maraton remarked. "Very soon after this is settled, I have promised to speak at Sheffield."

"In a way it is terrible," she said, with a sigh, "and yet it is so much better than the things we feared. Tell me about yourself a little, won't you? How have you been spending your time? You have a large, gloomy house here, they tell me, shrouded with mystery. Have you any amusements or have you been working all the time?"

"Half my days have been spent with your uncle," he reminded her. "The other half at home, working. So many of my facts were rusty. As to my house, is it really mysterious, I wonder? It is large and gloomy, at the extreme corner of an unfashionable square. It suits me because I love space and quietness, and yet I like to be near the heart of things."

"But do you do nothing but work?" she asked. "Have you no hobbies?"

He shook his head.

"I seem to have had no time for games. I like walking, walking in the country or even walking in the cities and watching the people. Only the London streets are so sad. Then I am fond of reading. I'm afraid I should be rather a strange figure if I were to be suddenly projected into your world, Lady Elisabeth."

"But I like to feel that you are in my world," she said gently. "Believe me, it isn't altogether made up of people who play games."

"I read the daily papers," he remarked. "Didn't I see something yesterday about Lady Elisabeth Landon having won the scratch prize at Ranelagh at a ladies' golf meeting?"

She laughed pleasantly.

"Oh! well," she protested, "you must make allowance for my bringing up. We begin to play

games in this country as soon as we can crawl about
the nursery. It all depends upon the value you set
upon these things."

A servant knocked at the door and announced the
service of luncheon. Elisabeth rose reluctantly to
her feet.

"Now, I suppose, I must hand you over to the
serious business of life," she sighed. "If you do
have a minute to spare when you have finished with
my uncle," she added in a lower tone, as they passed
down the wide staircase side by side, "come up and
see me before you go. I shall be in till four o'clock."

The familiarity of her words, half whispered in
his ear, the delightful suggestion of some confidential
understanding between them, were alike fascinating
to him. In her plain white serge coat and skirt, and
smart hat — she had just come in from walking in
the park — she seemed to him to represent so perfectly the very best and most delightful type of
womanhood. Her complexion was perfect, her skin
fresh as a child's. She carried herself with the
spring and grace of one who walks through life self-
confidently, fortified always with the knowledge that
she was a favourite with women as well as with men.
He sat by her side at luncheon and he could not help
admiring the delicate tact with which she prevented
the conversation from ever remaining more than a
few seconds in channels which might have made him
feel something of an alien. There was another
nephew of Mr. Foley's there, a famous polo player
and sportsman; Lord Carton, whose eyes seldom left
Elisabeth's face; Sir William Blend, the great law-

yer; Mr. Horrill and Lord Armley. These, with Elisabeth's mother and herself, made up the party.

"I think I am going to bar politics," Lady Grenside said, as she took her place.

"Impossible!" Mr. Foley retorted, in high good humour. "This is a political luncheon. We have great and weighty matters to discuss. You women are permitted to be present, but we allot to you the hardest task of all — silence."

"A sheer impossibility, so far as mother is concerned," Elisabeth observed. "As for me, I call myself a practical politician. I intend to take part in the discussion."

Mr. Foley looked across the round table with twinkling eyes.

"We are going to talk about Universal Manhood Suffrage," he announced.

"Scandalous," Elisabeth declared, "before we have our votes!"

"Perhaps," Maraton suggested, "it was Universal Suffrage that Mr. Foley meant."

"Including children and aliens," Lady Grenside remarked. "I am sure the children at the school I went over yesterday could have ruled the nation admirably. They seemed to know positively everything."

"Mother, you are too frivolous," Elisabeth insisted. "If this tone of levity is not dropped, I shall start another subject of conversation. Mr. Maraton, you, of course, are in favour of Universal Manhood Suffrage?"

"I am not at all sure about it," he replied. "It

gives the vote to a lot of people I'd sooner see deported."

" But you — you to talk like that! " she exclaimed. He smiled.

" Votes should belong to those who have a stake in the country, not to the flotsam and jetsam," he continued solemnly.

" But you're a Tory! " she cried.

" Not a bit," he answered. " If I had my way, you would very soon see that one man wouldn't have so much more stake in the country than another. Then Universal Suffrage follows automatically — in fact that's the way I'd arrive at it."

" Don't ever let Mr. Maraton be Prime Minister! " Elisabeth begged. " He's too iconoclastic."

" And just now I was a Tory," Maraton protested.

" It isn't my fault that you are a study in contraries," she laughed. " But then politicians are rather like that, aren't they? I think really that they should be like surgeons, specialise all the time."

" Come down to Ranelagh and play golf after luncheon," Lord Carton suggested abruptly from across the table. " I've got my little racing car outside and I'll take you down there like a rocket."

" Thanks," she answered, " I want particularly to stay in till four o'clock this afternoon. Besides, you can't play golf, you know."

" I don't think Elisabeth has improved," he remarked to her mother, turning deliberately away.

" And I am sure Jack's left his heart in Central America," Elisabeth declared. " He was always fond of dark-complexioned ladies. Mr. Maraton, have you been a great traveller?"

He shook his head.

"I have been in South America," he replied, "and I know most of the country between San Francisco and New York pretty well."

"And Europe?" she asked.

"I walked from Vienna to Paris when I was a boy," he told her. "It's years, though, since I was on the Continent."

Her cousin began to talk of his hunting experiences, and every one listened. As soon as the service of luncheon was concluded, Lady Grenside rose.

"I dare say we shall all meet again before you go," she said. "Coffee is being served to you in the library, Stephen. We won't say good-bye to anybody. Jack, don't forget that you are dining here to-night. You shall take in the blackest young lady I can pick out for you."

Elisabeth followed her mother. At the last moment, Maraton caught a little whisper which only just floated from her lips.

"Till four o'clock!"

The two younger men took their departure almost immediately. The others moved into the library. Mr. Foley plunged at once into the subject which was uppermost in their minds.

"Mr. Maraton," he began, "we want to talk about these strikes. Horrill here, and Blend, have an idea that you are working towards some definite result — that you have more in your mind than I have told them. It is only this morning," he went

on in a lower tone, and glancing towards the closed
door, " that I explained to them your Manchester
speech. They know now that England has you to
thank for the fact that we are not at this moment
preparing for war."

CHAPTER XXII

Between three and four o'clock, half a dozen people, on different devices, tried to draw Elisabeth from her retirement. Her particular friend called to suggest a round of the picture galleries, tea at the club, and a motor ride to Ranelagh. Lord Carton repeated his invitation to a game of golf. Two people invited her out into the country on various pretexts. Her dressmaker rang up and begged for her presence without delay. To all of these importunities Elisabeth remained deaf. She sat in her room in an easy-chair drawn up to the open window, with a book in her hand at which she scarcely glanced. Her thoughts were with the five men downstairs. Every now and then she glanced at the clock. She heard the conference break up. She sat quite still, listening. Presently there was the sound of a firm tread upon the stairs. She closed her book and breathed a little sigh. A servant ushered in Maraton.

"You have not forgotten, then," she said softly. "Come and sit in my favourite chair and rest for a few moments. I am sure that you must be tired."

He sank down with an air of content. She sat upon the end of the sofa, close to him, her head resting upon her hands.

"Well," she asked, "have you converted Sir William?"

"Up to a certain extent, I believe," he answered, after a momentary hesitation. "I don't think that he trusts me. Lawyers have a habit of not trusting people, you know. On the other hand, I don't think he means to give any trouble. Of course, they don't like what they have to face. No one does. It isn't every one who has the sagacity of your uncle."

"I am glad," she said, "that you appreciate him. Tell me now what is going to happen?"

"Mr. Foley will have his own way," Maraton declared. "The Manchester strike will be over in a few days. The Sheffield strike will be dealt with in the same manner. People will talk about the great loss of trade, the shocking depreciation of profits, the lowered incomes of the people, and all that sort of thing. What will really happen will be that the investor and the manufacturer are going to pay, and Labour is going to get just about a tithe of its own in these two cases. The country will be none the poorer. The money will be still there, only its distribution will be saner."

"And the end of it?" she murmured. "What will the end of it be?"

"We can none of us tell that," he answered gravely. "There are some, like Sir William, who insist that when Labour has once started, as it will have started after Sheffield, there will be no holding it. I can not answer for it. I only say that the course Mr. Foley has adopted is distinctly the best for the country. If an obstinate man had been in his place to-day, nothing could have saved you from civil war first and possibly from foreign conquest later."

" A month ago," she observed, " you seemed fully prepared for these things."

" I was," he admitted.

" But you are an Englishman, are you not? "

" I am English. I daresay that under other considerations I might even have called myself a patriotic Englishman. As it is, I have very little feeling of that sort. There has been too much self-glorification, and it's the wrong class of people who've revelled in it and enjoyed it. It's a fine thing to die for one's country. It's a shameful thing that that country should grind the life and brains and blood out of a hundred of her children, day by day."

A servant brought in tea, delightfully served. There were small yellow china cups, pale tea with a faint, aromatic odour, thick cream, strawberries and cakes.

" If only you would appreciate it," she declared, " you are really rather a privileged person. No one has tea with me here."

" I do appreciate it," he assured her, " perhaps more than you think."

There was a moment's silence. As he was taking his cup from her fingers, their eyes met, and she looked away again almost immediately.

" I wish," she said, " that you would tell me more about yourself — what you did in America, what your life has been? You are rather a mysterious person, aren't you? "

"In a sense, perhaps, I must seem so," he admitted. "You see, I was an orphan very early. There wasn't any one who cared how I grew up, and I wandered a good deal. The earlier part of my life I was over here — I was at Heidelberg University, bye the bye — and in Paris for two years studying art, of all things! Then something — I don't know what it was — called me to America, and I found it hard to come back. It's a big country, you know, Lady Elisabeth. It gets hold of you. If it hadn't driven me out, I doubt whether I should ever have left it."

"But what was it first inspired you with this — well, wouldn't you call it a passion — for championing the cause of the people?"

He shook his head.

"Born in me, I suppose. I have watched them, lived with them, and then I have been through the whole gamut of Socialistic literature. It is not worth reading, most of it. The essential facts are there to look at, half-a-dozen phrases, a single field of view. It's all very simple."

"Now I am going to ask you something else," she went on. "That first night when we talked together, you seemed so full of hope, so dauntless. Since then, is it my fancy — since you came back from Manchester — are you a little disappointed with life? Don't you know in your heart that you've done what's best?"

"I wish I did," he answered simply. "My common sense tells me that I have chosen well, and then sometimes, in the nights, or when I am alone, other thoughts come to me, and I feel almost as though I had been faithless, as though I had simply chosen the easier way. Look how pleasant it is all being made for me! I am no longer an outcast; I bask in the sun of your uncle's patronage; people ask me to dinner, seek my friendship, people whom I feel ought to hate me. I am not sure about it all."

"Listen," she said, "if you had indeed pulled down those pillars, don't you think that day by day and night by night you would have been haunted by the faces of those whom you had destroyed? Think of the children who would have died of starvation, the women who would have been torn from their husbands, the ruined homes, the sorrow and the misery all through the land. Yours would have been the hand which had dealt this blow. You would not have lived to have seen into the future. Would it have been enough for you to have believed that you had done it for the best — that that unborn generation of which you spoke would have benefitted? Oh, I do not think so! I believe that when you realise it, you must be glad."

"It is at any rate consoling to hear you say so," he remarked. "Yet, when you have made up your mind to play the martyr, it is a little hard," he added, helping himself to strawberries, "to be treated like a pampered being."

"In other words," she laughed, "you are discontented because you have been successful?"

"I suppose human nature never meant to let us rest satisfied."

"Don't you ever think of yourself," she asked,

" what your own life is going to be? You've settled
down now. You will be a Member of Parliament in
a few weeks, a Cabinet Minister before long. I know
what my uncle thinks of you. He believes in you.
To tell you the truth, so do I."

" I am glad."

" I believe," she went on, " that you will do the
work that you came here to do. There is no reason
why you should not do it from the Cabinet. But
there is the rest — your own life. Are you never
going to amuse yourself, to take holiday, to draw
some of the outside things into your scheme of
being? "

He sat quite silent for a little time. He was
inclined to struggle against the charm of her soft
voice, the easy intimacy with which she treated him.
In a sense he felt as though he were losing control
of himself.

" I don't know," he said. " I think one ought to
find one's work sufficient for a time. It is engross-
ing, isn't it? And that reminds me — I must go."

He rose almost abruptly to his feet. She was
quick to appreciate his slight confusion of thought,
his nervous self-impatience, and she smiled quietly.
She was content to let him escape. She held out
her hand, though, and his fingers seemed conscious
of the firm, delicate warmth of her clasp.

" Come and talk to me again soon," she begged.
" Come either as a politician or a friend, or however you like. It gives me so much pleasure to talk
with you. Uncle will tell you that every one spoils
me. Even Sir William comes and tells me about

his troubles with the Irish Members. Will you come? "

He made a half promise. His departure was a little hasty — almost abrupt; he was conscious of a distinct turmoil of feeling. He hurried away, as though anxious to rid himself of the influence of the place. At the corner of the street he was about to hail a taxicab when a man gripped him by the arm. He turned quickly around. The face was somehow familiar to him — the grey, untidy beard, long hairy eyebrows, sunken eyes, the shabby clothes. It was David Ross.

" Can I speak a word with you, Mr. Maraton? "

Maraton nodded.

" Of course. I don't remember your name. You were at Manchester, weren't you, and at my house with the others? "

" Ross, my name is," the man answered. " I'd no call to be at Manchester, for I'm not one of the delegates. I'm not an M.P. but I've done a lot of speaking for them lately, and Peter Dale, he said if I paid my own expenses I could come along. I borrowed the money. I had to come. I had to hear you speak. I wanted to know your message."

" Were you satisfied with it? " Maraton enquired.

" I don't know," was the doubtful reply. " You ask me a question I can't answer myself. I thought so at the time, but since then I've spent many sleepless nights and many tired hours, asking myself that question. Now I am here to ask you one. Did you speak that night what you had in your mind when you left America? — what you thought of on the

steamer coming over — what you meant to say when
first you set foot in this country?"

Maraton was interested. He walked slowly along
by the side of his companion.

"I did not," he admitted. "I came with other
views."

"I knew it!" Ross exclaimed, almost fiercely. "I
felt it, man. You came to preach redemption, even
though the means were sharp and short and sudden,
means of blood, means of death. Before you ever
came here, I seemed to hear your voice crying across
that great continent, crying even across the ocean.
It was a terrible cry, but it seemed as though it
must reach up into heaven and down into hell, for
it was aflame with truth. It seemed to me that I
could see the revolution upon us, the death that is
like sleep, the looking down once more from some
undiscovered place upon the new morning. You
never uttered that cry over here."

Maraton glanced at his companion curiously.

"Mine was an immense responsibility," he said.
"Granted that I had the power, do you think that
I had the right to stir up a civil war here in the
face of the help I was promised for our people?"

David Ross sighed.

"I don't know," he confessed. "I only know
that many years ago, Peter Dale, when he was a
young man, spoke as though the word of truth were
burning in his heart. He was for a revolution. He
would be content with nothing less. And Borden
was like that, and Graveling, and others whom you
don't know. And then the people gave them their

mandate, knocked a bit of money together, and sent
them to Parliament. There, somehow or other, they
seemed to fall into the easier ways. They worked
stolidly and honestly, no doubt, but something had
gone, something we've all missed, something that by
this time might have helped. When they told me —
it was Aaron who came and told me — rode his bicycle
like a madman, all the way from Soho. 'Maraton
is come!' he shouted. Then it seemed to me that
freedom was here; no more compromises, but battle
— the naked sword, battle with the wrongs of generations to requite. Is the sword sheathed?"

Maraton passed his arm through his companion's.
"It is not sheathed," he declared, "nor while I
have life will it be sheathed. If I have chosen the
quieter methods, it is because for the present I have
come to believe that they are the best. Six hundred
thousand people in Lancashire are going to start
life next Monday with an increase of between fifteen
and twenty per cent to their weekly wage. Isn't
that something to the good? And then, in a few
weeks, every forge and furnace in Sheffield will be
cold until the men's demands are granted there.
And when that is over, we go for every industry,
one by one, throughout the country. Before a year
is past, I reckon that many millions will have passed
from the pockets of the middle classes into the pockets
of the labouring man. I am going to set that stream
running faster and faster, and then I am going to
begin all over again. With prosperity, the labouring classes will gain strength. You will have more
time for thought, for education, for self-knowledge.

And as they gain strength, once more we raise our hands. Do they seem slow to you, our methods, David Ross? Believe me, they did to me. Yet in my heart I know that I have chosen the right."

The man drew a little sigh. There may have been disappointment mingled with it, yet there was a certain amount of relief.

" I was afraid for you, Maraton," he said. " I thought of those others when they stumbled upon the easy ways, and I was afraid. With you it may be different. Hold on your way, then. It is not for me to criticise. But if you slacken, if your hand droops, then I shall come again."

He turned abruptly away and disappeared, walking with quick, shambling footsteps. Maraton looked after him thoughtfully for several moments, then he continued on his way homewards.

CHAPTER XXIII

The last words had been spoken, the suspense of a few hours was at an end. Maraton was on his way back to London, a duly accredited Member of Parliament for the eastern division of Nottingham. From his place in the railway carriage he fancied that he could hear even now the roar of voices, feel the thrill of emotion with which he had waited for the result. An Independent Member, even when backed as Maraton had been backed, is never in a wholly safe position. On the whole, he had done well. He had increased the majority of four hundred to a majority of seven hundred. And this, too, in the face of unexpected difficulties. At the last minute a surprise had been sprung upon the constituency. A Labour candidate had entered the field. Maraton's telegram to Peter Dale had produced no reply. The man, if not officially recognised, was at least not officially discouraged. His intervention had been useless, however. Maraton had carried the working men with him. In a sense it was an election on the strangest issues which had ever been fought. Many of the most far-seeing journalists of the day predicted in this new alliance the redistribution of Parties which for some time had been inevitable. So far as Maraton was concerned, it was, without doubt, an unexpected phase in his career. He was Maraton, M.P., representative of a manufacturing town; elected, indeed, as an Independent, but with a weighty backing of the Unionist Party behind him. The next time he spoke, probably, if he did speak before his journey to Sheffield, would be in the House of Commons. Would he, like those others, feel the inertia of it, the slow decay of his ambitions, the fatal tendency towards compromise?

Arrived at St. Pancras, Maraton drove straight to his house in Russell Square and, letting himself in with his latch-key, made his way to the study. The lights were still burning there. Julia and Aaron were sitting opposite to one another at the end of the long table, a typewriter between them and a pile of papers by Aaron's side. Julia rose at once to her feet.

"You are in!" she cried. "We have been telephoning all the evening. We heard half an hour ago."

Maraton nodded.

"In by seven hundred. Not bad, I suppose, considering that I must have been rather a hard nut to crack. Has Peter Dale been here?"

Aaron shook his head.

"He hasn't been near the place."

Maraton's face hardened.

"You know that they sprang a Labour candidate upon me at the last moment? He did me no particular harm, but it was an infamous trick. I wired to Dale yesterday and had no reply."

"David Ross has been here," Aaron said. "We heard all about it from him. There is dissension in the camp. Dale was in favour of withdrawing their candidate, but Graveling wouldn't have it."

" He did me no harm, anyway," Maraton remarked. " The Labour vote was mine from the start."

" So it ought to have been," Aaron declared vigorously. " What could they do but vote for you, with Manchester staring them in the face? "

Maraton's expression lightened, a gleam of humour twinkled in his eyes.

" After all," he murmured, " it would have been almost Gilbertian if I had been returned to Parliament with the Labour vote against me! . . . Aaron, go and ring up Peter Dale. I want this matter cleared up. Ask him when we can meet."

Aaron left the room upon his errand. Maraton moved restlessly about the room for a moment or two. He mixed himself a drink at the sideboard, and lit a cigarette. Julia's eyes followed him all the time.

" So you are a Member of Parliament," she said at last.

" I hope you approve? " he queried.

Julia did not answer him at once. He looked across at her from the depth of the easy chair into which he had thrown himself. She was wearing a plain black dress, buttoned to her throat and unrelieved even by a linen collar or any touch of white. She was pale, and her eyes seemed all the more beautiful for the faint violet lines beneath them.

" Parliament has been the grave of so many men's careers," Maraton continued. " I am fully warned.

Nothing of the sort is going to happen to me. I wouldn't have gone in now but for Foley. It's only fair. It helps him, and he's sticking to his pledges like a man."

"When do you go to Sheffield?" she asked.

"Next Wednesday. No postponements."

Julia nodded.

"Mr. Elgood has been here this afternoon," she said, "from Sheffield. He is the secretary of the Union, you know. He is coming again to-morrow morning. He wants to talk to you about the boys' age limit."

"Any letters of consequence?"

Julia pointed a little disdainfully to a pile upon the table.

"All invitations," she observed coldly. "Perhaps you had better look them through."

Maraton shook his head.

"They are no use to me," he declared, "unless they're political?"

He rose and stood by Julia's side, glancing idly through the heap of papers by the side of her machine.

"You seem to have found plenty to do, anyway," he remarked.

"There was a great deal," she assured him. "I think I have collected all the possible information you can need on the steel works of Sheffield."

"Haven't been overworking, I hope?"

She laughed at him softly. Her parted lips seemed somehow to lighten her face.

"This doesn't quite compare with nine hours a

day over a sewing machine, with a hundred other girls packed into a small room," she reminded him. "No, I haven't been overworking. I almost wished, an hour ago, that I could find something more to do."

"Why didn't you go out?"

"To-morrow night is Guild night," she said. "I go out then to talk to my girls. Miss Stevens is coming from the Lyceum Club to lecture to us on Woman's Suffrage."

"Do you want a vote?" he asked.

"If it comes," she replied. "It isn't worth worrying about. I like my girls, though, to be taught to think."

There was a brief silence. Maraton was still examining the letters laid out for his inspection. Julia was standing by his side. As the last one slipped through his fingers, he turned quickly towards her, oppressed by some mysterious significance in her silence. Her eyes were luminous. She seemed to be trembling. She avoided his enquiring glance.

"Julia!" he exclaimed.

She lifted her head slowly, almost unwillingly. Though her lips were parted, she made no attempt at speech. Then the door was suddenly opened. Aaron entered in some excitement.

"Mr. Dale and some of the others are here now, sir," he announced. "I heard they were on their way when I telephoned. They would like to see you at once."

Maraton stood for a moment quite still, without replying. Aaron gazed across the table in some surprise.

" What shall I say to them? " he asked.   " They are here now."

Maraton shrugged his shoulders.

" Let them come in," he directed.

CHAPTER XXIV

The three men — Peter Dale, Abraham Weavel and Graveling filed into the room a little solemnly. Maraton shook hands with the two former, but Graveling, who kept his head turned away from Julia, affected not to notice Maraton's friendly overtures.

"So you managed it all right," Peter Dale remarked. "Pretty close fit, wasn't it?"

"Seven hundred," Maraton replied. "Not so bad, considering. You see, I was a complete stranger and I am not sure that I have learnt the knack yet of that sort of platform speaking."

"However that may be," Abraham Weavel declared, accepting a cigar from the box which Maraton had ordered, and standing with his hands underneath his coat-tails upon the hearthrug, "you've done the trick. You're an M.P., same as we are."

"You've no objection, I hope?" Maraton remarked lightly.

"That's as may be," Mr. Weavel observed sententiously. "We don't, so to speak, know exactly where we are just at this moment. There's all sorts of rumours going about, and we want them cleared up. Go on, Dale, ask him the first question. You're spokesman, you know."

Mr. Peter Dale threw away the match with which

he had just lit his pipe, sampled the whiskey and water to which he had helped himself with a most liberal hand, and deliberately selected the most comfortable chair within reach. With his hands in his trousers pockets, the thumbs protruding, his pipe in the left-hand corner of his mouth, his eyebrows drawn close together, he looked steadfastly towards Maraton.

"The first question," he began stolidly, "is this. You owe your seat in Parliament to the Unionists. What have you promised them in return? You haven't attempted to commit us to anything, I hope?"

"Certainly not," Maraton replied. "Such an idea never occurred to me. So far as I know," he went on, after a moment's hesitation, "Mr. Foley is not, at the moment, in need of your support. His majority is sufficient."

Peter Dale frowned ominously.

"That may or may not be," he remarked gruffly. "So long as you haven't taken it upon yourself to pledge us to anything, well, that disposes of question number one. The next is, where are you going to sit in the House?"

Maraton's eyebrows were slightly raised.

"Where am I going to sit?" he repeated. "Remember, if you please, that as a member I have never been inside your House of Commons. I am not acquainted with its procedure. Where, in your opinion, ought I to sit?"

"Your place is with us," Peter Dale declared. "I can't see that there's any doubt about that."

"And why?"

" You're a Labour man, aren't you? " Peter Dale asked. " You call yourself one, anyway."

" If I am a Labour man," Maraton said, " why did you put up a candidate to oppose me at Nottingham? "

Peter Dale smoked steadily for several moments.

" It was nowt to do with me," he announced. " The fellow sprung up all on his own, as it were. Graveling here may have known something of it, but so far as we are concerned he was not an authorised candidate."

Maraton shrugged his shoulders slightly.

" There was nothing," he objected, " to convey that idea to the electors. He made use of the Labour agent and the Labour committee rooms. My telegram to you remained unanswered. Under those circumstances, I really can scarcely see how you find it possible to disown him."

" In any case," Abraham Weavel intervened, with conciliation in his tone, " he didn't do himself a bit o' good nor you a bit of harm. Four hundred and thirty votes he polled out of eight thousand, and those were votes which otherwise would have gone to the Liberal. I should say myself that it did you good, if anything."

" You may be right," Maraton admitted. " At the same time, one thing is very clear. You did not offer me the slightest official support. It is true that I did not ask for it. I prefer, as I have told you all along, my independence. It will be my object to continue without direct association with any party. If I can find a place in the house allotted to Independent Members, I shall sit there. If not, I shall sit with the Unionists."

Peter Dale's face darkened. This was what they had feared.

"You mean that you're breaking away from us?" he exclaimed angrily. "There's no room in our little party for Independent Members, no sort of sense in a mere handful of us all pulling different ways."

"I never joined your party, Mr. Dale," Maraton reminded him. "I have never joined any man's party. I am for the people."

"And what about us?" Graveling demanded. "Aren't we for the people? Isn't that what we're in Parliament for? Isn't that why we are called Labour Members?"

Maraton regarded the last speaker steadily.

"Mr. Graveling," he said, "since you have mooted the question, I will admit that I do not consider you, as a body of men, entirely devoted to the cause of the people. You are each devoted to your own constituency. It is your business to look after the few thousand voters who sent you into Parliament, and in your eagerness to serve and please them, I think that you sometimes forget the greater, the more universal truths. I may be wrong. That is how the matter seems to me."

"Then since you're so frank," Peter Dale declared, with undiminished wrath, "I'll just imitate your candour! I'll tell you how you seem to us. You seem like a man with a gift, whose head has been turned by Mr. Foley and his fine friends.

You're full of great phrases, but there's nothing practical about them or you. You're on your way to an easy place for yourself in the world, and a seat in Foley's Cabinet."

"Have you any objection," Maraton asked, "to the people's cause being represented in the Cabinet?"

It was the last straw, this! Peter Dale's voice shook with passion.

"It's been a promise," he shouted, "for this many a year! A sop to the people it was, at the last election. There's one of us ought to be in the Cabinet —one of us, I say, not a carpetbagger!"

"We're the wrong type of man," Graveling broke in sarcastically. "That's what he said. He was heard to say it to the Home Secretary. The wrong type of man he called us."

Maraton suddenly changed his attitude. He was momentarily conscious of Julia listening, from her place in the background, to every word with strained attention. After all, these men had doubtless done good work according to their capacity.

"My friends," he protested, "why do we bandy words like this? Perhaps it is my fault. I have had a long and tiring day, and I must confess that I to some extent resented a Labour man being set up against me, without a word of explanation. You mean well, all of you, I am sure, even if we can't quite see the same way. Don't let's quarrel. I am not used to Parties. I can't serve under any one. My vote's my own, and I don't like the political juggery of selling it here and there for a *quid pro quo*. We may sit on opposite benches, but I give you my

word that there isn't anything in the world which
brings me into political life or will keep me there,
save the welfare of the people. Now shake hands,
all of you. Let us have a drink together and part
friends."

Peter Dale shook his head doggedly. He had
risen to his feet — a man filled with slow burning but
bitter anger.

" No, sir!" he declared. " Me and my mates
have stood for the people for this many a year, and
we've no fancy for a fine gentleman springing up
like a Jack-in-the-box from somewhere else in the
House, without any reference to us, and yet calling
himself and advertising himself as the champion of
our cause. Outside Parliament we can't stop you.
The Trades' Union men think more of you, maybe,
than they do of us. But inside you can plough your
own furrow, and for my part, when you're on your
legs, the smoking-room will be plenty good enough for
me!"

" And for the rest of us!" Graveling agreed
fiercely. " If you're so keen on being independent,
you shall see what you can do on your own."

Dale was already on his way to the door, but
Maraton checked him.

" Mr. Dale," he said, " you are an older man than
I am, a man of much experience. I beg you to
reflect. The feelings which prompt you towards this
action are unworthy. If you attempt to send me to
Coventry, you will simply bring ridicule upon a
Party which should be the broadest-minded in the
House."

He had risen to his feet — a man filled with slow burning but
bitter anger.   *Page* 224.

Mr. Dale turned around. He had already crammed his black, wide-awake hat on to his head. Like all men whose outlook upon life is limited, the idea of ridicule was hateful to him.

" You mark my words, young man," he growled. " The one that makes a fool of himself is the one that's going to play the toady to a master who will send him to heel with a kick, every time he opens his mouth to bark! Go your own way. I'm only sorry you ever set foot in this country."

He passed out, followed by Weavel. Graveling only lingered upon the threshold. He was looking towards Julia.

" Miss Thurnbrein," he said, " can I have a word with you? "

" You cannot," she replied steadily.

He remained there, dogged, full of suppressed wrath. The sight of her taking her place before the typewriter seemed to madden him. Already she was the better for the change of work and surroundings, for the improved conditions of her daily life. There was the promise of colour in her cheeks. Her plain black gown was as simple as ever, but her hair was arranged with care, and she carried herself with a new distinction, born of her immense contentment. Her supercilious attitude attracted while it infuriated him.

" It's only a word I want," he persisted. " I have a right to some sort of civility, at any rate."

" You have no rights at all," she retorted. " I thought that we had finished with that the last time we spoke together."

"I want to know," he went on obstinately, "why you haven't been to work lately?"

"Because I have left Weinberg's," she told him curtly. "It is no business of yours, but if it will help to get rid of you —"

"Left Weinberg's," he repeated. "Got another job, eh?"

"I am Mr. Maraton's assistant secretary," she announced.

His face for a moment was almost distorted with anger.

"You're living here — under this roof?" he demanded.

"It is no concern of yours where or how I am living," she answered.

"That's a lie!" Graveling exclaimed furiously. "You're my girl. I've hung around after you for six years. I've known you since you were a child. I'll be d — d if I'll be thrown on one side now and see you become another man's mistress — especially his!"

He came a step further into the room. Maraton, who had been standing with his back to them, arranging some papers on his desk, turned slowly around. Graveling was advancing towards him with the air of a bully.

"Do you hear — you — Maraton?" he cried. "I've had enough of you! You can flout us all at our work, if you like, but you go a bit too far when you think to make a plaything of my girl. Do you hear that?"

"Perfectly," Maraton replied.

"And what have you got to say about it?"

Maraton shrugged his shoulders slightly.

"I don't know that I have anything particular to say about it. If it interests you to be told my opinion of you, you are welcome to hear it."

Graveling advanced a step nearer still. His fists were clenched, an ugly scowl had parted his lips. Julia came swiftly from her seat. Her eyes were filled with fury. She faced Graveling.

"Richard Graveling," she exclaimed, "I am ashamed to think that I ever let you call yourself my friend! If you do not leave the room and the house at once, I swear that I will never speak to you again as long as I live!"

He pushed her aside roughly.

"I'll talk to you presently," he declared. "It's him that my business is with now."

Maraton's eyes flashed a little dangerously.

"Keep your hands off that young lady," he ordered.

"You'd like her to protect you, would you?" Graveling taunted. "Listen here. I'm not the sort of man to have my girl taken away and made another man's plaything. Is she going to stop here? Answer me quickly."

"As long as she chooses," Maraton replied.

"Then take that!" Graveling shouted.

Maraton stepped lightly to one side. Graveling was overbalanced by his fierce blow into the empty air. The next moment he was lying on his back, and the room seemed to be spinning around him. Maraton was standing with his finger upon the bell. Julia was by his side, her eyes blazing. She spoke never a word, but as Graveling struggled back to his senses he could see the scorn upon her face.

Aaron and a man servant entered the room simultaneously. Maraton pointed to the figure upon the floor.

" Aaron," he said, " your friend Mr. Graveling has met with a slight accident. You had better take him outside and put him in a taxicab."

Graveling rose painfully to his feet. He was very pale, and there was blood upon his cheek. He leaned on Aaron's arm and he looked towards Maraton and Julia.

" Better apologise and shake hands," Maraton advised quietly.

Graveling seemed not to have heard him. He looked towards them both, and his fingers gripped Aaron's shoulder so that the young man winced with pain. Then without a single word he turned towards the door.

" Let him go! " Julia cried fiercely. " I am only thankful that you punished him. We do not want his apologies. I hope that I may never see him again! "

Graveling, who had reached the door, leaning heavily upon Aaron, turned around. His face, with the streak of blood upon his cheek, was ghastly. He left the room between Aaron and the servant. They heard his unsteady footsteps in the hall, a whistle, the departure of the cab.

" Aaron has gone with him," Maraton remarked quietly. " Perhaps it is as well."

Her face suddenly relaxed and softened. The fury left her eyes; she sank back into the easy chair.

"I am ashamed," she moaned. "Oh, I am ashamed!"

CHAPTER XXV

The sound of traffic outside had died away. The silence became almost unnaturally prolonged. Only the echo of Julia's last words seemed, somehow or other, to remain, words which inspired Maraton with a curious and indefinable emotion, a pity which he could not altogether analyse. Twice he had turned softly as though to leave the room, and twice he had returned. He stood now upon the hearthrug, looking down at her, perplexed, himself in some degree agitated. She was not weeping, although every now and then her bosom rose and fell as though with some suppressed storm. It was simply a paroxysm of sensitiveness. She was afraid to look up, afraid to break a silence which to her was full of consolation. Maraton, a little ashamed of the scene in which he had been an unwilling participator, bitterly self-accusing, still found his thoughts diverted from his own humiliation as he watched the girl — a long, slim figure bent in one strangely graceful curve, her beautiful hair gleaming in the soft light, her face still half hidden by her strong, capable fingers — a figure exquisitely symbolic, full of pathos. Her elbows rested upon her knees; she was crouched a little forward.

" Julia ! " he ventured at last.

She looked up, without undue haste but without

hesitation. She had obviously been waiting for speech from him. He saw then that his impression had been a true one. There were no traces of tears in her eyes, which sought his at once — sought his with a look which warned him suddenly of his danger. Her cheeks were burning; she was still shaking with some internal passion.

"After all," he said soothingly, "there are such people in the world. One can't ignore the fact of their existence. They don't really count."

Her eyes flashed.

"It is terrible that they should be allowed to live."

He smiled at her sympathetically. Speech seemed somehow to lessen the tension between them.

"My dear Julia," he declared, "I am suffering just as much as you. I have the feeling that I have descended to the level of a common brawler. Yet what was I to do? He needed the lesson very badly indeed."

"I only hope that it will last him all his life. I only hope that he will not come near either of us again."

"Very doubtful whether he will want to, I should think," Maraton remarked, leaning against the table. "You certainly didn't mince your words."

"If I could have thought of harsher ones, I would have used them," she asserted.

"What a waste of time it has been this evening!" He sighed, as his fingers turned over the pile of letters by his side. "What with Mr. Peter Dale and his little deputation, and this idiotic person Graveling, I have scarcely done a thing since I got home."

"There's nothing that you need do until to-morrow," she told him softly.

There was another brief pause. She was sitting up now — leaning back in her chair, indeed — trembling no longer, although the colour still flamed in her cheeks. Her eyes, which seldom left his face, were strangely, almost liquidly soft. Maraton moved restlessly in his place. Perhaps he had been unwise not to have stolen out of the room during the first few moments. Julia, as he very well knew, was no ordinary person, and he felt a sense of growing uneasiness. The tension of silence became ominous and he spoke simply to dissipate it.

"I hope I really didn't hurt the fellow."

"If you had killed him," she replied, "he deserved it!"

"He was an insulting beast, of course," Maraton continued. "After all, though, one mustn't bring oneself down to the level of these creatures. He saw with his eyes, and what is seen from that point of view isn't of any account. Perhaps it isn't his fault that he hasn't learnt to govern himself. If I were you, Julia, I wouldn't bother about it any more, really."

"It wasn't altogether what he said," she whispered. "It wasn't altogether that."

He looked at her enquiringly.

"You mean?"

She shook her head.

"Tell me?" he begged.

Once more he saw that little quiver pass through her frame. Her lips were parted and closed again.

Maraton was puzzled, but did his best to follow her line of thought.

"The only way to treat such a person," he continued, "is to treat him as a lunatic. That is what he really is. I scarcely heard what he said; already I have forgotten every word."

"But I can't! I never can!"

He shrugged his shoulders.

"My dear Julia," he protested, "I appeal to your common sense!"

She looked at him almost angrily. Her foot beat upon the floor.

"What has common sense to do with it!" she exclaimed. "Of course, it was a foolish thing to say. He didn't even believe it — I am sure of that. It was simply mad, insensate jealousy; a vicious attempt to make me suffer. That isn't where he hurt. It was because — shall I tell you?"

A sudden instinct warned him. He held out his hand.

"It will only distress you. No, I don't want to hear."

The momentary silence seemed endowed with peculiar qualities. They heard the little clock ticking upon the mantelpiece, the tinkle of a hansom bell outside, the muffled sound of motor horns in the distance. Very slowly her head drooped back once more to the shelter of her hands.

"You don't understand," she said simply. "Why should you? I wasn't even angry — that is the terrible part of it. I wished — I found myself wishing — that it were true!"

Maraton's hands suddenly gripped the edge of the table against which he was leaning. Her face was still concealed; once more her long, slim body was shaken with quivering sobs.

"The shame of it!" she moaned. "That is where he hurt. The shame of hearing it and knowing it wasn't true and of wanting it to be true! I haven't ever thought of any one like that — he knows that well enough. He used to call me sexless. There isn't any man in the world has ever dared to touch my lips — he knows it."

Maraton left his place and quietly approached her. She heard him coming, and the trembling gradually ceased. He sat on the arm of her chair, and his hand rested gently upon her shoulder.

"Dear Julia," he said, "I am glad that you have been honest. Life is always full of these emotions, you know, especially for highly-strung people, and sometimes the atmosphere gets a little overcharged and they blaze out as they have done this evening, and perhaps one is the better for it."

She remained quite motionless during his brief pause. One hand had moved from before her face and had gripped his.

"There's our work, you know, Julia," he went on. "There isn't anything in the world must interfere with that. We can't divide our lives, can we? We ought not to want to. If I could make you understand — can I, I wonder? — how splendid it is to have some one here by my side who understands. It seems to me that I am going to be a little lonely. I shall have to stand on my own feet a good deal. I

rely so much upon you, Julia. You are a woman,
aren't you — I mean a real woman? I need you."

Very slowly she raised her head. Her eyes met
his freely. There was something of the childlike
adoration of an instinctive and triumphant purity in
the smile which parted her lips. Maraton understood
at once that the danger was past. The thunder had
left the air.

"You know that I am your slave," she murmured.
"Don't be afraid that I am becoming neurotic. You
see, this was all a little new to me, and for a moment
I felt that I wanted to go and hide myself. That
has all passed now. I am not even ashamed. I
suppose one gets terrified with receiving so much,
and wants to give. It's a very natural feminine
impulse, isn't it? And I shall give — my fingers,
my brain — all I possess."

She rose suddenly to her feet and glanced at the
clock.

"What a day you must have had!" she exclaimed.
"You are not going to look at my Sheffield figures,
even, before the morning. Oh, you'll be surprised
when you see them! You've a wonderful case.
Some of the fortunes that have been made there —
that are being made there now — are barbaric. I
mustn't talk about it, or I shall get angry. Listen,
there's Aaron."

They heard the sound of his latch-key. A moment later he entered the room. He looked anxiously
at Maraton; Julia he scarcely noticed.

"I took him home," he announced. "He never
spoke a word the whole way; seemed stupid. I

shouldn't be surprised if he hadn't got a little con-
cussion."

"Did you send for a doctor?" Maraton asked.

"His landlady was going to do that," Aaron continued. "It was all I could do to sit in the cab by
his side. I wish — yes, I almost wish that he'd never
got up from that carpet."

"Thanks," Maraton replied. "I didn't come
over here to fill the inside of an English prison!"

"Prison!"

Aaron's expression of contempt was sublime.

"There's nothing they could have done to you,
sir. All the same, I only wish that your blow had
killed him."

"Why?"

Aaron dropped his voice for a minute.

"Because wherever we go or move," he said, "there
will always be the snake in the grass. He will be
filled forever with a poisonous hatred for you. He
will never dare to raise his hand against you to your
face — he isn't that sort of man — but he'll have his
stab before he's finished. He was born a sneak."

Maraton smiled carelessly as he bade them good
night.

"The one thing in the world," he reminded them,
"worse than having no friends, is to have no
enemies."

CHAPTER XXVI

Eight days later, Maraton delivered his prelimi-
nary address to the ironworkers of Sheffield, and at
six o'clock the next morning the strike had been
unanimously proclaimed. The columns of the daily
newspapers, still hopelessly bound over to the interests of the capitalist, were full of solemn warnings
against this new and disturbing force in English
sociology. The *Daily Oracle* alone paused to present
a few words of appreciation of the splendid dramatic
force wielded by this revolutionary.

" If this man is sincere," the *Oracle* declared, " the
country needs him. If he is a charlatan, then for
heaven's sake, even at the expense of all the laws that
were ever framed, away with him! There is no man
breathing to-day who is developing a more potent,
a more wide-reaching influence upon the destinies of
our country."

Maraton's first address had been delivered to a
great multitude, but there was no building whose
roof could cover the hordes of men who had made up
their minds to hear his last words at Sheffield. From
far and wide, the people came that night in countless
streams. A platform had been arranged in the
middle of the principal pleasure park of the town,
and around this, from early in the afternoon, they
began to take up their places. When night fell, so

far as the eye could see, the ground was covered with
a black mass of humanity. The multitude filled the
park and crowded up the encircling streets. As the
darkness deepened, they lit torches. Beyond, down
in the valley and up on the hillside, were rows of
lights and the flare of furnaces soon to be quenched.
Even that little group of hard, unimaginative men
who stood with Maraton upon the platform felt the
strange thrill of the tense and swelling throng gathered together with this inspiring background.

It seemed to Maraton himself, as he stood there
listening to the roar of welcoming voices, as though
all their white faces were gathered into one, the
prototype of suffering humanity, the sad, hollow-
cheeked, hollow-eyed victim of birth and heritage.
His voice seemed to swell that night to something
greater than its usual volume; some peculiar gift
of penetration seemed to have been accorded him. A
hundred thousand men heard his passionate prayer to
them. They were hard-featured, hard-minded York-
shiremen, most of them, but they never forgot.

"You will get the half a crown a week which your
leaders demand," Maraton told them. "Your masters — may God forgive me for using the word! —
will pay to that extent. But — if there is any justice beyond this world, how, indeed, will they meet
the debt built upon your sufferings, your cramped
lives, and the graves of your little children. That
half a crown a week, I say, will come to you. Don't
dare, any of you, to be satisfied when it does come. It
isn't a few shillings only that are owing to you. It's
another social system, a rearrangement of your

whole scheme of life, under which you and your children, and your children's children, may live with the
dignity and freedom due to that strange and common
gift of life which beats in your pulses and in mine.
I am here to-night to show you the way to that extra
half-crown, but I don't want you for one moment
to think that these small increases in wages represent
the end and aim of myself and those who share my
beliefs. Your day may not see it, nor mine, but
history for the last thousand years has shown us the
slow emancipation of the peoples of the world.
There are many rungs in the ladder yet to be climbed.
Your children may have to take up the burden where
you have left it. A revolution may be necessary,
sorrows innumerable may lie between you and the
goal of your class. And yet I bid you hope. I
plead with each one of you to remember that he is
not only an individual; that he is a unit of humanity,
that he is the progenitor of unborn children, a force
from which will spring the happier and the freer
generation, if not in our time, in the days to come."

He passed on to speak for a few moments about
the reconstituted state of Society, which was his
favourite theme, and from that to a peroration unprepared — fiercely, passionately eloquent. When he
had finished speaking, the air seemed curiously dull
and lifeless; an extraordinary silence, like the silence
before a thunderstorm, brooded over the place.
Then the human sea broke its bounds. The smut-
blackened trees quivered with the thunder of their
voices. Showers of sparks rose into the air from
the torches they waved. It was a pandemonium of

sound. They came on like a mighty flood, before whose force the dam has suddenly yielded. The platform was crushed like a nutshell before their onslaught. They were mad with a great enthusiasm, beside themselves with a passion stirred only in such men once or twice in a lifetime. The roar of their voices, as they shouted his name, reached even to the station, to which Maraton had been smuggled secretly in a fast motor-car — a disappearance which a great journalist on the next morning alluded to as the one supremely dramatic touch in a night of wonders. The roar of voices indeed was still in his ears as he stood before the window of his compartment, looking out over the fire-hung city with its vaporous flames, its huge furnaces, its glare which was already becoming fainter. A myriad lights still twinkled upon the hillsides; the smoke-stained sky was red with the reflection of those thousand torches. Even as the train rushed on into the darkness, he could hear the echo of their cry as they sought for him.

"Maraton! Maraton!"

He threw himself at last into a corner seat of his compartment, and conscious of a somewhat rare physical exhaustion, he rang the bell for the attendant and ordered refreshments. The evening papers were by his side, but he had no fancy to read. The thrill of the last few hours was still upon him. He sat with folded arms, looking idly through the window at the chaotic prospect. Suddenly he was aware that the door of his compartment had been opened. A man had entered and was taking the seat opposite to him, a man whose appearance struck Maraton at once as being vaguely familiar, a man who smiled at him almost with the air of an old acquaintance.

" You don't recognise me, I can see," the newcomer said, smiling slightly, " yet we ought to know one another."

Maraton looked at the intruder curiously. It was, in many respects, a remarkable face; a low, heavy forehead; eyes in which shone the unmistakable light; broad, firm mouth; fair hair, left unusually long. In figure the man was short and stout. His collar had parted, and a black bow of unusual size was drooping from his shoulder. He was slightly out of breath, too, as though he had but recently recovered from some strenuous exercise.

" I will save you from speculations — I am Henry Selingman," he pronounced.

Maraton held out his hand.

" Selingman! " he exclaimed. " It is your photographs, of course, then. We have never met."

" Never until to-night," Selingman admitted. " When I heard that you were in England, I made up my mind to come over. To-night seemed to me propitious. I wanted to understand this marvellous power of yours of which so many people have written. Nothing has been exaggerated. The message which I have struggled to deliver to the world through my poetry, my plays, such prose as I have ventured upon, you yourself can tear from your heart and throw to the people's own ears. . . . Forgive me — I, too, will smoke. I will drink wine, also," he added, ringing the bell. " I had a dozen friends to help me, but every bone in my body aches with the struggle to escape. You maddened them, those people. It was magnificent."

He ordered champagne from the attendant and began to smoke a long black cigar, nervously and quickly.

" To-night I shall write of this," he went on.   " I have lived for forty-five years and I have hunted all over the world, and in my study I have conjured up all the visions a man may, but never yet has there been anything like this.   The black hillside a mass of soft black velvet, jewelled like a woman's gown, the red fires from the blasting furnaces, the shower of sparks from a thousand torches, the glow upon the fog-poisoned sky, those faces — God, how white!   Never in my life have I seen the writing of the finger of the Messiah as I saw it to-night!   It has been the hour of a lifetime.   Maraton, over there, man, our toilers are toilers indeed, but not like that.   It isn't stamped into them.   No, they're not branded."

" Over there? " Maraton repeated.

" Belgium, Germany," Selingman continued,— " Germany chiefly.   Our Socialism has done better for us than that.   It has kindled a little fire in the heart of the men, and from its warmth has sprung something of that self-respect which will be the seed of the new humanity.   I want you over there, Maraton.   I want to show you.   Your heart will warm with joy.   God, what food for hell are your manufacturers here! How they'll burn! "

" The curse of England is its terrible middle class," Maraton said slowly.   " The present generation is the first even to dimly realise it.   Our aristocracy is

no better nor any worse than the aristocracy of other
nations; rather better, perhaps, than worse. But our
middle class rules the land. They represent the vot-
ing power. They conceal their real sentiments under
the name of Liberalism, they keep their heel upon the
neck of Labour. I tell you, when the revolution
comes, it will be Hampstead and Kensington the mob
will sack and burn, not Park Lane and Grosvenor
Square."

" You're right," Selingman agreed; " of course
you're right. You and I make no mistakes. We are
of the order of those whose eyes were touched in the
cradle. Maraton, sometimes I am sorry I'm an artist;
sometimes I loathe this sense of beauty which drives
my pen into the pleasanter ways. There's only one
thing in the world for you and me to work for. The
world to-day doesn't deserve the offerings of the artist
until it has purged itself. I waste my time writing
plays, but then, after all, I am not English. If
those were my people, Maraton, I doubt whether my
pen could ever have wandered even for a moment into
the pleasant ways."

Maraton sighed.

" There is America, too," he groaned.

" A conglomeration," Selingman declared hastily,
" not to be reckoned with yet as a nation. What is
born amongst the older peoples must find its way there
by natural law. It is not a country for commence-
ments. England — it is England where the harvest
is ripe. What are you doing, man? "

Maraton looked thoughtfully out of the window.
The train was gathering speed; they were travelling

now at a great pace. Outside, the twilight was fading. A black cloud had passed across the rising moon. The electric light illuminated the carriage. It was almost as though they were passing through a tunnel.

" You ask me almost the saddest question one could ask," he replied gently. " I am working for posterity. There is no other course. I called those people together to-night at Sheffield for the sake of half a crown a week extra wages. It will make life a little easier for them, and I suppose every atom of prosperity must count in the sum of their future and their children's future."

" Spent in beer, most likely," Selingman muttered.

" Why not? " Maraton exclaimed. " The possession of money to spend in luxuries of any sort must add something, at least, to their dignity. It means a lightening of the heart for a moment, an impulse of gladness. Why should we judge? Beer is only a prototype of other things. Then, Selingman, mark this. I brought the men of Lancashire out on strike some few weeks ago, and Sheffield now is following suit. It is a matter of a few shillings a week only, it is true, but I am very careful to tell them always that it is simply a compromise which I am advocating. These small increases are nothing. The operatives have a nature-given right to a share in the product of their labour. In these days their slave hire is thrown at them by an interloping person who calls himself an employer. In the days to come it will be different."

" You beat time, then! " Selingman cried. " You

head the waves! My friend Maraton, they are right, those who turned me out of my villa at Versailles and sent me over to you. They were right, indeed! I have business with you, man — an inspiration to share. Ours is a great meeting. You know Maxendorf?"

" By name," Maraton admitted, a little startled.

" A profound thinker," Selingman declared, " a mighty thinker, a giant, a pioneer. I tell you that he sees, Maraton. He has pitched his tent upon the hill-top. What do you know of him?"

" Chiefly," Maraton replied, " that he is an aristocrat, a diplomatist, and the future ambassador here of a country I do not love."

Selingman drained a glass of champagne before he answered. He lit another of his long, thin cigars and smoked furiously.

" Aristocrat — yes," he assented, " but you do not know Maxendorf. He will be a joy to you, man. Oh, he sees! The day of the millions is coming, and he knows it. On the Continent our middle class isn't like yours. The conflict will never be so terrible. Thank God, our Labour stands already with its feet upon the ground. With us, development is all that is necessary. But you — you are up against a cul-de-sac, a black mountain of prejudice and custom. Nothing can save you but an earthquake or a revolution, and you know it. You came to England with those ideas, Maraton. You have turned opportunist. It was the only thing left for you. You didn't happen to see the one way out. To-morrow it will be a new day with you. To-morrow we will show you."

They were rushing into London now. Selingman rose to his feet.

"At seven o'clock to-morrow I shall fetch you," he announced, "that is, if I do not come in the morning. I may come before — I may give you the whole day for your own. I make no promise. Your address — write it down. I have no memory."

Maraton wrote it and passed it over. Selingman thrust it into his pocket.

"I go to work," he cried. "Some part of the genius of your voice shall tremble to-morrow in the genius of my prose. I promise you that. 'Listen,' our friend Maxendorf would say, ' to the vainest man in Europe!' But I know. No man knows himself save himself. Adieu!"

CHAPTER XXVII

The lengthy reports of his Sheffield visit and speeches, of which the newspapers made great capital, an extraordinary impression of the same in Selingman's wonderful prose, and the caprice of a halfpenny paper, made Maraton suddenly the most talked about man in England. A notoriety which he would have done much to have avoided was forced upon him. Early on the morning following his return, his house was besieged with a little stream of journalists, photographers, politicians, men and women of all orders and degrees, seeking for a few moments' interview with the man of the hour. Maraton retreated precipitately into his smaller study at the back of the house, and left Aaron to cope as well as he might with the assailing host. Every now and then the telephone bell rang, and Aaron made his report.

"There are fourteen men here who want to interview you," he announced, "all from good papers. If you won't be interviewed, some of them want a photograph."

"Send them away," Maraton directed. "Tell them the only photograph I ever had taken is in the hands of the Chicago police."

"There's the editor here himself from the *Bi-Weekly*."

" My compliments and excuses," Maraton replied.
" I will be interviewed by no one."

" There's a representative from the *Oracle* here,"
Aaron continued, " who wants to know your exact
position in connection with the Labour Party. What
shall I say? "

" Tell him to apply to Mr. Dale!" Maraton answered.

" Mr. Foley and Lady Elisabeth Landon are outside in a car. Mr. Foley's compliments, and if you
could spare a moment, they would be glad to come in
and see you."

Maraton hesitated.

" You had better let them come in."

" Shall I go? " Julia asked.

Maraton shook his head.

" Stay where you are," he enjoined. " Perhaps
they will go sooner, if they see that I am at work with
you."

Mr. Foley was in his best and happiest mood. He
shook hands heartily with Maraton. Elisabeth said
nothing at all, but Maraton was conscious of one
swift look into his eyes, and of the fact that her
fingers rested in his several seconds longer than was
necessary.

" We are profoundly mortified, both my niece and
I," Mr. Foley said. " Never have I had so many
journalists on my doorstep, even on that notorious
Thursday when they thought that I was going to
declare war. I really fancy, Maraton, that they are
going to make a celebrity of you. Have you seen the
papers? "

"I have read Selingman's sketch," Maraton replied.

"They say," Mr. Foley went on, "that he wrote all night at the office in Fleet Street, and that his sheets were flung into type as he wrote them. Selingman, too — the great Selingman! You know him?"

"He travelled down from Sheffield with me last night," Maraton answered.

"A more dangerous person even than you," Mr. Foley observed, "and an Anglophobe. Never mind, what did we call about, Elisabeth?"

"Well, we were really on our way to the city," his niece reminded him. "It was you who suggested, when we were at the top of the Square, that we should call in and see Mr. Maraton."

"There was something in my mind," Mr. Foley persisted. "I remember. Next Friday is the last day of the session, you know, Mr. Maraton. We want you to go down to Scotland with us for a week."

Maraton shook his head.

"It is very kind of you," he said, "but I shall take no holiday. I need none. I have endless work here during the vacation. There are some industries I have scarcely looked into at all. And there is my Bill, and the draft of another one to follow. Thank you very much, Mr. Foley, all the same."

Elisabeth set down the illustrated paper which she had picked up. She looked across at Maraton.

"Don't you think for one week, Mr. Maraton," she suggested softly, "that you could bring your work with you. You could have a study in a quiet corner of the house, and if you did not care to bring a secretary, I would promise you the services of an amateur one."

Perhaps by accident, as she spoke, she glanced across at Julia, and perhaps by accident Julia at that moment happened to glance up. Their eyes met. Julia, from the grim loneliness of her own world, looked steadfastly at this exquisite type of the things in life which she hated.

" You are very kind," Maraton repeated, " but indeed I must not think of it. It seems to me," he went on, after a slight hesitation, " that every time lately when I have stood at the halting of two ways, and have had to make up my mind which to follow, I have been forced by circumstances to choose the easier way. This time, at least, my duty is quite plain. I have work to do in London which I cannot neglect."

Elisabeth picked up the paper which she had set down the moment before. Her eyes had been quick to appreciate the smothered fierceness of Julia's gaze. At Maraton she did not glance.

" Well, I am sorry," Mr. Foley said. " You are a young man now, Maraton, but one works the better for a change. I didn't come to talk shop, but you've set a nice hornet's nest about our heads up in Sheffield."

" There are many more to follow," Maraton assured him.

Mr. Foley chuckled. His sense of humour was indomitable.

" If there is one thing in the Press this morning," he declared, " more pronounced than the diatribes upon your speech, it is the number of compliments

paid to me for my perspicuity in extending the hand
of friendship to the most dangerous political factor
at present existent,— vide the *Oracle*. I've wasted
many hours arguing with some of my colleagues. If
I had known what was coming, I might just as well
have sat tight and waited for to-day. I am vindi-
cated, whitewashed. Only the Opposition are furious.
They are trying to claim you as a natural member of
the Radical Party. Shouldn't be surprised if they
didn't approach you to-day sometime."

Maraton smiled.

" The people I am in the most disgrace with," he
observed, " are my own little lot."

" That needn't worry you," Mr. Foley rejoined.
" Our Labour Members are not a serious body. The
forces they represent are all right, but they seem to
have a perfectly devilish gift of selecting the wrong
representatives. . . . You'll be in the House this
afternoon? "

" Certainly ! "

" I shall be rather curious to see what sort of a
reception they give you," Mr. Foley continued.
" You couldn't manage to walk in with me, I suppose?
It would mean such a headline for the *Daily Oracle!* "

Elisabeth glanced up from her paper.

" I am afraid, uncle," she remarked, " that *Punch*
was right when it said that your sense of humour
would always prevent your becoming a great politician."

" Let *Punch* wait until I claim the title," Mr. Foley
retorted, smiling. " No man has ever consented to be
Premier who was a great politician — in these days,

at any rate. I doubt, even, whether our friend Maraton would be a successful Premier. I fancy that if
ever he aspires so high, it will be to the Dictatorship
of the new republic."

Maraton sighed.

" Even the *Oracle*," he reminded them, " is convinced that I have no personal ambitions."

Mr. Foley took up his hat. He had been in high
good humour throughout the interview. Already he
was looking forward to meeting his colleagues.

" Well, we'll be off, Maraton," he said. " We had
no right to come and disturb you at this time in the
morning, only we were really anxious to book you
for our quiet week in Scotland. Change your mind
about it, there's a good fellow. I shall be your helpless prey up there. You could make of me what you
would."

Maraton shook his head very firmly.

" It is not possible," he answered. " Please do not
think that I do not appreciate your hospitality — and
your kindness, Lady Elisabeth."

She looked at him for a moment rather curiously.
There was something of reproach in her eyes; something, too, which he failed to understand. She did
not speak at all.

" Miss Thurnbrein," Maraton begged, " will you
see Mr. Foley and Lady Elisabeth out? It sounds
cowardly, doesn't it," he added, " but I really don't
think that I dare show myself."

Julia rose slowly to her feet and passed towards
the door, which Maraton was holding open. She
lingered outside while Maraton shook hands with his

two visitors, then would have hurried on in advance, but that Elisabeth stopped her.

" Do tell me," she asked, " you are the Miss Thurnbrein who has written so much upon woman labour, aren't you? "

" I have written one or two articles," Julia replied, looking straight ahead of her.

" I read one in the *National Review*," Elisabeth continued, " and another in one of the evening papers. I can't tell you, Miss Thurnbrein, how interested I was."

Julia turned and looked slowly at her questioner. Her cheeks seemed more pallid than usual, her eyes were full of smouldering fire.

" I didn't write to interest people," she said calmly. " I wrote to punish them, to let them know a little of what they were guilty."

" But surely," Elisabeth protested, " you make some excuse for those who have really no opportunity for finding out?   There is a society now, I am told, for watching over the conditions of woman labour in the east end.   Is that so really? "

" There is such a society," Julia admitted.   " I am the secretary of it."

" You must let me join," Elisabeth begged. " Please do.   Won't you come and see me one afternoon — any afternoon — and tell me all about it? Indeed I am in earnest," she went on, a little puzzled at the other's unresponsiveness.   " This isn't just a whim.   I am really interested in these matters, but it is so hard to help, unless one is put in the right way."

" The time has passed," Julia pronounced, " when patronage is of any assistance to such societies as the one we were speaking of. Nothing is of any use now but hard, grim work. We don't want money. We don't need support of any kind whatever. We need work and brains."

" I am afraid," Elisabeth said, as she held out her hand, " that you think I am incapable of either."

Julia's lips were tightly compressed. She made no reply. Mr. Foley glanced back at her curiously as they stepped into the car.

" What a singularly forbidding young woman! " he remarked.

Elisabeth shrugged her shoulders. It is given to women to understand much! . . . The car glided off. As they neared the corner of the Square, they passed a stout, foreign-looking man with an enormous head, a soft grey hat set far back, a quantity of fair hair, and the ingenuous, eager look of a child. He was hurrying towards the corner house and scarcely glanced in their direction. Mr. Foley, however, leaned forward with interest.

" Who is that strange-looking person? " Elisabeth asked.

Mr. Foley became impressive.

" One of the greatest writers and philosophers of the day," he replied. " I expect he is on his way to see Maraton. That was Henry Selingman."

CHAPTER XXVIII

Selingman took little heed of the cordon around Maraton. He brushed them all to one side, and when at last confronted by the final barrier, in the shape of Julia, he only patted her gently upon the back.

" Ah, but my dear child," he exclaimed, " you do not understand! Listen. I raise my voice, I shout — like this —' Maraton, it is I who am here — Selingman! ' You see, he will come if he is within hearing. You know of me, you pale-faced child? You have heard of Selingman, is it not so? "

Before Julia could answer, the door of the study was opened.

" Come in," Maraton called out from an invisible place.

Selingman, with a little bow of triumph to Julia, passed down the passage and into the library. He threw his hat upon the sofa and held out both his hands to Maraton. Julia, who had followed him, sank into a chair before her typewriter.

" I have made you famous, my friend," he declared. " You may quote these words in after life as representing the full sublimity of my conceit, but it is true. Have you read my ' Appreciation ' in the *Oracle?* "

" I have," Maraton admitted, smiling.

"The real thing," Selingman continued, "crisp and crackling with genius. As they read it, the photographers took down their cameras, the editors whispered to their journalists to be off to Russell Square, the ladies began to pen their cards of invitation."

"That's all very well," Maraton remarked, a little grimly, "but where do I come in? I have no time for the journalists, I refuse to be photographed, and I am not likely to accept the invitations. It takes my two secretaries half their time to wade through my correspondence and to decide which of it is to be pitched into the waste-paper basket. I am not a dealer in quack remedies, or an actor. I don't want advertisement."

"Pooh, my friend! — pooh!" Selingman retorted, drawing out his worn leather case and thrusting one of the long black cigars into his mouth. "Everything that is spontaneous in life is good for you — even advertisement. But listen to my news. It is great news, believe me. . . . A match, please."

Maraton struck a vesta and handed it to him. Selingman transferred the flame to a piece of paper from the waste-paper basket and puffed contentedly at his cigar.

"I light not cigars with a flavour like this, with a wax vesta," he explained. "Where was I? Oh, I know — the news! This morning I have received a message. Maxendorf has left for England."

Maraton smiled.

"Is that all?" he said. "I could have told you that myself. The fact is announced in all the morning papers."

" He will be at the Ritz Hotel to-night," Selingman
continued, unruffled. " When he arrives, I shall be
there. We speak together for an hour and then I
come for you."

" I shall be glad to meet Maxendorf," Maraton
agreed quietly. " He is a great man. But don't
you think for his first few days in England it would
be better to leave him alone, so far as I am concerned? "

" Later I will remind you of those words," Selingman declared. " For a genius you see no further
than the end of your nose. They tell me that when
you landed, there were prophets in the East End
who rose up and shouted —' Maraton is come! Maraton is here!' No more — just the simple announcement — as though that fact alone were changing life.
Very well. I will be your prophet and you shall be
the people. I will say to you, as they cried to the
Children of Israel groaning under their toil — Maxendorf has come! Maxendorf is here!"

Maraton was silent for a moment. He was sitting
on the edge of the table, with folded arms. His
visitor was pacing up and down the room, blowing
out dense volumes of smoke.

" You have more in your mind, Selingman, than
you have told me," he said.

" What is there that is hidden from the eye of
genius? " Selingman cried, with a theatrical wave of
the hand. " More than I have told you indeed —
more than I shall tell you. One thing, at least, I
have learnt in my struggles with the pen, and that is
to avoid the anti-climax. It is a great thing to re-

member that.   So I am dumb, I speak no more. . . .
Why don't you send your poor little secretary out
for a walk?   Mademoiselle, forgive me, but he works
you too hard."

She looked up at him, smiling.

" I worked very much harder before I came here,"
she answered quietly.

" I am fortunate in my secretary," Maraton
interposed.   " This is Miss Julia Thurnbrein, Selingman.   I don't suppose you read our reviews, but Miss
Thurnbrein is an authority on woman labour."

" I read nothing," Selingman declared, moving
over and grasping her by the hand.   " I read nothing.
People are my books.   I am forty-five years old.
I have done with reading.   I know a great deal, I
have read a great deal; I read no more.   Miss Julia
Thurnbrein, you say.   Well, I like the name of
Julia.   Only, young lady, you would do better to
spend a little more time with the roses, and a little
less under the roofs of this grey city.   Youth, you
know, youth is everything.   You work best for others
by realising the joys of life yourself.   I, too, am a
philanthropist, Miss Julia — I don't like your other
name — I, too, think and write for others.   I, too,
have dreams of a millennium, of days when the huge
wheel shall be driven to a different tune, and faces
be lifted to the skies that hang now towards the
gutters.   But details annoy me, details I cannot master.   I do not want to know how many sufferers
there are in the world and what particular sum they
starve upon.   I leave others to do that work.   I only
point forward to the day of emancipation.   Put

your hand in mine and I will show you in time where the clouds will first break."

Julia smiled at him a little sadly.

" Perhaps it is as well," she said, " that we have champions who do not care for detail. It is detail and the sight of suffering which sap all the enthusiasms out of us before our time."

Selingman frowned at her angrily. He blew out another cloud of smoke.

" You make me angry," he asserted. " I love your sex, I adore womanhood. I look upon a beautiful woman as a gift to the world. Beauty is a gift to be made much of, to be nourished, to be glorified. You are tired, young woman. You work too hard. You have the rare gift — has any one ever told you that you are beautiful? "

Julia stared at him, her lips a little parted, half angry, half wondering.

" Look at her," Selingman continued, turning to Maraton. " She has the slim body, the long, delicate figure of those Botticellis we all love — except the Russians. I never yet met a Russian who could appreciate a Botticelli. And her eyes — look at them, man. And you let her sit there till the hollows are forming in her cheeks. Be ashamed of yourself. Take her out into the country. One works just as well in the sunshine. You do better work if you can smell flowers growing around you while your brain is active. Lend her to me for a week. I'll take her to my cottage in the Ardennes. There I live with the sun — breakfast at sunrise, to bed at sunset. I will dictate to you, Miss Julia — dictate beautiful

things. You shall be proud always. You shall say
—'I have worked for Selingman. Conceited ass!'
you will probably add. Thank Heavens that I am
conceited! Nothing is so splendid in life as to know
your own worth. Nothing makes so much for happiness. . . . Maraton, where shall I find you to-
night?"

"In the House of Commons, probably," Maraton
replied. "But take my advice. Leave Maxendorf
alone for a few days."

"We will see — we will see," Selingman went on,
a little impatiently. "Come, I have nothing to do —
nothing whatever. I came to London to see you,
Maraton. You must put up with me. Work — put
it away. The sun shines. Let us all go into the
country. I will get a car. Or what of the river?
Perhaps not. I am too restless, I cannot sit still. I
will walk about always. And I cannot swim. We
will take a car and sometimes we will walk. I go to
fetch it now, eh?"

Maraton glanced helplessly at Julia. They both
laughed.

"I have to be back at four o'clock," the former
said. "I have an appointment at the House of
Commons then."

"Excellent!" Selingman declared. "I go there
with you. Your House of Commons always fasci-
nates me. I hear you speak, perhaps? No? What
does it matter? I will hear the others drone. I go
to fetch a car."

Maraton held out his hand.

"I have a car," he observed. "It is waiting now

at the back entrance. You had better get your things
on, Miss Thurnbrein. I can see that we have come
under the influence of a master spirit."

She looked at the pile of letters by her side, but
Maraton only shook his head.

"We must parody his own phrase and declare that
' Selingman is here!' " he said. "Go and put your
things on and tell Aaron. We will steal out like
conspirators at the back door."

They lunched at a roadside inn in Buckingham-
shire, an inn ivy-covered, with a lawn behind, and a
garden full of cottage flowers. Selingman with his
own hands dragged out the table from the little sitting-room, through the open windows to a shaded
corner of the lawn, drew the cork from a bottle of
wine, and taking off his coat, started to make a
salad.

"Insects everywhere," he remarked cheerfully.
"Hold your parasol over my salad, please, Miss
Julia. So! What does it matter? Where there
are flowers and trees there must be insects. Let
them live their day of life."

"So long as we don't eat them!" Julia protested.

"I have tasted insects in South America which
were delicious," Selingman assured them. "There
— leave your parasol over the salad, and, Maraton,
move the ice-pail a little more into the shade. Now,
while they set the luncheon, we will walk in that
little flower garden, and I will tell you, if you like,
a story of mine I once wrote, the story of two roses.
I published it, alas! It is so hard to save even our
most beautiful thoughts from the vulgarity of print,

in these days where everything — love and wine, and even the roses themselves — cost money. Bah!"

"The story, please," Julia begged.

He walked in the middle and took an arm of each of his companions.

"So you would hear my little story?" he exclaimed. "Then listen."

They obeyed. Presently he forgot himself. His eyes were half-closed, his thoughts seemed to have wandered into the strangest places. As his allegory proceeded, he seemed to drift away from all knowledge of his immediate surroundings. He chose his words always with the most exquisite and precise care. They listened, entranced. Then suddenly he stopped short in the path.

"For half an hour have I been giving of myself," he declared. "Almost I faint. Come."

He tightened his grasp upon their arms and started walking with short, abrupt footsteps and great haste for the luncheon table.

"Fool that I am!" he muttered. "It is one o'clock, and I lunch always at half-past twelve. I must eat quickly. See, the waiter looks at us sorrowfully. What of the omelette, I wonder? Come, Miss Julia, at my right hand there. Ah! was I not right? The roses are creeping already — creeping into their proper place. Sit back in your chair and eat slowly and drink the yellow wine, and listen to the humming of those bees. So soon you will become normal, a woman, just what you should be. Heavens! It is well that I came to see Maraton. When I saw you this morning in that room, I said

to myself — 'There is a human creature who half
lives. What a sin to half live!' . . . Taste that
salad, Maraton. Taste it, man, and admit that it is
well that I came."

They were alone in the garden — the inn was a
little way off the main road and they had discovered
it entirely by accident. Both Julia and Maraton
yielded gracefully enough to the influence of their
companion's personality.

" Whether it is well for us or not," Maraton remarked, as he watched the wine flow into his glass,
" to yield up one's will like this, to become even as
a docile child, I do not know, but it is very pleasant.
It is an hour of detachment."

· " It is the secret of youth, the secret of life, the
secret of joy," Selingman declared. " Detachment
is the word. Life would make slaves of all of us,
if one did not sometimes square one's shoulders and
say — ' No, thank you, I have had enough! Good-
bye! I return presently.' One needs a will, perhaps, but then, what is life without will? I myself
was at work. The greatest theatrical manager in
the world kept sentry before my door. The greatest
genius who ever trod upon the stage sent me frantic
messages every few hours. Then they spoke to me
of Maraton. I heard the cry — ' Maraton is here! '
I heard the thunder from across the seas. Up from
my desk, out from my room — hysterics, entreaties,
nothing stopped me. No luggage worth mentioning.
Away I come, to London, to Sheffield — what a place!
To-morrow — to-morrow or the next day I return,
full of life and vigour. It is splendid. I broke

away. No one else could have done it. I left them in tears. What did I care? It is for myself — for myself I do these things. Unless I myself am at my best, what have I to give the world? Miss Julia, your health! To the roses, and may they never leave your cheeks! No, don't go yet. There are strawberries coming."

Maraton and his host sat together for a few moments in the garden before they started on their return journey. Selingman leaned across the table. He had forgotten to put on his coat, and he sat unabashed in his shirt sleeves. He had drunk a good deal of wine, and the little beads of perspiration stood out upon his forehead.

"Maraton," he said, "you need me. You are like the others. When the fire has touched their eyes and indeed they see the things that are, they fall on their knees and they tear away at the weeds and rubbish that cumber the earth, and they never lift their eyes, and soon their frame grows weary and their heart cold. Be wise, man. The mark is upon you. Those live best and work best in this world who have a soul for its beauties. Women, for instance," he went on, smoking furiously. "What help do you make of women? None! You sit at one end of the table, your secretary at the other. You don't look at her. She might have pig's eyes, for anything you know about it. Idiot! And she — not quite as bad, perhaps. Women feel a little, you know, that they don't show. Why not marry, Maraton? No? Perhaps you are right. And yet women are wonderful. You can't do your greatest work, Maraton,

you never will reach your greatest work, unless a
woman's hand is in yours."

They rode back to London in comparative silence.
Selingman frankly and openly slept, with his grey
hat on the back of his head, his untidy feet upon
the opposite cushions, his mouth wide open. Maraton more than once found himself watching Julia
covertly. There was no doubt that in her strange,
quiet way she was beautiful. As he sat and looked
at her, his thoughts travelled back to the little garden, the sheltered corner under the trees, the curious
sense of relaxation which in that short hour Selingman
had inspired. Was the man indeed right, his philosophy sound? Was there indeed wisdom in the loosen-
ing of the bonds? He met her eyes suddenly, and
she smiled at him. With her — well, he scarcely
dared to tell himself that he knew how it was. He
closed his eyes again. A thought had come to him
sweeter than any yet.

As they neared London, Selingman awoke, smiled
blandly upon them, brushed the cigar ash from his
coat and waistcoat, put on his hat and looked about
him with interest.

"So we are arrived," he said presently. " The
Houses of Parliament, eh? I enter with you, Maraton. You find me a corner where I sleep while the
others speak, and wake at the sound of your voice.
Afterwards, late to-night, we shall go to Maxendorf."

CHAPTER XXIX

It happened to be a quiet evening in the House, and Maraton and Selingman dined together at a little before eight o'clock. Selingman's personality was too unusual to escape attention, and as his identity became known, a good many passers-by looked at them curiously. Some one sent word to Mr. Foley of their presence, and very soon he came in and joined them.

" Six years ago this month, Mr. Selingman," the Prime Minister reminded him, " we met at Madame Hermene's in Paris. You were often there in those days."

Selingman nodded vigorously.

" I remember it perfectly," he said —" perfectly. It was a wonderful evening. An English Cabinet Minister, the President of France, Coquelin, Rostand, and I myself were there. A clever woman! She knew how to attract. In England there is nothing of the sort, eh? "

" Nothing," Mr. Foley admitted. " I am going to beg you both to come on to me to-night. My niece is receiving a few friends. But I can promise you nothing of the same class of attraction, Mr. Selingman."

" We cannot come," Selingman declared, without hesitation. " I take my friend Maraton somewhere.

As we sit here, Mr. Foley, we have spoken of politics. You are a great man. If any one can lift your country from the rut along which she is travelling, you will do it. A Unionist Prime Minister and you hold out the hand to Maraton! But what foresight! What acumen! You see beyond the thunderclouds the things that we have seen. Not only do you see them, but you have the courage to follow your convictions. What a mess you are making of Parties!"

Mr. Foley smiled.

"Ah, well, you see," he said, "I am no politician. It is the one claim I have upon posterity that I am the first non-politician who ever became Prime Minister."

"Excellent! Excellent!" Selingman murmured.

"Maraton, alas!" Mr. Foley continued, "is only half a convert. As yet he wears his yoke heavily."

"A queer place for him," Selingman declared. "I looked down and saw him there this evening. I listened to the dozen words he spoke. He seemed to me rather like a lawyer, who, having a dull case, says what he has to say and sits down. Does he do any real good here, Mr. Foley?"

"It is from these walls," the Prime Minister reminded him, "that the laws of the country are framed."

Selingman shook his head slowly.

"Academically correct," he admitted, "and yet, walls of brick and stone may crumble and split. The laws which endure come into being through the power of the people."

"Don't throw cold water upon my compromise,"
Mr. Foley begged. "We are hoping for great
things. We are fighting the class against which you
have written so splendidly; we are fighting the bourgeoisie, tooth and nail. One thing is certainly
written — that if Maraton here stands by my side
for the next seven years, Labour will have thrown
off one, at least, of the shackles that bind her. Isn't
it better to release her slowly and gradually, than to
destroy her altogether by trying more violent
means?"

"Ah, who knows!" Selingman remarked enig-
matically. "Who knows! . . . And what of the rest
of the evening? Are there more laws to be made —
more speeches?"

"Finished," Mr. Foley replied. "There is nothing more to be done. That is why I am proposing
that you two men go to your rooms, make yourselves
look as much like Philistines as you can, and come
and pay your respects to my niece. Lady Elisabeth
is complaining a little about you, Maraton," he went
on. "You are a rare visitor."

"Lady Elisabeth is very kind," Maraton murmured.

"I wish that we could come," Selingman said.
"If I lived here long, I would bustle our friend
Maraton about. To-day I have had him a little
way into the country, him and his pale-faced secretary, and I have poured sunshine down upon them,
and wine, and good things to eat. Oh, they are very
narrow, both of them, when they look out at life!
Not so am I. I love to feel the great thoughts

swinging through my brain, but I love also the good
things of life. I love the interludes of careless joys,
I love all the pleasant things our bodies were meant
to appreciate. Those who do not, they wither early.
I do not like pale cheeks. Therefore, I wish that I
could stay a little time with this friend of ours. I
would see that he paid his respects to all the charming ladies who were ready to welcome him."

Mr. Foley laughed softly.

" What a marvellous mixture you would make,
you two! " he observed. " Your prose and Maraton's
eloquence, your philosophy and his tenacity. So
you won't come? Well, I am disappointed."

" We go to see a friend of mine," Selingman announced. " We go to pay our respects to a man
famous indeed, a man who will make history in your
country."

Mr. Foley's expression suddenly changed. He
leaned a little across the table.

" Are you speaking of Maxendorf? "

Selingman nodded vigorously.

" Since you have guessed it — yes," he admitted.
" We go to Maxendorf. I take Maraton there. It
will be a great meeting. We three — we represent
much. A great meeting, indeed."

Mr. Foley's face was troubled.

" Maxendorf only arrives to-night," he remarked
presently.

" What matter? " Selingman replied. " He is like
me — he is tireless, and though his body be weary,
his brain is ever working."

" What do they say on the Continent about his

coming?" Mr. Foley enquired. "We thought that
he was settled for life in Rome."

Selingman shook his head portentously.

"Politics," he declared, "ah! in the abstract they
are wonderful, but in the concrete they do not interest me. Maxendorf has come here, doubtless, with
great schemes in his mind."

"Schemes of friendship or of enmity?" Mr. Foley
asked swiftly.

Selingman's shoulders were hunched.

"Who can tell? Who can tell the thoughts which
his brain has conceived? Maxendorf is a silent man.
He is the first people's champion who has ever held
high office in his country. You see, he has the gifts
which no one can deny. He moves forward to whatever place he would occupy, and he takes it. He
is in politics as I in literature."

The man's magnificent egotism passed unnoticed.
Curiously enough, the truth of it was so apparent
that its expression seemed natural.

"I must confess," Mr. Foley said quietly, "to
you two alone, that I had rather he had come at some
other time. Selingman, you are indeed one of the
happiest of the earth. You have no responsibilities
save the responsibilities you owe to your genius.
The only call to which you need listen is the call
to give to the world the thoughts and music which
beat in your brain. And with us, things are different. There is the future of a country, the future
of an Empire, always at stake, when one sleeps and
when one wakes."

Selingman nodded his head vigorously.

"Frankly," he admitted, "I sympathise with you. Responsibility I hate. And yours, Mr. Foley," he added, "is a great one. I am a friend of England. I am a friend of the England who should be. As your country is to-day, I fear that she has very few friends indeed, apart from her own shores. You may gain allies from reasons of policy, but you have not the national gifts which win friendship."

"How do you account for it?" Mr. Foley asked him.

"Your Press, for one thing," Selingman replied; "your Press, written for and inspired with the whole spirit of the bourgeoisie. You prate about your Empire, but you've never learnt yet to think imperially. But there, it is not for this I crossed the Channel. It is to be with Maraton."

"So long as you do not take him from me, I will not grudge you his company," Mr. Foley remarked, rising. "On the other hand, I would very much rather that you made your bow to my niece to-night than went to Maxendorf."

Maraton felt suddenly a twinge of something which was almost compunction. Mr. Foley's face was white and tired. He had the air of a man oppressed with anxieties which he was doing his best to conceal.

"If I can," he said, "I should like very much to see Lady Elisabeth. Perhaps I shall be in time after our interview with Maxendorf, or before. I will go home and change, on the chance."

The Prime Minister nodded, but his slightly relaxed expression seemed to show that he appreciated

Maraton's intention. Selingman looked after him gloomily as he left the room.

"What devilish impulse," he muttered, "leads these men to pass into your rotten English politics! It is like a poet trying to navigate a dredger. Bah! . . . Need you go into that gloomy chamber again, my friend?"

Maraton shook his head.

"I have finished," he declared. "There will be no division."

"But do you never speak there?"

"Up to now I have not uttered more than a dozen words or so," Maraton replied. "You try it yourself — try speaking to a crowd of well-dressed, well-fed, smug units of respectability, each with his mind full of his own affairs or the affairs of his constituency. You try it. You wouldn't find the words stream, I can tell you."

Selingman grunted.

"And now — what now?"

"To my rooms — to my house," Maraton announced, "while I change."

"It is good. I shall talk to your secretary. I shall talk to Miss Julia while you disappear. Shall I rob you, my friend?"

"You would rob me of a great deal if you took her away," Maraton answered, "but —"

Selingman interrupted him with a fiercely contemptuous exclamation.

"You have it — the rotten, insular conceit of these Englishmen! You think that she would not come? Do you think that if I were to say to her,

— 'Come and listen while I make garlands of words, while I take you through the golden doors!' — do you think that she would not put her hand in mine? Fancy — to live in my fairy chamber, to listen while I give shape and substance to all that I conceive — what woman would refuse!"

Maraton laughed softly as they passed out into the Palace yard.

"Try Julia," he suggested.

CHAPTER XXX

Selingman had the air of one who has achieved a personal triumph as, with his arm in Maraton's, he led him towards the man whom they had come to visit.

" Behold! " he exclaimed. " It is a triumph, this! It is a thing to be remembered! I have brought you two together! "

Maraton's first impressions of Maxendorf were curiously mixed. He saw before him a tall, lanky figure of a man, dressed in sombre black, a man of dark complexion, with beardless face and tanned skin plentifully freckled. His hair and eyes were coal black. He held out his hand to Maraton, but the smile with which he had welcomed Selingman had passed from his lips.

" You are not the Maraton I expected some day to meet," he said, a little bluntly, " and yet I am glad to know you."

Selingman shrugged his shoulders.

" Max — my friend Max, do not be peevish," he begged. " I tell you that he is the Maraton of whom we have spoken together. I have heard him. I have been to Sheffield and listened. Don't be prejudiced, Max. Wait."

Maxendorf motioned them to seats and stood with his finger upon the bell.

"Yes," Selingman assented, "we will drink with you. You breathe of the Rhine, my friend. I see myself sitting with you in your terraced garden, drinking Moselle wine out of cut glasses. So it shall be. We will fall into the atmosphere. What a palace you live in, Max! Is it because you are an ambassador that they must house you so splendidly?"

Maxendorf glanced around him. He was in one of the best suites in the hotel, but he had the air of one who was only then, for the first time, made aware of the fact.

"These things are done for me," he said carelessly. "It seems I have come before I was expected. The Embassy is scarcely ready for occupation."

He ordered wine from the waiter and exchanged personal reminiscences with Selingman until it was brought. Selingman grunted with satisfaction.

"Two bottles," he remarked. "Come, I like that. A less thoughtful man would have ordered one first and the other afterwards. The period of waiting for the second bottle would have destroyed the appetite. Quite an artist, my friend Max. And the wine — well, we shall see."

He raised the glass to his lips with the air of a connoisseur.

"It will do," he decided, setting it down empty and lighting one of his black cigars. "Now let us talk. Or shall I, for a change, be silent and let you talk? To-day my tongue has been busy. Maraton is a silent man, and he has a silent secretary with great eyes behind which lurk fancies and dreams the poor little thing has never been encouraged to speak of. A silent man — Maraton. Rather like you, Max. Which of you will talk the more, I wonder? I shall be dumb."

"It will be I who will talk," Maxendorf asserted. "I, because I have a mission, things to explain to our friend here, if he will but listen."

"Listen — of course he will listen!" Selingman interrupted. "You two — what was it the *Oracle* called you both — the world's deliverers. Put your heads together and decide how you are going to do it. The people over here, Max, are rotting in their kennels. Sink-holes they live in. Live! What a word!"

"If you indeed have something to say to me," Maraton proposed, "let us each remember who we are. There is no need for preambles. I know you to be a people's man. We have all watched your rise. We have all marvelled at it."

"A Socialist statesman in the stiffest-necked country of Europe," Selingman muttered. "Marvelled at it, indeed!"

"I am where I am," Maxendorf declared, "because the world is governed by laws, and in the main they are laws of justice and right. The people of my country fifty years ago were as deep in the mire as the people of your country to-day. Their liberation has already dawned. That is why I stand where I do. Your people, alas! are still dwellers in the caves. The moment for you has not yet arrived. When I heard that Maraton had come to England, I changed all my plans. I said to myself — 'I will go to Maraton and I will show him how he may lead his people to the light.' And then I heard other things."

" Continue," Maraton said simply.

Maxendorf rose to his feet. He came a little nearer to Maraton. He stood looking down at him with folded arms — a lank, gaunt figure, the angular lines of his body and limbs accentuated by his black clothes and black tie.

" It came upon me like a thunderbolt," Maxendorf proceeded. " I heard unexpectedly that Maraton had entered Parliament, had placed his hand in the hand of a Minister — not even the leader of the people's Party. You do not read the Press of my country, perhaps. You did not hear across the seas the groan which came from the hearts of my children. I said to myself — ' The Maraton whom we knew of exists no longer, yet I will go and see.' "

Maraton moved in his chair a little uneasily. He felt suddenly as though he were a prisoner at the bar, and this man his judge.

" You do not understand the circumstances which I found existing on my arrival here," Maraton explained. " You do not understand the promises which I have received from Mr. Foley, and which he is already carrying into effect. You read of the Lancashire strike? "

Maxendorf nodded his long head slowly but said nothing.

" The settlement of that," Maraton continued, " was arranged before I spoke to the people. It is the same with Sheffield. For the first time, the Parliament of this country has passed a measure compelling the manufacturers to recognise and treat with the demands of the people. Trade Unionism has been lifted to an entirely different level. There are three Bills now being drafted — people's Bills. Revolutionary measures they would have been called, a thousand years ago. Every industry in the country will have its day. In the next ten years Capital will have earned many millions less, and those many millions will have gone to the labouring classes."

"Is it you who speak," Maxendorf asked grimly, "or is this another man — a sophist living in the shadow of Maraton's fame? Is there anything of the truth, anything of the great compelling truth in this piecemeal legislation? Is it in this way that the freedom of a country can be gained? One gathered that the Maraton who sent his message across the seas had different plans."

"I had," Maraton admitted, "but the time came when I was forced to ask myself whether they were not rather the plans of the dreamer and the theorist, when I was forced to ask myself whether I was justified in destroying this generation for the sake of those to come. Life, after all, is a marvellous gift. You and I may believe in immortality, but who can be sure? It is easy enough to play chess, but when the pawns are human lives, who would not hesitate?"

Maxendorf sighed.

"I cannot talk with you, Maraton," he said. "You will not speak with me honestly. You came, you landed on these shores with an inspired idea — something magnificent, something worthy. You have substituted for it the time-worn methods of all the reformers since the days of Adam, who have parted with their principles and dabbled in sentimental altruism. Piecemeal legislation — what can it do?"

"It can build," Maraton declared. "It can build, generation by generation. It can produce a saner race, and as the light comes, so the truth will flow in upon the minds of all."

"An illusion!" Selingman interrupted, with a sudden fierceness in his tone. "Once, Maraton, you looked at life sanely enough. Are you sure that to-day you have not put on the poisoned spectacles? Don't you know the end of these spasmodic reforms? You pass, your influence passes, your mantle is buried in your grave, and the country slips back, and the people suffer, and the great wheel grinds them into bone and powder just as surely a century hence as a century ago. Man, you don't start right. If you would restore a ruined and neglected garden, you must first destroy, make a bonfire of the weeds, prepare your soil. Then, in the springtime, fresh flowers will blossom, the trees will give leaf, the birds who have deserted a ruined and fruitless waste will return and sing once more the song of life. But there must be destruction, Maraton. You yourself preached it once, preached fire and the sword. Something has gone from you since those days. Compromise — the spirit of compromise you call it. How one hates the sound of it! Bah! Man, you are on a lower level, when you talk the smug talk of to-day. I am disappointed in you. Maxendorf is disappointed in you. You are riding down the easy way on to the sandbanks of failure."

" Your garden," Maraton rejoined, with an answering note of passion in his tone, " would never have blossomed again if you had driven the plough across it, ripped up its fruit trees, torn up its neglected plants by ruthless force. You must plant fresh seed and grow new trees. Then there's another nation, another world. What about your responsibilities to the present one? Isn't it great to save what is, rather than to destroy for the sake of those who have neither toiled nor suffered? I thought as you once. The philosopher thinks like that in his study. Stand before those people, look into their white, labour-worn faces, feel with them, sorrow with them for a little time, and I tell you that your hand will falter before it drives the plough. You will raise your eyes to heaven and pray that you may see some way of bringing help to them — to them who live — the help for which they crave. Haven't they a right to their lives? Who gives us a mandate to sweep them away for the sake of the unborn? "

" You have become a sentimentalist, Maraton," Maxendorf declared grimly. " The soft places in your heart have led you to forget for a moment the inexorable laws. Let us pass from these generalities. Let us speak of things such as you had at first intended. I know what was in your heart. You meant to pass from Birmingham to Glasgow, to preach the holy war of Labour, a giant crusade. You meant to close the mills, to stop the wheels, to blank the forges and rake out the furnaces of the country. You meant to place your finger upon its arteries and stop their beating. You meant to turn the people loose upon their oppressors. Though they must perish in their thousands, yet you meant to show them the naked truth, to show them of what they are being deprived, to show them the irresistible laws of justice, so that for very shame they must drop their tools and stand for their rights. Why didn't you do it?"

"I have told you," Maraton answered.

"Yes, you have told us," Maxendorf continued. "Supposing there were still a way by which even this present generation could reap the benefit? Are you great enough, Maraton, to listen to me, I wonder? That is what I ask myself since you have become a Party politician, a friend of Ministers, since you have joined in the puppet dance of the world. See to what I have brought my people. In ten years' time I tell you that nearly every industry in my country will be conducted upon a profit-sharing basis."

"You have brought them to this," Maraton reminded him swiftly, "by peaceful methods."

"For me there were no other needed," Maxendorf urged. "For you the case is different. If you are one of those who love to strut about and boast of your nationality, if you are one of those in whom lingers the smallest particle of the falsest sentiment which the age of romance has ever handed down to us — what they call patriotism — then my words will be wasted. But here is the message which I have brought to you and to your people. This is the dream of my life which he, Selingman, alone has known of — the fusion of our races."

" Magnificent! " Selingman cried, springing to his feet. " The dream of a god! Listen to it, Maraton. My brain has realised it. I, too, have seen it. Your country is bound in the everlasting shackles. Generations must pass before you can even weaken the hold of your bourgeoisie upon the soul and spirit of your land. You are tied hard and fast, and withal you are on the downward grade. The work which you do to-day, the next generation will undo. Give up this foolish legislation. Listen to Maxendorf. He will show you the way."

" When you speak of fusion," Maraton asked, " you mean conquest? "

" There is no such word," Maxendorf insisted. " The hearts of our people are close together. Put aside all these artificial ententes and alliances. There are no two people whose ideals and whose aims and whose destiny are so close together as your country's and mine. It is for that very reason that these periods of distrust and suspicion continually occur, suspicions which impoverish two countries with the millions we spend on senseless schemes of defence. Away with them all. Stop the pendulum of your country. Declare your coal strike, your railway strike, your ironfounders' strike. Let the revolution come. I tell you then that we shall appear not as invaders, but as friends and liberators. Your industries shall start again on a new basis, the basis which you and I know of, the basis which gives to the toilers their just and legitimate share of what they produce. Your trade shall flourish just as it flourished before, but away to dust and powder with your streets of pig-sties, the rat-holes into which your weary labourers creep after their hours of senseless slavery. You and I, Maraton, know how industries should be conducted. You and I know the just share which Capital should claim. You and I together will make the laws. Oh, what does it matter whether you are English or Icelanders, Fins or Turks! Humanity is so much greater than nationality. Your men shall work side by side with mine, and what each produces, each shall have. What is being done for my country shall surely be done for yours. Can't you see, Maraton — can't you see, my prophet who gropes in the darkness, that I am showing you the only way?"

Maraton rose to his feet. He came and stood by Maxendorf's side.

"Maxendorf," he said, "you may be speaking to me from your heart. Yes, I will admit that you are speaking to me from your heart. But you ask me to take an awful risk. You stand first in your country to-day, but in your country there are other powerful influences at work. So much of what you say is true. If I believed, Maxendorf — if I believed that this fusion, as you call it, of our people could come about in the way you suggest, if I believed that the building up of our prosperity could start again on the real and rational basis of many of your institutions, if I believed this, Maxendorf, no false sentiment would stand in my way. I would risk the eternal shame of the historians. So far as I could do it, I would give you this country. But there is always the doubt, the awful doubt. You have a ruler whose ideas are not your ideas. You have a people behind you who are strange to me. I have not travelled in your country, I know little of it. What if your people should assume the guise of conquerors, should garrison our towns with foreign soldiers, demand a huge indemnity, and then, withdrawing, leave us to our fate? You have no guarantees to offer me, Maxendorf."

"None but my word," Maxendorf confessed quietly.

"You bargain like a politician!" Selingman cried. "Man, can't you see the glory of it?"

"I can see the glory," Maraton answered, turning around, "but I can see also the ineffaceable ignominy of it. Is your country great enough, Maxendorf, to follow where your finger points? I do not know."

"Yet you, too," Maxendorf persisted, "must sometimes have looked into futurity. You must have seen the slow decay of national pride, the nations of the world growing closer and closer together. Can't you bear to strike a blow for the great things? You and I see so well the utter barbarism of warfare, the hideous waste of our mighty armaments, draining the money like blood from our countries, and all for senselessness, all just to keep alive that strange spirit which belongs to the days of romance, and the days of romance only. It's a workaday world now, Maraton. We draw nearer to the last bend in the world's history. Oh, this is the truth! I have seen it for so long. It's my religion, Maraton. The time may not have come to preach it broadcast, but it's there in my heart."

Selingman struck the table with the palm of his hand.

"Enough!" he said. "The words have been spoken. To-morrow or the next day we meet again. Go to your study, Maraton, and think. Lock the door. Turn out the Julia I shall some day rob you of. Hold your head, look into the future. Think! Think! No more words now. They do no good. Come. I stay with Maxendorf. I go with you to the lift."

Maxendorf held out his hand.

"Selingman is, as usual, right," he confessed. "We are speaking in a great language, Maraton. It is enough for to-night, perhaps. Come back to me when you will within the next forty-eight hours."

They left him there, a curious figure, straight and motionless, standing upon the threshold of his room. Selingman gripped Maraton by the arm as he hurried him along the corridor.

"You've doubts, Maraton," he muttered. "Doubts! Curse them! They are not worthy. You should see the truth. You're big enough. You will see it to-morrow. Get out of the fog. Maxendorf is the most profound thinker of these days. He is over here with that scheme of his deep in his heart. It's become a passion with him. We have talked of it by the hour, spoken of you, prayed for some prophet on your side with eyes to see the truth. Into the lift with you, man. Look for me to-morrow. Farewell!"

CHAPTER XXXI

Maraton was more than ever conscious, as he climbed the stairs of the house in Downing Street an hour or so later, of a certain fragility of appearance in Mr. Foley, markedly apparent during these last few weeks. He was standing talking to Lord Armley, who was one of the late arrivals, as Maraton entered, talking in a low tone and with an obviously serious manner. At the sound of Maraton's name, however, he turned swiftly around. His face seemed to lighten. He held out his hand with an air almost of relief.

"So you have come!" he exclaimed. "I am glad."

Maraton shook hands and would have passed on, but Mr. Foley detained him.

"Armley and I were talking about this afternoon's decision," he continued. "There will be no secret about it to-morrow. It has been decided to carry out our autumn manœuvres as usual in Southern waters."

Maraton nodded.

"I am afraid that is one of the things the significance of which fails to reach me," he remarked. "You were against it, were you not?"

Mr. Foley groaned softly.

"My friend," he said, "there is only one fault

with the Members of my Government, only one fault
with this country. We are all foolishly and blindly
sanguine. We are optimistic by persuasion and
self-persuasion. We like the comfortable creed. I
suppose that the bogey of war has strutted with us
for so long that we have grown used to it."

Maraton looked at his companion thoughtfully.

"Do you seriously believe, Mr. Foley," he asked
in an undertone, "in the possibility, in the imminent
possibility of war?"

Mr. Foley half-closed his eyes and sighed.

"Oh, my dear Maraton," he murmured, "it isn't
a question of belief! It's like asking me whether
I believe I can see from here into my own drawing-
room. The figures in there are real enough, aren't
they? So is the cloud I can see gathering all the
time over our heads. It is a question only of the
propitious moment — of that there is no manner of
doubt."

"You speak of affairs," Maraton admitted, "of
which I know nothing. I do not even understand
the balance of power. I always thought, though,
that every great nation, our own included, paid a
certain amount of insurance in the shape of huge
contributions towards a navy and army; that we paid
such insurance as was necessary and were rewarded
with adequate results."

Mr. Foley forgot his depression for an instant,
and smiled.

"What a theorist you are! It all depends upon
the amount of insurance you take up, whether the
risk is covered. We've under-insured for many

years, thanks to that little kink in our disposition. We got a nasty knock in South Africa and we had to pay our own loss. It did us good for a year or two. Now the pendulum has just reached the other extreme. We've swung back once more into our silly dream. Oh, Maraton, it's true enough that we have great problems to face sociologically! Don't think that I underrate them. You know I don't. But every time I sit and talk to you, I have always at the back of my mind that other fear. . . . Have you seen Maxendorf to-night?"

"I have just left him," Maraton replied.

"An interesting interview?"

"Very!"

Mr. Foley gripped his arm.

"My friend," he said,— "you see, I am beginning to call you that — you have talked to-night with one of the most wonderful and the most dangerous enemies of our country. You won't think me drivelling, will you, or presuming, if I beg you to remember that fact, and that you are, notwithstanding your foreign birth, one of us? You are an Englishman, a member of the English House of Parliament."

"I do not forget that," Maraton declared gravely.

"Go and find Lady Elisabeth," Mr. Foley directed. "She was a little hurt at the idea that you were not coming. I have a few more words to say to Armley."

Maraton passed on into the rooms, which were only half filled. Some fancy possessed him to pause for a moment in the spot where he had stood alone for some time on his first visit to this house, and as he lingered there, Lady Elisabeth came into the room,

leaning on the arm of a great lawyer. She saw him
almost at once — her eyes, indeed, seemed to glance
instinctively towards the spot where he was standing.
Maraton felt the change in her expression. With
a whisper she left her escort and came immediately
in his direction. He watched her, step by step.
Was it his fancy or had she lost some of the haughti-
ness of carriage which he had noticed that night not
many months ago; the slight coldness which in those
first moments had half attracted and half repelled
him? Perhaps it was because he was now admitted
within the circle of her friends. She came to him,
at any rate, quickly, almost eagerly, and the smile
about her lips as she took his hand was one of real
and natural pleasure.

"How good of you!" she murmured. "I scarcely
hoped that you would come. You have been with
Maxendorf?"

He nodded.

"Is it a confession?" he asked. "It was Mr.
Foley's first question to me."

"It is because we hate and distrust the man," she
replied. "You aren't a politician, you see, Mr.
Maraton. You don't quite appreciate some of the
forces which are making an old man of my uncle
to-day, which make life almost intolerable for many
of us when we think seriously," she went on simply.

"Aren't you exaggerating that sentiment just a
little?" he suggested.

"Not a particle," she assured him. "However,
you came here to be entertained, didn't you? I
won't croak to you any more. I think I have done

my duty for this evening. Let us find a corner and talk like ordinary human beings. Are you going in to supper?"

"I hadn't thought of it," he admitted.

"I dined at seven o'clock," she told him. "We seem to have provided supper for hundreds of people, and I am sure not half of them are coming."

They passed through two of the rooms into a long, low apartment which led into the winter gardens. At one end refreshments were being served, and the rest of the space was taken up with little tables. Elisabeth led him to one placed just inside the winter garden. A footman filled their glasses with champagne.

"Now we are going to be normal human beings," she declared. "How much I wish that you really were a normal human being!"

"In what respect am I different?"

"You know quite well," she answered. "I should like you to be what you seem to be — just a capable, clever, rising politician, with a place in the Cabinet before you, working for your country, sincere, free from all these strange notions."

"Working for my country," he repeated. "That is just the difficult part of the whole situation, nowadays. I know that I am rather a trouble to your uncle. Sometimes I fear that I may become even a greater trouble. It is so hard to adopt the attitude which you suggest when one feels the intolerable situation which exists in that country."

"But we are on the highroad now to great reforms," she reminded him. "Another decade of

years, and the people whom you worship will surely
be lifting their heads."

He smiled as she looked across at him with a puzzled air.

"It is strange," she remarked, "that you, too,
have the appearance of a man dissatisfied with himself. I wonder why? Surely you must feel that
everything has gone your way since you came to
England?"

"I am not sure how I feel about it," he replied.
"Think! I came with different ideas. I came with
a religion which admitted no compromises, and I
have accepted a compromise."

"A wise and a sane one," she declared, almost
passionately. "And to-night — tell me, am I not
right? — to-night there have been those who have
sought to upset it in your mind."

"You are clairvoyant."

"Not I, but it is so easy to see! It is the dream
of Maxendorf's life to bring England to the verge
of a revolution by paralysing her industries. Better
for him, that, than any violent scheme of conquest.
If he can stop the engine that drives the wheels of
the country, they can come over in tourist steamers
and tell us how to govern it better."

"And if they did," he asked quickly, "isn't it
possible that their rule over the people might be
better than the rule of this stubborn generation?"

She drew herself up. Her eyes flashed with anger.

"Haven't you a single gleam of patriotism?" she
demanded.

He sighed.

"I think that I have," he replied, "and yet, it lies at the back of my thoughts, at the back of my heart. It is more like an artistic· inspiration, one of those things that lie among the pleasant impulses of life. Right in the foreground I see the great groaning cycle of humanity being flung from the everlasting wheels into the bottomless abyss. I cannot take my eyes from the people, you see."

She sat almost rigid for some brief space of time. A servant was arranging plates in front of them, their glasses were refilled, the music of a waltz stole in through the open door. Around them many other people were sitting. An atmosphere of gaiety began gradually to develop. Maraton watched his companion closely. Her eyes were full of trouble, her sensitive mouth quivering a little. There was a straight line across her forehead. Her fair hair was arranged in great coils, without a single ornament. She wore no jewels at all save a single string of pearls around her slim white neck. Maraton, as the moments passed, was conscious of a curious weakening, a return of that same thrill which the sound of her voice that first day — half imperious, half gracious — had incited in him. He waved his hand towards the crowd of those who supped around them.

"Let us forget," he begged. "I, too, feel that I have more in my mind to-night than my brain can cope with. Let us rest for a little time."

Her face lightened.

"We will," she assented gladly. "Only, do remember what my constant prayer about you is. Things, you know, in some respects must go on as they are, and the country needs its strongest sons. Mr. Foley would like to bring you even closer to him. I know he is simply aching with impatience to have you in the Cabinet. Don't do anything rash, Mr. Maraton. Don't do anything which would make it impossible. There are many beautiful theories in life which would be simply hateful failures if one tried to bring them into practice. Try to remember that experience goes for something. And now — finished! Tell me about Sheffield? I read Selingman's marvellous article. One could almost see the whole scene there. How I should love to hear you speak! Not in Parliament — I don't mean that. I almost realise how impossible you find that."

"It is only a matter of earnestness," he replied, " and a certain aptitude for forming phrases quickly. No one can feel deeply about anything and not find themselves more or less eloquent when they come to talk about it. By the bye, have you ever met Selingman?"

She shook her head.

"My uncle knew him. He tells me that he asked him here to-night. I wish that he had come. And yet, I am not sure. Some of his writings I have hated. He, too, is a theorist, isn't he? I wonder —"

She paused, and looked expectant.

"I often wonder," she went on, " is there nothing else in your life at all except this passionate altruism? In your younger life, for instance, weren't there ever any sports or occupations that you cared for?"

"Yes," he admitted slowly, "for some years I did a good many of the usual things."

"And now the desire for them has all gone," she asked, "haven't you any personal hopes or dreams in connection with life? Isn't there anything you look forward to or desire for yourself?"

"I seem to have so little time. And yet, one has dreams — one always must have dreams, you know."

"Tell me about yours?" she insisted.

He sat up abruptly. Her fingers fell upon his arm.

"We will go and sit under my rose tree," she suggested.

They moved back into the winter garden until they came to a seat at its furthest extremity. A fountain was playing a few yards away, and clusters of great pink roses were drooping down from some trellis-work before them.

"Here, at least," she continued, as she leaned back, "we will not be tempted to talk seriously. Tell me about yourself? Do you never look forward into the future? Have you no personal ambitions or hopes?"

He looked steadily ahead of him.

"I am only a very ordinary man," he replied. "Like every one else, sometimes I look up to the clouds."

"Tell me what you see there?" she begged.

He was silent. The sound of voices now came to them like a distant murmur, a background to the slow falling of the water into the fountain basin.

"Lady Elisabeth," he said, "it is not always possible to tell even one's own self what the thoughts mean which come into one's brain."

" You will not even try to tell me, then? "

" I must not," he answered.

She sat with her hands folded in front of her, her head drooped a little. Maraton felt himself suddenly at war with a whole multitude of emotions. Was it possible that this thing had come to him, that a woman could take the great place in his life, a woman not of his kind, one who could not even share the passion which was to have absorbed every impulse of his existence to the end? She was of a different world. Perhaps it had all been a mistake. Perhaps it would have been better for him to have stayed outside, to have never crossed the little borderland which led into the land of compromises. And all the time, while his brain was at work, something stronger, more wonderful, was throbbing in his heart. He moved restlessly in his place. Her ungloved hand lay within a few inches of him. He suddenly caught it.

" Lady Elisabeth," he whispered, " I feel like a traitor. I feel myself moved to say things to you under false pretences. I ought not to have come here."

" What do you mean? " she demanded. " You can't mean —"

Their eyes met. He read the truth unerringly.

" No, not that," he answered. " There is no one. What I feel is, at any rate, consecrate. But I have no right. I am not sure, even at this moment, whether it is not in my heart to take a step which you would look upon as the blackest ingratitude. My life, Lady Elisabeth, holds issues in it far apart, and it is vowed, dedicate."

"You are going to break away?" she asked quietly.

"I may," he admitted. "That is the truth. That is why I hesitated about coming here to-night. And yet, I wanted to come. I wasn't sure why. I know now — it was to see you."

"Oh, don't be rash!" she begged. "Don't! I may talk to you now really from my heart, mayn't I?" she went on, looking steadfastly into his face. "Don't imagine that that great gulf exists. It doesn't. If you break away, it will be a mistake. You want to feel your feet upon the clouds. You don't know how much safer you will be if you keep them upon the earth. You may bring incalculable suffering and misery upon the very people whom you wish to benefit. You think that I am a woman, perhaps, and I know little. Yes, but sometimes we who are outside see much, and it is dangerous, you know, to act upon theories. I haven't spoken a single selfish word, have I? I haven't tried to tell you how much I should hate to lose you."

He rose to his feet.

"I am going away," he said hoarsely. "I must fight this thing out alone. But —"

He looked around. The words seemed to fail him. Their little corner of the winter garden was still uninvaded.

"But, Lady Elisabeth," he continued, "you know the thing which makes it harder for me than ever. You know very well that if I decide to do what must

"I am going away," he said hoarsely.   *Page* 296.

make me a stranger in this household, I shall do it at a personal sacrifice which I never dreamed could exist."

She swayed a little towards him. Her face was suddenly changed, alluring; her eyes pleaded with him.

" You mustn't go away," she whispered. " If you go now, you must come back — do you hear? — you must come back! "

CHAPTER XXXII

It was the eve of the reopening of Parliament. Maraton, who had been absent from London — no one knew where — during the last six weeks, had suddenly reappeared. Once more he had invited the committee of the Labour Party to meet at his house. His invitation was accepted, but it was obvious that this time their attitude towards the man who welcomed them was one of declared and pronounced hostility. Graveling was there, with sullen, evil face. He made no attempt to shake hands with Maraton, and he sat at the table provided for them with folded arms and dour, uncompromising aspect. Dale came late and he, too, greeted Maraton with bluff unfriendliness. Borden's attitude was non-committal. Weavel shook hands, but his frown and manner were portentous. Culvain, the diplomat of the party, was quiet and reserved. David Ross alone had never lost his attitude of unwavering fidelity. He sat at Maraton's left hand, his head a little drooped, his eyes almost hidden beneath his shaggy grey eyebrows, his lower lip protuberant. He had, somehow, the air of a guarding dog, ready to spring into bitter words if his master were touched.

"Gentlemen," Maraton began, when at last they were all assembled, "I have asked you, the committee who were appointed to meet me on my arrival in

England, to meet me once more here on the eve of
the reopening of Parliament."

There was a grim silence. No one spoke. Their
general attitude was one of suspicious waiting.

" You all know," Maraton went on, " with what
ideas I first came to England. I found, however,
that circumstances here were in many respects different from anything I had imagined. You all know
that I modified my plans. I decided to adopt a middle course."

" A seat in Parliament," Graveling muttered,
" and a place at the Prime Minister's dinner table."

" For some reason or other," Maraton continued,
unruffled, " my coming into Parliament seemed ob-
noxious to Mr. Dale and most of you. I decided in
favour of that course, however, because the offer
made me by Mr. Foley was one which, in the interests
of the people, I could not refuse. Mr. Foley has
done his best to keep to the terms of his compact
with me. Perhaps I ought to say that he has kept
to it. The successful termination of the Lancashire
strike is due entirely to his efforts. The prolong-
ation of the Sheffield strike is in no way his fault.
The blind stupidity of the masters was too much
even for him. The position has developed very
much as I feared it might. You cannot make employers see reason by Act of Parliament. Mr. Foley
kept his word. He has been on the side of the men
throughout this struggle. He has used every atom
of influence he possesses to compel the employers to
give in. Temporarily he has failed — only temporarily, mind, for a Bill will be introduced into

Parliament during this session which will very much
alter the position of the employers. But this partial
failure has convinced me of one thing. This is too
law-abiding a country for compromises. For the last
six weeks I have been travelling on the Continent.
I have realised how splendidly Labour has emanci-
pated itself there compared to its slow progress in
this country. From town to town in northern Europe I passed, and found the great industries of the
various districts in the hands of a composite body
of men, embracing the boy learning the simplest
machine and the financier in the office, every man
there working like a single part of one huge machine,
each for the profit of the whole. A genuine scheme
of profit-sharing is there being successfully carried
out. It is owing to this visit, and the convictions
which have come to me from the same, that I have
called you together to-day."

"You invited us," Peter Dale remarked deliberately, "and here we are. As to what good's likely
to come of our meeting, that's another matter.
There's no denying the fact that we've not been able
to work together up till now, and whether we shall
in the future is by no means clear."

"I am sorry to hear you say so, Mr. Dale," Maraton declared. "I only hope that before you go you
will have changed your mind."

"Not in the least likely, that I can see," Peter
Dale retorted. "For my part, I can't reckon up
what you want with us. You've gone into the House
on your own and you've chosen to sit in a place by
yourself. You've tried your best to manage things

according to your own way of thinking, without us. Now, all of a sudden, you invite us here. I wonder whether this has anything to do with it."

With some deliberation, Peter Dale produced from his pocket a letter, which he smoothed out upon the table before him. He had the air of a man who prepares a bombshell. Maraton stretched out his hand toward it.

" Is that for me? " he asked.

Peter Dale kept his fingers upon it.

" Its contents concern you," he announced. " I'll read it, if you'll be so good as to listen. Came as a bit of a shock to us, I must confess."

" Anonymous? " Maraton murmured.

" If its contents are untrue," Peter Dale said, " you will be able to contradict them. With your kind permission, then. Listen, everybody:

" ' *Dear Sir:*

" ' The following facts concerning a recent addition to the ranks of your Party should, I think, be of some interest to you.

" ' The proper name of Mr. Maraton is Mr. Maraton Lawes.

" ' Mr. Maraton Lawes and a younger brother were once the possessors of the world-famous Lawes Oil Springs, and are now the principal shareholders in the Lawes Oil Company.

" ' The person in question is a millionaire.

" ' A Socialist millionaire who conceals the fact of his wealth and keeps his purse closed, is a person, I think, open to criticism.

" ' A sketch of Mr. Maraton Lawes' career will shortly appear in an evening paper.' "

Maraton listened without change of countenance. All eyes were turned upon him.

" Well? " he enquired nonchalantly.

" Is this true? " Peter Dale demanded.

Maraton inclined his head.

" The writer," he said, " a man named Beldeman, I am sure has been singularly moderate in his statements. I have been expecting the article to appear for some time."

They were all of them apparently afflicted with a curious combination of emotions. They were angry, and yet — with the exception of Graveling — there was beneath their anger some evidence of that curious respect for wealth prevalent amongst their order. They looked at Maraton with a new interest.

" A millionaire! " Peter Dale exclaimed impressively. " You admit it! You — a Socialist — a people's man, as you've called yourself! And never a word to one of us! Never a copper of your money to the Party! I repeat it — not one copper have we seen! "

The man's cheeks were flushed with anger, his brows lowered. Something of his indignation was reflected in the faces of all of them — momentarily a queer sort of cupidity seemed to have stolen into their expressions. Maraton shrugged his shoulders slightly.

" Why should I subscribe to your Party funds? " he asked calmly. " Some of you do good work, no

doubt, and yet there is no such destroyer of good
work as money. Work, individual effort, unselfish enthusiasm, are the torches which should light on your
cause. Money would only serve the purpose of a
slow poison amongst you."

"Prattle!" Abraham Weavel muttered.

"Rot!" Peter Dale agreed. "Just another question, Mr. Maraton: Why have you kept this secret
from us?"

"I will make a statement," Maraton replied coolly.
"Perhaps it will save needless questions. My money
is derived from oil springs. I prospected for them
myself, and I have had to fight for them. It was
in wilder days than you know of here. I have a
younger brother, or rather a half-brother, whom I
was sorry to see over here the other day, who is my
partner. My average profits are twenty-eight thousand pounds a year. Ten thousand pounds goes to
the support of a children's home in New York; the
remainder is distributed in other directions amongst
institutions for the rescue of children. Five thousand a year I keep for myself."

"Five thousand a year!" Peter Dale gasped indignantly. "Did you hear that?" he added, turning
to the others.

"Four hundred a year and a hundred and fifty
from subscriptions, and that's every penny I have
to bring up seven children upon," Weavel declared
with disgust.

"And mine's less than that, and the subscriptions
falling off," Borden grunted.

"What sort of a Socialist is a man with five thousand a year who keeps his pockets tightly buttoned up, I should like to know?" Graveling exclaimed angrily.

Maraton smiled.

"You have common sense, I am sure, all of you," he said. "In fact, no one could possibly accuse you of being dreamers. Every effort of my life will be devoted towards the promulgation of my beliefs, absolutely without regard to my pecuniary position. I admit that the possession of wealth is contrary to the principles of life which I should like to see established. Still, until conditions alter, it would be even more contrary to my principles to distribute my money in charity which I abominate, or to weaken good causes by unwholesome and unearned contributions to them. Shall we now proceed to the subject of our discussion?"

"What is it, anyway?" Peter Dale demanded gruffly. "Do you find that after being so plaguey independent you need our help after all? Is that what it is?"

"I want no one's help," Maraton replied quietly. "I only want to give you this earliest notice — because, in your way, you do represent the people — that it is my intention to revert to my first ideas. I have arranged a tour in the potteries next week. I go straight on to Newcastle, and from there to Glasgow. I intend to preach a universal strike. I intend, if I can, to bring the shipbuilders, the coal-miners, the dockers, the railroad men, out on strike, while the Sheffield trouble is as yet unsolved. Whatever may come of it, I intend that the Government of this country shall realise how much their prosperity is dependent upon the people's will."

There was a little murmur. Peter Dale, who had filled his pipe, was puffing away steadily.

" Look here," he said slowly, " Newcastle's my job."

" Is it? " Maraton replied. " There are a million and a quarter of miners to be considered. You may be the representative of a few of them. I am not sure that in this matter you represent their wishes, if you are for peace. I am going to see."

" As for the potteries," Mr. Borden declared, " a strike there's overdue, and that's certain, but if all the others are going to strike at the same time, why, what's the good of it? The Unions can't stand it."

" We have tried striking piecemeal," Maraton pointed out. " It doesn't seem to me that it's a success. What is called the Government here can deal with one strike at a time. They've soldiers enough, and law enough, for that. They haven't for a universal strike."

Peter Dale struck the table with his clenched fist. His expression was grim and his tone truculent.

" What I say is this," he pronounced. " I'm dead against any interference from outsiders. If I think a strike's good for my people, well, I'll blow the whistle. If you're for Newcastle next week, Mr. Maraton, so am I. If you're for preaching a strike, well, I'm for preaching against it."

" Hear, hear! " Graveling exclaimed. " I'm with you."

Maraton smiled a little bitterly.

"As you will, Mr. Dale," he replied. "But remember, you'll have to seek another constituency next time you want to come into Parliament. Do be reasonable," he went on. "Do you suppose the people will listen to you preaching peace and contentment? They'll whip you out of the town."

"It's the carpet-bagger that will have to go first!" Dale declared vigorously. "There's no two ways about that."

Maraton sighed.

"Sometimes," he said, looking around at them, "I feel that it must be my fault that there has never been any sympathy between us. Sometimes I am sure that it is yours. Don't you ever look a little way beyond the actual wants of your own constituents? Don't you ever peer over the edge and realise that the real cause of the people is no local matter? It is a great blow for their freedom, this which I mean to strike. I'd like to have had you all with me. It's a huge responsibility for one."

"It's revolution," Culvain muttered. "You may call that a responsibility, indeed. Who's going to feed the people? Who's going to keep them from pillaging and rioting?"

"No one," Maraton replied quietly. "A revolution is inevitable. Perhaps after that we may have to face the coming of a foreign enemy. And yet, even with this contingency in view, I want you to ask yourselves: What have the people to lose? Those who will suffer by anything that could possibly happen, will be the wealthy. From those who have not, nothing can be taken. What I prophesy is that

in the next phase of our history, a new era will dawn.
Our industries will be re-established upon different
lines. The loss entailed by the revolution, by the
dislocating of all our industries, will fall upon the
people who are able and who deserve to pay for it."

There was a moment's grim silence. Then David
Ross suddenly lifted his head.

"It's a great blow!" he cried. "It's the hand
of the Lord falling upon the land, long overdue —
too long overdue. The man's right! This people
have had a century to set their house in order. The
warning has been in their ears long enough. The
thunder has muttered so long, it's time the storm
should break. Let ruin come, I say!"

"You can talk any silly nonsense you like, David
Ross," Dale declared angrily, "but what I say is
that we are listening to the most dangerous stuff
any man ever spouted. What's to become of us,
I'd like to know, with a revolution in the country?"

"You would probably lose your jobs," Maraton
answered calmly. "What does it matter? There
are others to follow you. The first whom the people
will turn upon will be those who have pulled down
the pillars. Our names will be hated by every one
of them. What does it matter? It is for their
good."

Peter Dale doubled up his fist and once more he
smote the table before him.

"I am dead against you, Maraton," he announced.
"Put that in your pipe and smoke it. If you go to
Newcastle, I go there to fight you. If you go to
any of the places in this country represented by us,

our Member will be there to fight. We are in Parliament to do our best for the people we represent, bit by bit as we can. We are not there to plunge the country into a revolution and run the risk of a foreign invasion. There isn't one of us Englishmen here who'll agree with you or side with you for one moment."

" Hear, hear! " they all echoed.

" Not one," Graveling interposed, " and for my part, I go further. I say that the man who stands there and talks about the risk of a foreign invasion like that, is no Englishman. I call him a traitor, and if the thing comes he speaks of, may he be hung from the nearest lamp-post! That's all I've got to say."

Maraton opened his lips and closed them again. He looked slowly down that wall of blank, unsympathetic faces and he merely shrugged his shoulders. Words were wasted upon them.

" Very well, gentlemen," he said, " let it be war. Perhaps we'd better let this be the end of our deliberations."

Graveling rose slowly to his feet. His face was filled with evil things. He pointed to Maraton.

" There's a word more to be spoken! " he exclaimed. " There's more behind this scheme of Maraton's than he's willing to have us understand! It looks to me and it sounds to me like a piece of dirty, underhand business. I'll ask you a question, Maraton. Were you at the Ritz Hotel one night about two months ago, with the ambassador of a foreign country? "

" I was," Maraton admitted coolly.

Graveling looked around with a little cry of triumph.

" It's a plot, this; nothing more nor less than a plot! " he declared vigorously. " What sort of an Englishman does he call himself, I wonder? It's the foreigners that are at the bottom of the lot of it! They want our trade, they'd be glad of our country. They've bribed this man Maraton to get it without the trouble of fighting for it, even! "

Maraton moved towards the door. Holding it open, he turned and faced them.

" Before I came," he said, " I hoped that you might be men. I find you just the usual sort of pigmies. You call yourselves people's men! You haven't mastered the elementary truths of your religion. What's England, or France, or any other country in the world, by the side of humanity? Be off! I'll go my own way. Go yours, and take your little tinsel of jingoism with you. Whenever you want to fight me, I shall be ready."

" And fight you we shall," Peter Dale thundered, " mark you that! There's limits, even to us. The Government of this country mayn't be all it should be, but, after all, it's our English Government, and there is a point at which every man has to support it. The law is the law, and so you may find out, my friend! "

They filed out. Maraton closed the door after them. He was alone. He threw open the window to get rid of the odour of tobacco smoke which still hung about. The echo of their raucous voices seemed still in the air. These were the men who should have been his friends and associates! These were the men to whom he had the right to look for sympathy! They treated him like a dangerous lunatic. Their own small interests, their own small careers were threatened, and they were up in arms without a moment's hesitation. Not one of them had made the slightest attempt to see the whole truth. The word " revolution " had terrified them. The approach of a crisis had driven their thoughts into one narrow focus: what would it mean for them?

He resumed his seat. The empty chairs pushed back seemed, somehow or other, allegorical. He was alone. The man for whose friendship he had indeed felt some desire, the man who had opened his hands and heart to him — Stephen Foley — would know him henceforth no more. He drew his thoughts resolutely away from that side of his life, closed his ears to the music which beat there, crushed down the fancies which sprang up so easily if ever he relaxed his hold upon his will. He was lonely; for the first time in his life, perhaps, intensely lonely. In all the country there was scarcely a human being who would not soon look upon him as a madman. What did one live for, after all? Just to continue the dull, hopeless struggle — to fight without hope of reward, to fight with oneself as well as with the world?

The door was opened softly. Julia came in. Perhaps she guessed from his attitude something of his trouble, for she moved at once to his side.

" They have gone? " she asked.

" They have gone," he admitted.

She sighed.

"I shall not ask you anything," she said, "because I know. Pigs of men — pigs with their noses to the ground! How can they lift their heads! You could not make them understand!"

"I scarcely tried," he confessed. "They have found out, for one thing, that I am wealthy, a fact that does not concern them in the least, and they accused me of it as though it were a crime. It was all so hopeless. You cannot make men understand who have not the capacity for understanding. You cannot make the blind see. They even reminded me that they were Englishmen. They talked the usual rubbish about conquest and foreign enemies and patriotism."

"Clods!" she muttered. "But you?"

She sat down beside him, her eyes full of light. She laid her hands boldly upon his.

"You will not let yourself be discouraged?" she pleaded. "Remember that even if you are alone in the world, you are right. You fight without hope of reward, without hope of appreciation. You will be the enemy of every one, and yet you know in your heart that you have the truth. You know it, and I know it, and Aaron knows it, and David Ross believes it. There are millions of others, if you could only find them, who understand, too — men too great to come out from their studies and talk claptrap to the mob. There are other people in the world who understand, who will sympathise. What does it matter that you cannot hear their spoken voices? And we — well, you know about us."

Her voice was almost a caress, the loneliness in his heart was so intense.

"Oh, you know about us!" she continued. "I — oh, I am your slave! And Aaron! We believe, we understand. There isn't anything in this world," she went on, with a little sob, "there isn't anything I wouldn't gladly do to help you! If only one could help!"

He returned very gently the pressure of her burning fingers. She drew his eyes towards hers, and he was startled to see in those few minutes how beautiful she was. There was inspiration in her splendidly modelled face — the high forehead, the eyes brilliantly clear, kindled now with the light of enthusiasm and all the softer burning of her exquisite sympathy. Her lips — full and red they seemed — were slightly parted. She was breathing quickly, like one who has run a race.

"Oh, dear master," she whispered,—"let me call you that — don't, even for a moment, be faint-hearted!"

The door was suddenly thrown open. Selingman entered, an enormous bunch of roses in his hand, a green hat on the back of his head.

"Faint-hearted?" he exclaimed. "What a word! Who is faint-hearted? Julia, I have brought you flowers. You would have to kiss me for them if he were not here. Don't glower at me. Every one kisses me. Great ladies would if I asked them to. That's the best of being a genius. Lord, what a wreck he looks! What's wrong with you, man? I know! I met them at the corner of the street. There

was the rat-faced fellow with the red tie, and the
miner — Labour Members, they call themselves. I
would like to see them with a spade! Have you been
trying to get at their brains, Maraton? What's
that to make a man like you depressed? Did you
think they had any? Did you think you could draw
a single spark of fire out of dull pap like that?
Bah!"

Julia was moving quietly about the room, putting
the flowers in water. Aaron had slipped in and was
seated before his desk. Selingman, his broad face
set suddenly into hard lines, plumped himself into
the chair which Peter Dale had occupied.

"Man alive, lift your head — lift your head to
the skies!" he ordered. "You're the biggest man
in this country. Will you treat the prick of a pin
like a mortal wound? What did you expect from
them? Lord Almighty! . . . I've packed my bag.
I'm ready for the road. Two hundred and fifty
pounds a time from the *Daily Oracle* for thumbnail
sketches of the Human Firebrand! Lord, what is
any one depressed for in this country! It's chock-
full of humour. If I lived here long, I should be
fat."

He looked downward at his figure with compla-
cency. Julia laughed softly.

"Aren't you fat now?" she asked.

"Immense," he confessed, "but it's nothing to
what I could be. It agrees with me," he went on.
"You see, I have learnt the art of being satisfied
with myself. I know what I am. I am content.
That is where you, my friend Maraton, need to grow

a little older. Oh, you are great enough, great enough if you only knew it! Even Maxendorf admits that, and he told me frankly he's disappointed in you. Don't sit there like a dumb figure any longer. We are all coming with you, aren't we? I have brought my car over from Belgium. It is a caravan. It will hold us all — Aaron, too. Let us start; let us get out of this accursed city. Where is the first move? "

"We can't leave to-night," Maraton said. "I am addressing a meeting of the representatives of the Amalgamated Railway Workers — that is, if Peter Dale doesn't manage to stop it. He'll do his best."

"He won't succeed," Aaron declared eagerly. "I saw Ernshaw two hours ago. They're on to Peter Dale and his move. Do you know why Peter Dale was late here this afternoon? He'd been to Downing Street. I heard. Foley's lost you, but he's holding on to the Labour Party. He's pitting the Labour Party against you in the country."

Selingman laughed heartily.

"He's got it!" he exclaimed. "That's the scheme. I am all for a fight, spoiling for it. Fighting and eating are the grandest things in the world! What time is the meeting? "

"Seven o'clock," Maraton replied.

"Two hours we will give you," Selingman continued. "Nine o'clock, a little restaurant I know in the West End, the four of us before we start. We will do ourselves well."

"Before I leave London," Maraton said, "I must see Maxendorf once more."

Selingman stroked his face thoughtfully.

" Your risk," he remarked. " Don't you let these chaps think you are mixed up with Maxendorf."

" I must see Maxendorf," Maraton insisted. " When I leave London to-night, the die is cast. I have cut myself adrift from everything in life. I shall make enemies with every class of society. There must be one word more pass between Maxendorf and me before I hold up the torch."

" He's got it," Selingman declared. " The trick is on him already. Maxendorf he shall see. I will arrange a meeting somewhere — not at the hotel. Miss Julia, write down this address. This is where we all meet at nine. Half-past six now. I will take you round to your meeting, Maraton. Do you want any papers? "

" I want no papers," Maraton answered. " I speak to these men to-night as I shall speak to them in the north. I take no papers from London with me, no figures, nothing. It is just the things I see I want to tell them."

Selingman nodded.

" You shall speak immortal words," he declared. " And I — I am the one man in the world to transcribe them, to write in the background, to give them colour and point. What giants we are, Maraton — you with your stream of words, and I with my pen! Miss Julia," he added, " remember that you are to be our inspiration as well as my secretary. Put on your prettiest clothes to-night. It is our last holiday."

She looked at him coldly.

"I do not wear pretty clothes," she said.

"Little fool!" he exclaimed. "Just because you've the big things beating in your brain, you'd like to close your eyes to the fact that your sex is the most wonderful thing on God's earth. That's the worst of a woman. If ever she begins to think seriously, she does her hair in a lump, changes silk for cotton, forgets her corsets, and leaves off ribbons. Silly, silly child!" he went on, shaking his forefinger at her. "I tell you women have done their greatest work in the world when their brains have been covered with a pretty hat. . . . There she goes," he growled, as she left the room. "Thinks I'm a flippant old windbag, I know. And I'm not. Why don't you fall in love with her, Maraton? It would be the making of you. Even a prophet needs relaxation. She is yours, body and soul. One can tell it with every sentence she speaks. And she is for the cause," he concluded with a graver note in his tone. "She has found the fire somewhere. There were women like her who held Robespierre's hand. . . . Eh?"

Maraton glanced up. Selingman was leaning forward and his eyes were fixed steadily upon his friend.

"I was afraid, just a little afraid," he said slowly, "of the other woman. I am glad she didn't count enough. Women are the very devil sometimes when they come between us and the right thing!"

CHAPTER XXXIII

Selingman came into the restaurant with a huge rose in his buttonhole and another bunch of flowers — carnations this time — in his hands. He made his way to the little round table where Julia and Aaron were seated.

"For you, Miss Julia," he declared, depositing them by her side. "Pin them in the front of your frock. Drink wine to-night. Be gay. Let us see pink, also, in your cheeks. It is a great evening, this. Maraton is here?"

"Not yet," Jula answered, smiling.

Selingman sat down between them. He gave a lengthy order to a waiter; then he turned abruptly to Julia.

"He will keep to it, you think? This time you believe that he has made up his mind?"

"I do," she asserted vigorously.

"What is he made of, that man?" Selingman continued, sipping the Vermouth which he had just ordered. "He makes love to you, eh? Ach! never mind your brother. For a man like Maraton, what does it matter? You are of the right stuff. You would be proud."

She looked steadily out of the restaurant.

"I have been a worker," she said, "in a clothing factory since I was old enough to stand up, and what little time I have had to spare, I have spent in study, in trying to fit myself for the fight against those things that you and I and all of us know of. There has been no opportunity," she went on, more slowly, " I have not allowed myself —"

" Ah, but it comes — it must come!" Selingman interrupted. " You have the instinct — I am sure of that. Use your power a little. It will be for his good. Every man who neglects his passions, weakens. You have the gifts, Julia. I tell you that — I, Selingman, who know much about woman and more about love and life. You've felt it, too, yourself sometimes in the quiet hours. Haven't you lain in your bed with your eyes wide open, and seen the ceiling roll away and the skies lean down, and felt the thoughts come stealing into your brain, till all of a sudden you found that your pulses were beating fast, and your heart was trembling, and there was a sort of faint music in your blood and in your ears? Ah, well, one knows! Suffer yourself to think of these hours when he is with you sometimes. Don't make an ice maiden of yourself. You've done good work. I know all about you. You could do more splendid work still if you could weave that little spell which you and I know of."

" It is too late," she sighed, " too late now. He has become used to me. I am a machine — nothing more, to him. He does not even realise that I am a woman."

" What do you expect?" Aaron asked harshly. " Why should a man, with great things in his brain, waste a moment in thinking of women?"

Selingman's under-lip shot out, a queer little way he had of showing his contempt.

"Little man," he told Aaron, "you are a fanatic. You do not understand. It is a quarter past nine and I am hungry. . . . Ah!"

Maraton came in just then. He had the air of a man who has been through a crisis, but his eyes were bright as though with triumph. Selingman stood up and filled a glass with wine.

"The first rivet has been driven home," he cried. "I see it."

"It has indeed," Maraton answered. "For good or for evil, the railway strike is decided upon. There is civil war waging now, I can tell you," he added, as he sat down. "Graveling was there with a message. The whole of the Labour Party is against the strike. The leaders of the men are hot for it, and the men themselves. There wasn't a single one of them who hesitated. Ernshaw, who represents the Union, told me that there wasn't one of them who wouldn't get the sack if he dared to waver. They know what the Government did in Lancashire and they know what they tried to do at Sheffield. With the railway companies they'll have even more influence."

"Let us dine," Selingman insisted, welcoming the approach of the waiters. "You see me, a man of forty-five, robust, the picture of health. How do I do it? In this manner. When I dine, all cares go to the winds. When I dine, I forget the hard places, I let my brain free of its burden. I talk nonsense I love best with a pretty woman. To-night we will

talk with Miss Julia.   You see, I have brought her
more flowers.   She does not wear them, but they lie
by her plate."

"I have never worn an ornament in my life," Julia
told him, " and I don't think that any one has ever
given me flowers."

Selingman groaned.

" Oh, what pitiful words! " he exclaimed.   " If
there is one thing sadder in life than the slavery of
the people, it is to find a woman who has forgotten
her sex.   Almost you inspire me, young lady, with
the desire to take you by the hand and offer you
my escort into the gentler ways.   If I were sure of
success, not even my fair friends on the other side
of the Channel could keep me from your feet.   Maraton, look away from the walls.   There's nothing beyond — just a world full of fancies.   There's some
Sole Otèro on your plate which is worth tasting, and
there's champagne in your glass.   What matter if
there are troubles outside?   That's good — there is
music."

He beckoned to the *chef d'orchestre,* engaged him
for a few moments in conversation, poured him out
a glass of wine, and slipped something into his hand.
Then he recommenced his dinner with a chuckle of
satisfaction.

" The little man can play," he declared.   " He has
it in his fingers.   We shall hear now the waltzes
that I love.   Ah, Miss Julia, why is this not Paris!
Why can I not get up and put my arm around your
waist and whisper in your ear as we float round and
round in a waltz?   Stupid questions!   I am too short

to dance with you, for one thing, and much too fat.
But one loves to imagine. Listen."

Maraton had already set down his knife and fork.
The strains of the waltz had come to him with a queer
note of familiarity, a familiarity which at first he
found elusive. Then, as the movement progressed,
he remembered. Once more he was sitting in that
distant corner of the winter garden, hearing every
now and then the faint sound of the orchestra from
the ballroom. It was the same waltz; alas, the same
music was warming his blood! And it was too late
now. He had passed into the other world. In his
pocket lay the letter which he had received that evening from Mr. Foley — a few dignified lines of bitter
disappointment. He was an outcast, one who might
even soon be regarded as the wrecker of his own country. And still the music grew and faded and grew
again.

It was late before they had finished dinner, and
Maraton took Selingman to one side.

"Remember," he insisted, "it is a bargain. Before I go north I must see Maxendorf."

Selingman nodded.

"It is arranged," he said. "We both agreed that
it was better for you not to go to the hotel. Wait."

He glanced at his watch and nodded.

"Stay with your brother, little one," he directed,
turning to Julia. "We shall be away only a few
moments. Come."

"Where are we going?" Maraton enquired, as
they passed through the restaurant and ascended the
stairs.

Selingman placed his finger by the side of his nose.

"A plan of mine," he whispered. "Maxendorf is here, in a private room."

Selingman hurried his companion into a small private dining-room. Maxendorf was sitting there alone, smoking a cigarette over the remnants of an unpretentious feast. He welcomed them without a smile; his aspect, indeed, as he waved his hand towards a chair, was almost forbidding.

"What do you want with me, Maraton?" he asked. "They tell me — Selingman tells me — there was a word you had to say before you press the levers. Say it, then, and remember that hereafter, the less communication between you and me the better."

Maraton ignored the chair. He stood a little way inside the room. Through the partially opened window came the ceaseless roar of traffic from the busy street below.

"Maxendorf," he began, "there isn't much to be said. You know — Selingman has told you — what my decision is. It took me some time to make up my mind — only because I doubted one thing, and one thing alone, in the world. That one thing, Maxendorf, was your good faith."

Maxendorf lifted his eyes swiftly.

"You doubted me," he repeated.

"You're a people's man, I know," Maraton went one, "but here and there one finds queer traits in your character. They say that you are also a patriot and a schemer."

"They say truly," Maxendorf admitted, "yet

these things are by the way. They occupy a little
cell of life — no more. It is for the people I live
and breathe."

" For the people of the world," Maraton persisted
slowly —" for humanity? Is there any difference in
your mind, Maxendorf, between the people of one
country and the people of another? "

Maxendorf never faltered. His long narrow face
was turned steadily towards Maraton. His eyebrows
were drawn together. He spoke slowly and with
great distinctness.

" I am for humanity," he declared. " Many of
the people of my country I have already freed. It
is for the sufferers in other lands that I toil in these
days. If I am a patriot, it is because it is part of
my political outfit, and a political outfit is necessary
to the man who labours as I have laboured."

" So be it, then," Maraton decided. " I accept
your words. Within a month from this time, the revolution will be here. This land will be laid waste, the
terror will be brewed. I fear nothing, Maxendorf,
but as one man to another I have come to tell you,
before I start north, that if in your heart there is
a single grain of deceit, if ever it shall be made clear
to me that I have been made the cat's-paw of what
you have called patriotism, if the people of this country have left a breath of life in my body, I shall
dedicate it to a purpose at which you can guess."

" It is to threaten me that you have come? " Maxendorf asked quietly.

" Don't put it like that," Maraton replied.
" These are just the words which you yourself can-

not fail to understand. Neither you nor I hold life so dearly that the thought of losing it need make us quaver. I am here only to say this one word — to tell you that the heavens have never opened more surely to let out the lightning, than will your death be a charge upon me if you should vary even a hair's-breadth from our contract. If Maxendorf, the people's man, hides himself for only a moment in the shadow of Maxendorf the politician, he shall die!"

Maxendorf held out his hand.

"Death," he said scornfully, "is not the greatest ill with which you could threaten me, but let it be so. Humanity shall be our motto — no other."

"You spar at one another," Selingman declared, "like a couple of sophists. You are both men of the truth, you are both on your way to the light. I give you my benediction. I watch over you — I, Selingman. I am the witness of the joining of your hands. Unlock the gates without fear, Maraton. Maxendorf will do his work."

CHAPTER XXXIV

About seven miles from London, Selingman gave the signal for the car to pull up. They drew in by the side of the road and they all stood up in their places. Before them, the red glow which hung over the city was almost lurid; strange volumes of smoke were rising to the sky.

" Rioters," Selingman muttered.

Julia looked around with a little shiver. There were no trams running, and a great many of the shops were closed. Some of the people lounging about in the streets had the air of holiday makers. Little bands of men were marching arm in arm, shouting. Occasionally one of them picked up a stone and threw it through a shop window. They had not seen a policeman for miles.

" It is the beginning of the end," Maraton said slowly. " The only pity is that one must see it at all."

Julia pointed down the road.

" What is that? " she asked.

A long, grey-looking line was slowly unwinding itself into the level road. It came into sight like a serpent. It reached as far as the eye could see. From somewhere behind, they heard the sound of music.

" Soldiers," Maraton replied —" marching, too."

They moved the car over to the other side of the road. Presently a mounted officer galloped on ahead and rode up to them.

" Your name and address, please? "

Maraton hesitated.

" Why do you ask for it? " he demanded.

" I am sorry to inform you that your car must be surrendered at once," was the reply. " I hope we shall not inconvenience you very much but those are the general orders. Every motor car is to be commandeered. Sorry for the lady. Give me your name and address, please, at once, the cost price of your car, and how long it has been in your possession? "

Selingman gasped.

" Is the country at war? " he asked. " We have come from South Wales to-day. We heard nothing en route."

" There are no newspapers being issued," the officer told them. " The telegraph is abandoned to the Government, and also the telephone. Even we have no idea what is happening. We are trying to run a few trains through to the north but we have had a couple of hundred men killed already. They are to start again the other side of Romford. In the meantime, I am sorry, but I am bound to take possession of your car at once."

" My name is Selingman."

The officer looked at him curiously.

" Are you Henry Selingman," he enquired —" I mean the fellow who has been writing about Maraton? "

Selingman nodded.

"Then I am afraid I can't say I do feel so sorry to inconvenience you," the officer continued grimly. "Alight at once, if you please — all of you."

"But how are we to get into London?" Selingman protested.

"Walk," the officer replied promptly. "Be thankful if you reach there at all; and keep to the main streets, especially if the lady is going with you."

"Are there no police left?" Maraton demanded.

"We drafted most of them away to the riot centres. Then the train service ceased, too, and they haven't been able to come back. Now we have had an alarm from somewhere — I don't know where — and we've got orders to push troops towards the east coast. If you'll take my advice, Mr. Selingman," the officer concluded, "you'll keep your name to yourself for a little time. People who've been associated in any way with Maraton are not too popular just now around here."

Some more officers had ridden up. Two were already in the car. Soon it vanished in a cloud of dust on its way back. Julia, Selingman, Aaron and Maraton were left in the road, along which the soldiers were still marching. They started out to walk. Now and then a motor-car rattled by, full of soldiers, but for the most part the streets were almost empty. No one spoke to them or attempted to molest them in any way. As they drew nearer London, however, the streets became more and more crowded. Men in the middle of the road were addressing little knots of listeners. There was a complete row of shops, the plate-glass windows of which had been knocked in and the contents raided. They pushed steadily onwards. Here and there, little groups of loiterers assumed a threatening aspect. They came across the dead body of a man lying upon the pavement. No one seemed to mind. Very few of the passers-by even glanced at him. Selingman shivered.

"Ghastly!" he muttered. "This reminds me of the first days of the French troubles. How quiet the people keep! They are tired of robbing for money. It is food they want. A sandwich just now would be a dangerous possession."

They reached Algate. There were still no trams running, and nearly all the houses were tightly shuttered.

"Six weeks!" Maraton murmured to himself as he looked around. "Could any one believe that this might happen in six weeks!"

"Why not?" Selingman demanded. "You stop the arteries of life when you stop all communication from centre to centre. It's the most merciful way, after all. Everything will be over the sooner."

They passed down Threadneedle Street, a wilderness with boards nailed up in front of the great bank windows. A little further on there was the usual crowd of people, but they were all hanging about, uncertain what to do. There was no Stock Exchange business being transacted, simply because there were no buyers. At the Mansion House they found a few 'buses running, and managed to board one which was going westwards. It set them down in New Oxford Street, not far from Russell Square.

Here there were denser crowds than ever. The entance to the square itself was almost blocked.

"What's going on here?" Maraton asked a loiterer.

They heard a loud, hoarse yell, repeated several times. The man pointed with his finger.

"They are round Maraton's house," he answered. "They have broken in all his windows. He's not there or they'd have had him out and flayed him alive."

A brief silence ensued. There seemed something ominous in this message, delivered apparently from one typical of his class, a worker out of work, a pipe in his mouth, a generally aimless air about his movements.

"But forgive me," Selingman remarked, "I am a stranger in this country. I have been told that Maraton is a friend of the people."

The man nodded gloomily.

"There's plenty that calls him so in other parts of the country," he assented. "I belong to a Working Man's Club and what we can't see is what's the bally use of a job like this? He's bitten off more than he can chew — that's what Maraton's done. He's stopped the railways and the coal, and even you can tell what that means, I suppose, sir? Pretty well every factory in the country is shutting down or has shut down. Well, supposing the Government make terms, which they say they can't. The miners and railway men may get a bit more. What about all the rest of us? We're more likely to get a bit less. Then what if the Germans get over here?

There's all sorts of rumours about this morning. They say that three-quarters of the fleet is hung up for want of coal. . . . My! Look there, they've fired his house! I wouldn't be in his shoes for something! They say he's hiding up in Northumberland."

The man passed on. Maraton was the first to speak.

" Come," he said quietly, " there is nothing here to be discouraged at. We knew very well that for the first few months — years, perhaps — this thing had to be faced. We must get rooms somewhere. I have to meet the railway men to-night. Young Ernshaw rode up from Derby on a motor-cycle to make the appointment. As for you, Selingman," Maraton went on, as they turned back towards New Oxford Street, " why do you stay here? Your coming has been splendid. It has been a joy to have you near. But between ourselves," he added, lowering his voice, " you know what mobs are. Take my advice and get back home for a time. We shall meet again."

Selingman shook his head.

" I helped to light the torch," he declared. " I'll see it burn for a while. I was in Paris through the last riots — a dirty sight it was! You'll pull through this. Maybe we're better apart for a time. But we'll see one another housed first," he added. " I want to know where you all are."

There was no difficulty about shelter of a sort. The private hotels, which were plentiful in the neighbourhood, were half empty, and supplied rooms readily enough, although they were curiously apathetic about the matter. At each one of them the charges for food were enormous. Maraton divided a bundle of notes into half and made Aaron take one portion.

"Look after Julia," he directed, "and I think you'd better keep away from me. A good many of them knew that you were my secretary. Look after your sister. Keep quiet for a time. Wait."

He tore a sheet of paper from his pocket-book, wrote a few lines upon it and twisted it up.

"You will find an address in New York there," he said. "If anything happens to me, go over and present it in person."

Aaron took it almost mechanically. His eyes scarcely for a second had left his master's face.

"Let me stay here," he begged, "if it's only an attic. There may be work to be done. Let me stay, sir. My little bit of life is of no more account to me than a snap of the fingers. Don't send me away. Julia's a woman — they won't hurt her. She can go back to her old rooms. The streets are quite orderly. Let me stay, sir!"

"No one seemed to notice us come in," Julia pleaded. "Let me stay, too. You heard what the porter said — we could choose what rooms we liked. It is safer in this part of London than in the East End, and you know," she added, looking at him steadily, "that if there is trouble to come, I have no fear."

Maraton hesitated. Perhaps they were as well where they were, under shelter. He nodded.

"Very well," he agreed. "There seems to be no one to show us about. We will go and select rooms."

In the hall they passed a man in the livery of the hotel. Maraton enquired the way to the telephone, but he only shook his head.

"Telephone isn't working, sir," he announced, "not to private subscribers, at any rate. They haven't answered a call for two days."

"Are any meals being served in the restaurant?" Maraton asked.

The man shook his head.

"Not regular meals, sir," he replied. "What food we've got is all locked up. You can get something between eight and nine. We close the hotel doors then."

"They tell me I can select any room I like upstairs that isn't occupied," Maraton remarked.

The porter nodded.

"Nearly all the servants have gone," he explained, "so they can't try to run the hotel. Gone out to find food somewhere. They couldn't feed them here."

"Is there wine in the place?" Selingman asked.

"Plenty," the man answered.

"If needs be, then, we will carouse," Selingman declared. "First, a wash. Then I will forage. Leave it to me to forage, you others. I know the tricks. I shall not go away. I shall stay here with you."

They selected rooms — Maraton and Selingman adjoining ones on the first floor; the others higher up. Then Selingman departed on his expedition, and

Maraton sat down before the window in the sitting-room. He drew aside the curtain and stared. They had been in the hotel rather less than half an hour, but the autumn twilight had deepened rapidly. Darkness had fallen upon the city — a strange, un-redeemed darkness. The street lamps were unlit. It was as though a black hand had been laid upon the place. Only here and there the sky was reddened as though with conflagration. Maraton's head sunk upon his arms. These, indeed, were the days when he would need all his courage. He threw open the window. There was a curious silence without. The roar of traffic had ceased entirely. The only sound was the footfall of the people upon the pavement. He looked down into the street, crowded with little knots of men, one or two of them carrying torches. He watched them stream by. It was the breaking up of the crowd which had gathered together to sack and burn his house.

The door was softly opened and closed again. He turned half around. Through the shadows he saw Julia's pale face as she came swiftly towards him. With a sudden gesture she fell on her knees by his side. Her fingers clasped him, she clung to his arm.

"Ah, I knew that I should find you like this!" she cried. "Don't look down into the street, don't look at those unlit places! Look up to the skies. See, there is a star there already. Nothing up there — nothing which really matters — is altered. This is only the destruction that must come before the dawn. It was you yourself who prophesied it, you yourself who saw it so clearly. Oh, don't be sad because you have pulled down the pillars! It isn't so very long before the morning."

He passed his arm around her and gripped her fingers tightly. So they were sitting when, by and by, Selingman burst into the room.

CHAPTER XXXV

Selingman was once more entirely his old self. He staggered into the room with a tin of biscuits under one arm, and three bottles of hock under the other, all of which he deposited noisily upon the round table in the middle of the room.

"I am the prince of caterers," he declared. "I surpass myself. Come out of the shadows, you dreamer. There is work to be done, food to be eaten, wine to be drunk."

From his left-hand pocket he produced three candles, which he placed at intervals along the mantelpiece and lit. Then for the first time he saw Julia.

"Ah," he cried, "our inspiration! Congratulate yourself, dear Miss Julia. After all, you are going to dine or sup, or whatever meal you may choose to call it. Behold!"

From his other pocket he produced two great jars of potted meat, a jar of jam, a handful of miscellaneous knives and forks, and a corkscrew.

"I have found an intelligent person here," he confided to them. "He has shown me the way to the wine cellar. Only the landlord and he are permitted to fetch wine. They fear a raid. *Niersteiner*, of a reasonable vintage."

"I will fetch Aaron," Julia said as she left the room.

" The girl worships you, and you're a beast to her," Selingman exclaimed, his eyes fixed upon the door through which she had vanished. " A man, indeed! A creature of wood and sawdust! Listen! "

His hand flashed out, his hand which grasped still the corkscrew.

" Listen, you man from the clouds," he continued. " I shall rob you of her. I adore her. To-day she may think me merely fat and eccentric. Don't rely upon that. I have the gift when I choose. I can tell fairy tales, I can creep a little way into her mind and fill her brain with delicate fancies, build images there and destroy them, play softly upon the keynote of her emotions, until one day she will wake up and what will have happened? She will be mine! "

He banged the table with the bottle of wine he was holding. Then, with great care and accuracy, he drew the cork.

" Your health! " he cried, raising his glass. " Ah, no! I have not sipped the wine. I change the toast. To Julia! "

Maraton rose to his feet, and turned his back upon the gloomy darkness which brooded over the city. He took the glass of wine which Selingman was holding out and leaned towards him earnestly.

" My friend," he said, " it seems strange to me that we speak of these things at such an hour. Yet let me tell you something. I don't know why I want to tell you, but I do. I am not, perhaps, quite what you think me. Only, the night you and I went north together, the gates of that world which you speak of so easily were closed behind me."

"It was the other woman," Selingman exclaimed.

"It was the other woman," Maraton echoed.

Selingman set down the bottle upon the table. Two great tears rolled down from his blue eyes. He held out both his hands and gripped Maraton's.

"My friend," he said, "now indeed I love you! We are twin souls. You, too, are human as you are wonderful. You see what an old woman I am. This sentiment — oh, it will be the end of me! But tell me — I must know. It was because you went north that it was ended?"

Maraton nodded slowly.

"I chose the opposite camp," he answered. "What could I do?"

"Nature," Selingman declared, brandishing a great silk handkerchief, "is the queerest mistress who ever played pranks with us. Here, in the same camp, dwells a divinity, and you — you must peer down into the lower world. . . . Never mind, potted meat and hock are good. Julia," he added, turning his head at the sound of the opening door, "to genius in adversity all gentle familiarities are permitted. I grant myself the privilege of your Christian name. Come and grace our feast. I have found food and wine. I am your self-appointed caterer. There is no butter, but that is simply one of those pleasant tests for us, a test of will and fortitude. All my life until to-night I have loved butter. From henceforth — until we can get it again — I detest it. Let us eat, drink and be merry. Where is Aaron?"

"He went out into the streets," Julia replied. "He will be back presently."

Aaron came in a few minutes later, struggling with the weight of the parcels he was carrying. He laid them down upon the sideboard, and turned towards Maraton with an air of triumph.

"I've been there, sir," he announced. "I've got the letters, your private dispatch box, and a lot of papers we needed. It's only the outside walls of the house that are charred. The fire was put out almost at once. And I've seen Ernshaw."

Maraton's eyes were lit with pleasure.

"You're a fine fellow, Aaron," he commended.

"I've got my bicycle, too," Aaron continued. "I can get half over London, if necessary, while you stay here."

"Tell me about Ernshaw?" Maraton begged quickly.

"He's loyal — they all are," Aaron cried. "Oh, you should hear him talk about Peter Dale and Graveling, and that lot! They're spread up north now, all of them, trying to kill the strike. And the men won't move anywhere. His own miners wouldn't listen to Dale. Mr. Foley sent him up to Newcastle in his motor-car. They played a garden hose on him and burned an effigy of himself, dressed in old woman's clothes. Mr. Foley's had the railway men to Downing Street twice, but they've never wavered. Ernshaw is splendid. There are seven of them, and Ernshaw's own words were that they've made up their minds that grass could grow in the tracks and hell fires scorch up the land before they'd go back to slavery. They're for you, sir, body and soul. They won't give in."

" Thank God! " Maraton muttered. " What about the mob? "

" Loafers and wastrels," Aaron exclaimed indignantly, " dirty parasites of humanity, thieves; not an honest worker amongst them! They're the sort who shouted themselves hoarse on Mafeking night and hid in their holes when the war drums were calling. The authorities got a hundred police from somewhere, and they crumbled away like rats running for their holes. Ernshaw asks you not to go back to Russell Square because of the difficulty of getting at you, but this was his message to you, sir, when I told him of your arrival. He begged me to tell you that they were the scum of the earth; that from Newcastle to the Thames the men who stand idle to-day wait in faith and trust for your word and yours only. He will be here before long."

Selingman nodded ponderously. His mouth was very full, but he did not delay his speech.

" You have brought a splendid message, young man," he pronounced. " Sit down and eat with us. Exercise your imagination but a little and you will indeed believe that you have been bidden to a feast of Lucullus. Has any one, I wonder, ever appreciated the marvellous and yet subtle sympathy which can exist between potted meat and biscuits — especially when washed down with hock? Join us, my young friend Aaron. Abandon yourself with us to the pleasure of the table. We will discuss any subject upon the earth — except butter! Miss Julia, do you know where I shall go when I leave here? No? I go to seek chocolates and flowers for you."

She laughed gaily.

"Chocolates and flowers," she repeated, "at ten o'clock at night! And for me, too!"

"And why not for you?" Selingman demanded, almost indignantly. "You are like all enthusiasts of your sex. You are too intense, you concentrate too much. You have lived in a cold and austere atmosphere. You have waited a long time for the hand which is to lead you into the sunshine."

She laughed at him once more, yet perhaps this time a little wistfully.

"Very well," she promised, "I will reform. I will eat all the chocolates you can bring me, and I will sleep with your flowers at my bedside. There! Am I improving?"

Selingman rose to his feet. He drained his glass of wine and lit one of his long black cigars by the flame of the candle.

"Dear Julia," he said, "you have spoken. I start on the quest of my life."

CHAPTER XXXVI

Selingman had scarcely left the place when Ernshaw arrived, piloted into the room by Aaron, who had been waiting for him below. Maraton and he gripped hands heartily. During the first few days of the campaign they had been constant companions.

"At least," he declared, as he looked into Maraton's face, "whatever the world may think of the justice of their cause, no one will ever any longer deny the might of the people."

"None but fools ever did deny it," Maraton answered.

"How are they in the north?" Ernshaw asked.

"United and confident," Maraton assured him. "Up there I don't think they realise the position so much as here. In Nottingham and Leicester, people are leading their usual daily lives. It was only as we neared London that one began to understand."

"London is paralysed with fear," Ernshaw asserted, "perhaps with reason. The Government are working the telephones and telegraph to a very small extent. The army engineers are doing the best they can with the East Coast railways."

"What about Dale and his friends?"

Ernshaw's dark, sallow face was lit with triumph.

"They are flustered to death like a lot of rabbits in the middle of a cornfield, with the reapers at work!" he exclaimed. "Heckled and terrified to death! Cecil was at them the other night. 'Are you not,' he cried, 'the representatives of the people?' Wilmott was in the House — one of us — treasurer for the Amalgamated Society, and while Dale was hesitating, he sprang up. 'Before God, no!' he answered. 'There isn't a Labour Member in this House who stands for more than the constituency he represents, or is here for more than the salary he draws. The cause of the people is in safer hands.' Then they called for you. There have been questions about your whereabouts every day. They wanted to impeach you for high treason. Through all the storm, Foley is the only man who has kept quiet. He sent for me. I referred him to you."

"The time for conferences is past," Maraton said firmly.

"We know it," Ernshaw replied. "What's the good of them? A sop for the men, a pat on the back for their leaders, a buttering Press, and a public who cares only how much or how little they are inconvenienced. We have had enough of that. My men must wake into a new life, or sleep for ever."

"What is the foreign news?" Maraton asked.

"All uncertain. The air is full of rumours. Several Atlantic liners are late, and reports have come by wireless of a number of strange cruisers off Queenstown. Personally, I don't think that anything definite has been done. The moment to strike isn't yet. The Admiralty have been working like slaves to get coal to their fleet."

"You came alone?" Maraton enquired.

Ernshaw nodded.

"I came alone because the seven of us are as men with one heart. We are with you into hell!"

"And the men," Maraton continued,— "I wonder how many of them realise what they may have to go through."

"You stirred something up in them," Ernshaw said slowly, "something they have never felt before. You made them feel that they have the right of nature to live a dignified life, and to enjoy a certain share of the profits of their labour, not as a grudgingly given wage but as a law-established right. There's a feeling born in them that's new — it's done them good already. I never heard so little grumbling at the pay. I think it's in their heart that they're fighting for a principle this time, and not for an extra coin dragged from the unwilling pockets of men who have no human right to be the janitors of what their labour produces. They've got the proper feeling at last, sir. You've touched something which is as near the religious sense as anything a man can feel who has no call that way. It's something that will last, too! Their womenkind have laid hold of it. When they start life again, they mean to start on a different plane."

"How are the accounts lasting out?" Maraton asked.

Ernshaw produced some books from his pocket and they sat down at the table.

"We're not so badly off for money," he declared. "It's the purchasing power of it that's making things difficult. I have spread the people out as much as I can. It's the best chance, but next week will be a black one."

They pored over the figures for a time. Outside, the streets were almost as silent as death. Suddenly the door was thrown open, and they both looked up hastily. Selingman stood there, but Selingman transformed. All the colour seemed to have left his cheeks; his eyes were burning with a steely fire. He closed the door behind him and he shivered where he stood. Maraton sprang to his feet.

"What, in God's name, has happened, man?" he cried. "Quick!"

Selingman came a little further into the room. He raised his hands above his head; his voice was thick with horror.

"I have betrayed you!" he moaned. "I have betrayed the people!"

He stood there, still trembling. Maraton poured him out wine, but he swept it away.

"No more of those things for me!" he continued. "Listen to my tale. If there is a God, may he hear me! By every line I have written, by every world of fancy into which I have been led, by every particle of what nations have called my genius, I swear that I speak the truth!"

"I believe you," Maraton said. "Go on. Tell me quickly."

"I trusted Maxendorf," Selingman proceeded, his voice shaking, "trusted and loved him as a brother. I have been his tool and his dupe!"

Maraton felt himself suddenly at the edge of the world. He leaned over and looked into the abyss

called hell.   For a moment he shivered; then he set
his teeth.

"Go on," he repeated.

"Maxendorf and I have spoken many times of
the future of this country. The dream which he
outlined for you, he has spoken of to me with glit-
tering eyes, with heaving chest, with trembling voice.
It was his scheme that I should take you to him.
You, too, believed as I did. To-night I visited him.
I stepped in upon the one weak moment of his life.
He needed a confidant. He was bursting with joy
and triumph. He showed me his heart; he showed me
the great and terrible hatred which burns there for
England and everything English. The people's man,
he calls himself! He is for the people of his own
country and his own country only! You and I have
been the tools of his crafty schemes. This country,
if he possesses it, he will occupy as a conqueror. He
will set his heel upon it. He will demand the greatest indemnity of all times. And every penny of it
will flow into his beloved land. We thought that the
dawn had come, we poor, miserable and deluded victims of his craft. We are dooming the people of
this country to generations of slavery!"

Maraton for a moment sat quite still. When he
spoke, his tone was singularly matter-of-fact.

"Where is Maxendorf?" he asked.

"Still at the hotel. The Embassy was not ready,
and he has made excuses. He is more his own master there."

Maraton turned to Ernshaw.

"Ernshaw," he begged, "wait here for me. Wait."

He took up his hat and left the room. Selingman stood almost as though he were praying.

"Now," he muttered, "is the time for the strong man!"

CHAPTER XXXVII

Into the salon of Maxendorf's suite at the Ritz Hotel, freed for a moment from its constant stream of callers, came suddenly, without announcement — from a place of hiding, indeed — Maraton. He stepped into the room swiftly and closed the door. Maxendorf was standing with his back to his visitor, bending over a map.

"Who's that?" he asked, without looking up. "You, Franz? You, Beldeman?"

There was no reply. Maxendorf straightened his gaunt figure and turned around. He stood there motionless, the palm of one hand covering the map at which he had been gazing, the lamplight shining on his gaunt, strangely freckled face.

"You!" he muttered.

Maraton remained still speechless. Maxendorf stretched out his hand for the telephone, but before he could grasp it, his hand was struck into the air. He wasted no time asking useless questions. His visitor's face was enough.

"What have you to gain by this?" he demanded. "Even if you could take my life, it will alter nothing."

Maraton caught him fiercely by the throat. Maxendorf, notwithstanding his superior height, was powerless. He was forced slowly backwards across the couch, on to the floor. Maraton knelt by his side. His grasp was never for a second relaxed.

"I leave you to-night," Maraton whispered, "with a gasp or two of life in you, but remember this. If I fail to undo your work, as sure as I live, I will keep my word. My hand shall find your throat again — your throat, do you hear? — and shall hold you there, tighter and tighter, until the life slips out of your body, just as it is almost slipping now!"

Maxendorf was unconscious. Maraton suddenly threw him away. Then he left the room, rang for the lift and made his way once more out into the street. Piccadilly was a shadowy wilderness. St. James's Street was thronged with soldiers marching into the Park. Maraton pursued his way steadily into Pall Mall and Downing Street. Even here there were very few people, and the front of Mr. Foley's house was almost deserted, save for one or two curious loiterers and a couple of policemen. Maraton rang the bell and found no trouble in obtaining admittance. The butler, however, shook his head when asked if Mr. Foley was at home.

"Mr. Foley is at the War Office, sir," he announced. "We cannot tell what time to expect him."

"I shall wait," Maraton replied. "My business is of urgent importance."

The butler made no difficulty. He recognised Maraton as a guest of the house and he showed him into the smaller library, which was generally used as a waiting-room for more important visitors. It was the room in which Maraton had had his first conversation with Mr. Foley. He looked around him with faint, half painful curiosity. It was like a place which he had known well in some other life. It seemed impossible to believe that he was the same man, or that this was the same room. Yet it was barely four months ago! Too restless to sit still, he walked up and down the apartment with quick, unsteady footsteps. Then suddenly the door opened. Elisabeth appeared. She recognised Maraton and started. She looked at him with a fixed, incredulous stare.

"You?" she exclaimed. "You here? What do you want?"

"Your uncle," he answered. "How long will he be?"

She closed the door behind her with trembling fingers. Then she came further into the room and confronted him.

"Why are you here?" she demanded. "To gloat over your work?"

"To undo it, if I can," he replied quickly,— "a part of it, at any rate. I fell into a trap — Selingman and I. I've a way out, if there's time. I want your uncle."

"You mean it?" she begged feverishly, her face lightening. "Oh, don't raise our hopes again just to disappoint us!"

"I mean it," he reiterated. "I want your uncle. With his help, if he has the courage, if he dare face the inevitable, I'll break the railway strike to-night and the coal strike to-morrow."

She sat down suddenly. She, too, had changed during the last few months. Her face was thinner; there were lines under her eyes. She had lost something of the fresh, delicate splendour of youth which had made her seem so dazzling.

"I can't believe that you are in earnest," she faltered.

"There isn't any doubt about it," he assured her. "Send round and hurry your uncle."

She moved to the writing-table and wrote a few lines hastily. Then she rang the bell and gave them to a servant. She was still without a vestige of colour.

"I can't dare to feel hopeful," she observed gloomily, when the door had been closed and they were once more alone. "We trusted you before, we believed that everything would be well. You were brutal to us both — to me as well as to my uncle."

"I made no promises," he reminded her. "I broke no ties. I was a people's man; I still am. I took the course I thought best. I thought I saw a way to real freedom."

"It was Maxendorf!" she exclaimed, under her breath.

He nodded.

"Maxendorf was too clever for me," he confessed. "Perhaps, just at this moment, he is a little sorry for it."

"What do you mean?" she asked hastily.

Maraton shrugged his shoulders.

"Oh, he's alive — only just, though! I shook the life nearly out of him. He knows that if we fail within these next twenty-four hours, your uncle and I, I am going to take what's left. I promised him that."

Her eyes glowed.

"You are a strange person," she declared. "How did you come to see the truth — to know that you had been misled by Maxendorf?"

"It was Selingman who told me," he explained. "Selingman, too, was deceived, but Selingman was nearer to him. He discovered the truth and he came to me. It was a matter of two hours ago. I made my way first to Maxendorf. I remembered my promise. I waited about in the corridors outside his room until I saw an opportunity. Then I slipped in and took him by the throat. Oh, he's alive, but not very much alive to-night!"

"Tell me about your wonderful journey north?" she begged.

He shook his head.

"Just at present it is like a nightmare," he replied. "We went from place to place and I preached the new salvation. I told them to trust in me and I would lead them to the light. I believed it. Though the way I knew must be strewn with difficulties, though there were great risks and much suffering, I believed it. I saw the dawn of the millennium. I made them believe that I saw it. They placed their trust in me. I have led them to the brink of God knows what!"

"You have led them to the brink of war," she said gravely. "We wait for its declaration every hour, my uncle and I. They know our plight. They are waiting for the exactly correct minute."

"They may wait a day too long," Maraton muttered. "For myself, I believe that they have already waited a day too long. Maxendorf was too certain. He never dreamed that I might learn the truth. Listen!"

A car stopped outside. They heard the sound of footsteps in the hall, the door was quickly opened. Mr. Foley stood there. He was looking very grave and white, but his eyes flashed at the sight of Maraton.

"You!" he exclaimed.

He gave his coat and hat to the servant; then he closed the door behind him. He remained standing — he offered no form of greeting to his unexpected visitor.

"What do you want?" he demanded. "Why have you come to me?"

"To give you your chance," Maraton replied, with swift emphasis. "You are the only statesman I know who would have courage to accept it. Dare you?"

Mr. Foley remained speechless. He stood perfectly still, with folded arms.

"This isn't an hour for recriminations," Maraton continued. "I have played into Maxendorf's hands — I admit it. There's time to checkmate him. I'll free every railroad in the country to-morrow, and the coal-pits next day, with your help."

"I have forced your delegates to come to me," Mr. Foley answered. "To all my offers they have but one reply: they await your word; they are not seeking for terms."

"Accept mine," Maraton begged, "and I swear to you that they shall consent. Mind, it isn't a small thing, but it's salvation, and it's the only salvation."

"Go on," Mr. Foley commanded.

"Pledge your word," Maraton proceeded deliberately, "pledge me your word that next Session you will nationalise the railways on the basis of three per cent for capital, a minimum wage of two pounds ten, a maximum salary of eight hundred pounds, contracts to be *pro rata* if profits are not earned. Pledge me that, and the railway strike is over."

"It's Socialism," Elisabeth gasped.

"It's common sense," Mr. Foley declared. "I accept. What about the coal?"

"You don't need to ask me that," Maraton replied swiftly. "Our coalfields are the blood and sinews of the country. They belong to the Government more naturally even than the labour-made railways. Take them. Pay your fair price and take them. Do away with the horde of money-bloated parvenus, who fatten and decay on the immoral profits they drag from Labour. We are at the parting of the ways. We wait for the strong man. Raise your standard, and the battle is already won."

"And you?" Mr. Foley muttered.

"I am your man," Maraton answered.

Mr. Foley held out his hand.

"If you mean it," he said gravely, "we'll get through yet. But are you sure about the others — Ernshaw and his Union men? We've tried all human means, and Ernshaw is like a rock. Dale and Graveling and all the rest have done what they could. Ernshaw remains outside. I thought that I had won the Labour Party. It seems to me, when the trouble came, that they represented nothing."

"They don't," Maraton agreed, "but Ernshaw represents the people, and I represent Ernshaw. He was with me only a little time ago. There won't be a Labour Party any longer. It will be a National Party, and you will make it."

"I am an old man," Mr. Foley murmured slowly, but his eyes kindled as he spoke.

They both laughed at him.

"Young enough to found a new Party," Maraton insisted, "young enough to bring the country into safety once more."

The atmosphere seemed heavily charged with emotion. Elisabeth's eyes were shining. She held out her hands to Maraton, and he kept them reverently in his.

"To-night," he announced, "with Ernshaw's help I start for the north. In a few hours we shall have freed the railway lines. I leave the Press to you, Mr. Foley. I shall go on to the mines."

"And I?" Lady Elisabeth asked. "What is my share? Is there nothing I can do?"

Their eyes met for one long moment.

"When I return," he said quietly, "I will tell you."

CHAPTER XXXVIII

From town to town, travelling for the most part on the platform of an engine, Maraton sped on his splendid mission. It was Ernshaw himself who drove, with the help of an assistant, but as they passed from place to place the veto was lifted. The men in some districts were a little querulous, but at Maraton's coming they were subdued. It was peace, a peace how splendid they were soon to know. By mid-day, trains laden with coal were rushing to several of the Channel ports. Maraton found his task with the miners more difficult, and yet in a way his triumph here was still more complete. He travelled down the backbone of England, preaching peace where war had reigned, promising great things in the name of the new Government. Although he had been absent barely forty-eight hours, it was a new London into which he travelled on his return. The streets were crowded once more with taxicabs, the evening papers were being sold, the shops were all open, the policemen were once more in the streets. Selingman, who had scarcely once left Maraton's side, gazed about him with wonder.

"It is a miracle, this," he declared. "There is no aftermath."

"The people are waiting," Maraton said. "We

have given them serious pledges. Their day is to come."

"You believe that Foley will keep his word?" Selingman asked.

"I know that he will," Maraton replied. "As soon as the Bills are drafted, he will go to the country. It will be a new Party — the National Party. Stay and see it, Selingman — a new era in the politics of the world, a very wonderful era. The country is going to be governed for the people that are worth while."

"If one could but live long enough!" Selingman sighed. "All over the universe it comes. Where was it one read of footsteps that sounded amongst the hills like footsteps upon wool? In the night-watches you can hear those footsteps. The world trembles with them."

"And after all," Maraton continued, "the sun of the world's happiness is made up of the happiness of units. Presently we shall have time to think of those things."

"It is true," Selingman said disconsolately. "I find myself rejoicing in the good which is coming to humanity and forgetting personal sorrows. There is that wonderful, that adorable secretary of yours — Julia. What should you say to me, my friend Maraton, if I were indeed to rob you of her? For once I am in earnest."

Maraton started for a moment. The idea at first was ludicrous.

"I suppose," he admitted, "I should reconcile myself to the inevitable. Times are going to be

different. I dare say that Aaron will be the only
secretary I shall need. But will she go? Remember, she is a woman of the people. I think that she
will never settle down, even with your splendid work
to control. She is less a poet than a humanitarian."

"What am I, man," Selingman retorted, striking
himself on the chest, "but a humanitarian? Listen
to the wonderful proof — it is not a secretary I re-
quire; it is a wife!"

Maraton was staggered.

"Have you told her?"

"What is the use?" Selingman growled. "She is
yours, body and soul. You have but to lift up your
finger, and she would follow you to the end of the
world. I don't idealise women, you know, Maraton,
and virtue isn't a fetish with me. But I know that
girl. If you hold out your hands, she is yours, but
if you withhold them, she is the most virginal creature that ever breathed."

"She is a splendid character," Maraton said
softly.

"Why don't you marry her yourself?" Selingman
asked abruptly. "How can you look at her, hear
her speak, watch her, without wanting to marry her?
What are you made of?"

Maraton sighed.

"I am one of the victims, I suppose, of that curious
instinct of selection. I care for some one else; I
have cared for some one else ever since the first night
I set foot in England."

"Then I'll get her," Selingman declared. "In
time I'll get her."

They all dined together at the little restaurant on the borders of Soho. Selingman was the giver of the feast and his spirits were both wonderful and infectious. The roar of London was recommencing. Newspapers were being sold on the streets. The strange cruisers seemed mysteriously to have disappeared from the Atlantic. The fleet, imprisoned no longer, was on its way to the North Sea. There was none of the foolish, over-exuberant rejoicing of bibulous jingoism, but a genuine, deep spirit of thankfulness abroad. Men and women were glad but thoughtful. There were new times to come, great promises had been made. There were rumours everywhere of a new political Party.

"We pause to-night," Selingman declared, "at the end of the first chapter. Almost I am tempted to linger in this wonderful country — at any rate until the headlines of the next are in type. You go down to the House to-night?"

"At nine o'clock," Maraton replied, glancing at the clock.

"Will they remember," Selingman continued thoughtfully, "that you were the Samson who pulled down the pillars, or will they merely hail you as the deliverer? Will they think of that ghostly ride of yours on the locomotive, I wonder, when you tore screaming through the darkness, with the risk of a buffer on the line at every mile; stepped from the engine, grimy, with your breath sucked out of you by the wind, and the roar of the locomotive still throbbing in your ears — stepped out to deliver your message to the waiting throngs? Magnificent! A

subject worthy of me and my prose! I shall write
of it, Maraton. I shall sing the glory of it in verse
or script, when your fame as a politician of the moment has passed. You will live because of the gar-
land that I shall weave."

Maraton sipped his wine thoughtfully.

"But for your overweening humility, Selingman,"
he began —

Selingman struck the table with his fist.

"It is a night for rejoicings, this," he thundered.
"I will not have my weaknesses exposed. Let us, for
to-night, at any rate, see the best in each other.
Glance, for instance, at Miss Julia. Admire the exquisite pink of my carnations which she has conde-
scended to wear; see how well they become her."

"I feel like a flower shop," Julia laughed.

"And you look like the spirit of the flowers herself," Selingman declared, "the wonderful Power on
the other side of the sun, who draws them out of the
ground and touches their petals with colour, shakes
perfume into their blossoms and makes this England
of yours, in springtime, like a beautiful, sweet-smell-
ing carpet."

"Don't listen to him, Julia," Maraton warned her.
"It was only a month ago that he told me that no
civilised man should live in this country because of
the women and the beer."

"A man changes," Selingman insisted fiercely.
"Your beer I will never drink, but Miss Julia knows
that she hasn't in the world a slave so abject as I."

Maraton rose to his feet.

"I must go," he announced. "I have to talk with

Mr. Foley for a few minutes. You had better come with me, Aaron. Selingman will see Julia back."

They watched him depart. Julia sighed as he passed through the door.

"I can read your thoughts," Selingman said quickly. "You are feeling, are you not, that to-night his leaving us has in it something allegorical. He was made for the storms of life, to fight in them and rejoice in them, and Fate has taken him by the hand and is leading him now towards the quieter places."

"It is not his choice," Julia murmured. "It is destiny."

"Can't you look a little way into the future?" Selingman continued, peering through half-closed eyes into his wine glass. "He represents the only possible link between the only possible political party of this country and the people. He will win for them in twelve months what they might have waited for through many weary years. He will sit in the high places. History will speak well of him. I will wager you half a dozen pairs of gloves that within a week the *Daily Oracle* will call him the modern Rienzi. And yet, with the end of the struggle, with the end of the fierce fighting, comes something — what is it? — disappointment? We have no right to be disappointed, and yet, somehow, one feels that it is the cold and the storm and the wind which keep the best in us — the fighting best — alive."

Julia's eyes were soft, for a moment, with tears. She, too, was following him a little way into the future.

"They will make a politician of him," she sighed. "So much the better for politics. But there is one thing which I do not think that he will ever forget. So long as he lives he will be a people's man."

Selingman became curiously silent. Soon he paid the bill.

"Will you put me in a cab?" she asked him outside.

He shook his head.

"I shall ride home with you."

"It is rather a long way," she reminded him. "I am down at my old rooms again. The house in Russell Square is full of workmen, after the fire."

"It does not matter how far," he said simply.

His fit of silence continued. When at last they arrived at their destination, she held out her hand. Again he shook his head.

"I am coming in," he announced.

She hesitated.

"My rooms are very tiny."

"I am coming in," he repeated.

He followed her up the stairs. Her little sitting-room was in darkness. She struck a match and lit the lamp. She would have pulled down the blind, but he checked her.

"No," he objected, "let us stand and look down together upon this wilderness. So!"

They were high up and they looked upon a treeless waste — rows of houses, tall factories, the line of the river beyond, the murky glow westwards.

"Here I can talk to you," he said. "Here it is silent. Soon I go back to my life and my life's work. You, Julia, must go with me."

She drew a little away from him, speechless with a queer sort of surprise, and a little indignant. He held her wrist firmly.

"I am a man who has written much of love," he continued, " of love and life and all the tangled skein of emotions which make of it a complex thing. And yet so few of us know what love is, so few of us know what companionship is, so few of us know the world in which those others dwell. You have looked at me with your great eyes, Julia, and at first you saw nothing but a fat, plain old man, with plenty of conceit and a humour for idle speeches. And to-day you think a little differently, and as the days go on you will think more differently still, for I am going to take you with me, Julia, and I am going to keep you with me, and I am going to keep the light in your eyes and the laughter at your lips, in the only way that counts. You will sit with me in my study, you shall see my work come and hear it grow. I shall take you into the world where the music is born, and your eyes will be closed there, and you will only know that there is another soul there who is your guide, and in whom you trust, and for whom you have a strange feeling. That is how love comes, Julia — the only sort of love which lasts. It isn't born in this land, it doesn't even flourish in this universe. If you don't come up in the clouds to find it, it isn't the sort that lasts. You are going to find it with me, dear."

She had begun to tremble a little, the tears were in her eyes.

"Oh, I know!" he faltered, with a break in his

own voice. " But you'll leave your sorrows behind
in my world."

It was midnight when Maraton left the House.
He came out with Mr. Foley, and they stood for a
moment at the entrance. An electric coupé rolled
swiftly up.

" You must come home with me for a minute or
two, Maraton," Mr. Foley urged. " It is on your
way."

The coupé, however, was already occupied. Elisabeth leaned out of the window. She held the door
open.

" I am going to take Mr. Maraton back with me,"
she insisted. " The car is there for you, uncle."

Mr. Foley smiled.

" Quite right," he assented. " Get in, Maraton.
I shall be home before you."

Maraton obeyed, and they glided out of the Palace
yard.

" I was there all the time," Elisabeth told him
quietly. " I heard everything. I was so glad, so
proud. Even your Labour Members had to come
and shake hands with you."

" I don't think Mr. Dale liked it," he remarked,
smiling. " They are not bad fellows at heart, but
they've got the poison in their systems which seems,
somehow or other, to become part of the equipment
of the politician — self-interest, over-egotism, con-
traction of interest. It makes one almost afraid."

She leaned a little towards him.

" You will not fear anything," she whispered confidently. " To-night, as I looked down, it seemed to me that as a looker-on I saw more, perhaps, of the real significance if it all than you who were there. It is a new force, you know, which has come into politics, a new Party. I suppose historians will call to-night, the fusion of Parties which is going to happen, an extraordinary triumph for Mr. Foley. Perhaps he deserves it — in my heart I believe that he does — but not in the way they would try to make out."

" His heart is right," Maraton declared. " He has wide sympathies and splendid understanding."

" It is a new chapter which begins to-night," she repeated. " You will have many disappointments to face, both of you."

" But isn't it a glorious fight ! " he exclaimed enthusiastically. " A great cause at one's back, a future filled with magnificent possibilities ! Lady Elisabeth," he went on, " you can't imagine what this hour means. Sometimes I have had moments of horrible depression. It is so easy to feel the sorrows of the people in one's heart, so easy to stir them into a passionate apprehension of their position. And then comes the dull, sickening doubt whether, after all, it had not been better to leave them as they were. Of what use are words — that is what I have felt so often. And now there has come the power to do great things for them. Life couldn't hold anything more splendid."

Her hand touched his. She had withdrawn her glove.

" You will let me help ? " she begged.

He turned towards her then, and she saw the light in his face for which she had longed. With a little cry her head sank upon his shoulder, and his arms closed around her.

"I am almost jealous of the people," she murmured. "Only I want you to teach me to love them and feel for them as you do. I want to feel that the same thing in our lives is bringing us always closer together."

THE END

www.ingramcontent.com/pod-product-compliance
Lightning Source LLC
Chambersburg PA
CBHW032225010726
47494CB00002B/358